the
beach
house

BOOKS BY JENNY HALE

the
beach
house

JENNY HALE

bookouture

Published by Bookouture in 2021

An imprint of Storyfire Ltd.
Carmelite House
50 Victoria Embankment
London EC4Y 0DZ

www.bookouture.com

ISBN: 978-1-80019-651-3
eBook ISBN: 978-1-80019-650-6

Prologue

Melanie Simpson sat across from her mother and her older sister Kathryn, staring at the page she'd pulled from Gram's will that was sandwiched between her thumb and the balled-up tissue in her fist. "This doesn't make any sense," she said, bewilderment flooding her.

Her mother shrugged with an empathetic shake of her head from the other side of the table, over the bowl of M&M's that Kathryn had been using as rewards to potty train her two-year-old son, Ryan. "I know."

"I thought Gram would leave me her own house, and I'd live here in Spring Hill with you all—fix it up, make it my own... We'd talked about it before—" Her throat closed up with emotion and her eyes filled with tears as she tried to squeeze the image of Gram's empty hospital bed from her mind. She'd never imagined that when they went into that room to pack up her grandmother's things to go home, Gram wouldn't be going with them.

Melanie ran her nails through her dark chestnut hair along her scalp, to tuck back the runaway strands that had escaped her ponytail. She couldn't remember the last time she'd done her hair or put makeup on, having spent the last three years taking care of Gram. Even now that she didn't have to look after anyone anymore, she still couldn't bring herself to do it. She could barely get out of bed in the morning.

"It could be a fresh start," her mother said with forced positivity. "You've always loved that little village in Florida, and you'd still get to fix up a house."

Melanie's green eyes grew round. "Have you *seen* that house?" she said, new tears forming at the thought of the shambles of a building Gram was proposing that Melanie buy with her inheritance. They'd walked past it every year that they'd gone to the village of Rosemary Bay on vacation, but Melanie had never taken their musings about fixing it up seriously. "It's a black hole financially. It might be cheaper just to level it."

Kathryn's eyebrows bounced. "That's an idea," she said, snagging an M&M and popping it into her mouth. Her sister scooted the bowl toward Melanie but she waved away the gesture with a teary smile.

Melanie's gaze fell back on the words in the will: *...provided you make the necessary repairs to the structure and maintain the intended style of the home.*

"I told Gram once that I thought the house would be an amazing bed and breakfast. We'd daydreamed about what it would be like to own it, but I never thought in a million years that she'd actually want me to buy it." Her lip wobbled.

She'd lost everything to take care of Gram. It was as if her life were split into two parts and if she tried really hard, she could just about remember the girl who'd run off to live in the city to work at Starcross Creative, a trendy marketing firm with lounge-style offices and direct access to the rooftop bar above them.

She and her fiancé Adam had lived in a swanky high rise not too far away, in an upscale area of Nashville. Melanie's father had been killed in a car crash when Melanie was three, and her grieving mother had always prayed for her girls to find lasting love, so Mama had been delighted when Adam popped the question after a year of dating. It was laughable now; Melanie remembered her and Adam's heartfelt conversations about starting a family, but how they didn't even have time with their schedules to care for a dog. They were busy professionals on their way to their own happy ending.

And then Gram got sick, and everything changed.

"This inheritance will be barely enough to cover repairs on that house," Melanie said on an inhale, rubbing her temples.

The Ellis house, as the locals in the quaint Florida village of Rosemary Bay knew it, was supposedly haunted. And it looked that way. On the market for decades, it sat in ruins off the beaten path, just waiting for some developer to knock it down, and superstition loomed. She'd read a Halloween article about it once that claimed dark figures were seen behind the windows, and the chandelier in the parlor would swing out of nowhere.

Melanie remembered that chandelier. Despite the local legend, it took her back to happier times.

"Come here." Gram had beckoned Melanie over to the window of the old house, her hand pressed against the murky glass to shield her eyes from the sun.

Skittish, Melanie had crept across the wiry, overgrown weeds of the yard, coming up behind her grandmother, glancing over her shoulder for any apparitions that wanted to terrify the daylights out of her. She put her hands against the window, a shiver running through her as she peered into the old parlor.

"Isn't that chandelier just divine?" Gram said, her voice a dreamy whisper.

Melanie peered at the enormous fixture of beaded glass that dripped from the ceiling, like a ghostly *Titanic* version of Gatsby's mansion.

"It's so pretty," she said, losing her breath at both the grandeur of the room and the decay of it. "If you like ghosts," she added quietly.

"Boo!" Gram shocked her with two hands on her shoulders, causing her to let out a blood-curdling scream that could probably be heard by the sailboats out on the turquoise gulf that lapped onto the shore behind the house. "Sorry," Gram said, falling into a fit of laughter. "I couldn't resist."

After she'd settled back down, Melanie playfully cut her eyes at Gram. "Do you believe in ghosts?" she'd asked.

Gram lifted her large sunglasses to make eye contact and, turning her attention back to the house, her grin sliding into a serious expression, she nodded. "Ghosts are whispers of the past," she said thoughtfully. "They only stick around when they want to tell us something that we need to know."

"Think so?" Melanie put her hands on her hips and took in the chipped shingles, the missing siding, and the broken railings. "I read that a loner named Alfred Ellis owned this house. Is that true?"

"Mm hm." Gram pursed her lips while she pressed a loose window molding back into place.

"He lived all by himself his whole life, apparently, clouded in secrets, dying here alone."

"That's what I hear," Gram said.

"They say that he came from a wealthy family with a large inheritance from his grandfather's success in the shipping industry."

Gram nodded.

"Did you know him, growing up?"

"He moved into town and built this after your granddaddy and I got married. We'd already moved away by then."

Melanie considered this as she peeked into another window. The hallway was empty and full of dust. "Think he haunts it?"

Gram smacked her hands together to get the dirt off them. "Perhaps. If he has something to say." Her gaze roamed the house as if she were looking for evidence that he did.

"Melanie?" Her sister's waving hand came into focus in front of her face, pulling Melanie from the memory. "I know it's not a lot of money, but we wanted to tell you that if you decide to follow Gram's wishes and buy the house, we'll give you whatever's left from selling Gram's rancher after we've settled her debts. You can use it to open the bed and breakfast."

"Thank you," she said, grateful for her little family. They always had her back.

"Does that thank you mean you *are* going to buy the Ellis house?" her mother asked. "A bed and breakfast is a great way to get back out there, Melanie," she said. "And the way you are with people, you'd be amazing at it."

Melanie sat, quietly thoughtful. She gazed out the window into the Tennessee sunshine. Kathryn's husband Toby had taken their toddler outside to give them time to talk. He chased Ryan around the yard while the little boy's giggles floated into the air like feathers.

"You don't have to decide right now," her mother continued. "The house isn't the only reason we've brought you here today."

Melanie tossed her tissue into the kitchen trashcan and turned to her family. "What is it?"

"I wasn't sure if you'd be ready to hear from her just yet," her mother began, looking uneasily at Kathryn. Melanie's sister offered an encouraging nod. "Gram wrote you a letter. We found it in her things at the hospital." Her mother pulled the letter from her purse and slid it across the table.

Melanie's vision blurred with tears at the sight of Gram's swooping lettering spelling out her name.

"Wait to read it if you aren't ready," her mother said, reaching out and patting Melanie's hand, her face clouded in worry for her daughter.

Melanie swallowed, trying to keep herself from falling apart. She set down the page of Gram's will she'd been holding, the paper crumpled from her tight grip, and picked up the envelope.

"Like Mom said, don't feel like you have to read it now," Kathryn told her. "Unless you want us here for support. I know how hard this is for you."

Melanie ran her finger over the seal of the envelope. "For three years, I spent every single moment with her. I endured her endless chattering about her garden and her worries that this was the year the fruitworms were going to totally take over her tomato plants."

Her mother let out a little chuckle and grabbed a tissue from the box on the windowsill.

"I know she kept her favorite cookies to the right of the breadbox," Melanie continued, her voice breaking, "and that, by her bedside, she had a jar of ten-dollar bills that she added to every month in the hopes of one day going on a cruise, because she'd never been on one. I find myself still calling out, 'Do you need any help to get to the kitchen?' right at noon when she usually has her lunch."

"I thought it might be too soon," her mother said under her breath to her sister.

Melanie looked up from the envelope. "I'm okay," she assured them, wiping another tear with the back of her hand. "What I'm saying is that, after three years of it, the silence is deafening." She picked up the letter. "It'll be comforting to hear her voice again—even if it's in my head."

Her mother gave her hand an encouraging squeeze.

Melanie opened the envelope, her movements slow to prolong the moment, knowing that when she'd read the final word of this letter, the silence would stretch on for an eternity. She cast her eyes lovingly over the opening line and then began to read:

My dear Melanie,

I'll bet you thought you'd finally shut me up. You're wondering what more I could possibly have to say that I haven't already told you, during the three years we lived together...

She tipped her head back and laughed through her tears. That was so Gram.

Well, there is something. I wanted to tell you that you did a good thing, taking care of me through my cancer and helping me hang in there. I've had a long life, and you're to thank for the last three years of it. But I've watched that vibrant girl that showed up with her moving boxes three years ago wither into a reserved, contemplative person, and that risk-taker has been slowly stripped away. I worry that I robbed you of who you are. I need you to figure out how to get back to that firecracker you were when you got here. Remember what I told you about ghosts? If you don't take life by the horns, and swing it around, I'm gonna drive you crazy until you do.

"Oh, Gram. I hope you do," Melanie said, swallowing the lump in her throat.

Life is all about risks, Melanie. Playing it safe doesn't get you anywhere but where you are now. Go. Find that life that's floating around the universe just waiting for you to grab it and never let go. And if I have any say in heaven, I'll be right there, pushing it toward you the whole way. I love you, baby girl. Catch ya on the other side!

Gram

Melanie folded the letter and placed it back in the envelope, tears now spilling over the puffy rims of her eyes. Her mother handed her a new tissue, all of them sniffling.

"So whatcha gonna do, sugar bean?" her mom asked, clearly trying to keep the mood as light as possible.

Melanie pushed a big smile across her face. "I'm gonna move to Rosemary Bay and buy the Ellis house."

Gram always knew best, and if she thought that there might be life for Melanie in the village where they had so many fond memories together, then that was exactly where she'd go. It was time for a change.

Chapter One

Rosemary Bay Village, The Gulf Coast

September 1956

Miss Andrews, as she was known in the village, dragged her dainty fingertips along the back of the bench at Willow Pier, overlooking the sparkling Gulf of Mexico, and sat down beside the handsome sailor in uniform. She crossed her legs at the ankle and ran her hands down her pencil skirt to straighten it across her thighs.

"What are you thinking about?" she asked, trying not to swallow him with her gaze. After spending the summer together, she'd decided that he was everything she'd ever dreamed of in a man.

"You," he replied, and then he smiled that smile she'd become so fond of, his affection for her undeniable.

"You're early," she said warmly, working hard to keep her fondness from bubbling up, for fear that acknowledging it would tear her heart out when he left.

The sailor whom she'd come to know as the dashing Alfred Ellis turned her way, his chiseled features dropping with his sultry stare, his dark brown eyes making her feel like she could see his soul right through them. "I didn't want to miss a minute with you." He took her hand from her lap and laced his fingers in hers, causing her breathing to become shallow.

The woman ran her other hand unsteadily over the light brown curls of her soft bob that she'd gotten styled just today so she could look her best for him. She'd powdered her face to a milky white, her red lips lined in a fashionable pout. "How long before you deploy?" she asked, cutting right to the chase to prepare herself for the ache she would inevitably feel the minute he walked off the pier.

"Thirty minutes," he said, his voice breaking.

He swallowed, and she wondered if his reaction had been due to leaving her or nerves about heading off to his next destination. He stood up and took her other hand, pulling her to a standing position. "I adore you," he blurted, sending a burst of excitement through her. "Let's spend our last moments together in each other's arms. And then, when I come back, marry me."

Her mother had warned her about the men passing through town, coming in for a whirlwind getaway, then leaving as quickly as they came, never to return. It was one of the downsides of living in a tropical destination. While her heart told her otherwise, she had to adhere to the expectations of being a lady. But she knew in her heart that all she'd have to do was ask and Alfred would come back for her.

"I'll tell you what," she said, staring into his eyes with purpose, just the sight of him filling her with a kind of joy she'd never felt before. "Send me a letter after you're gone and tell me again that you'll marry me, and I'll wait for you. If you still want to be with me after months at sea, then it's meant to be."

"I want to kiss you now. I love you," he whispered.

But she shook her head. "It will make it all the sweeter when you return," she said, kissing her finger and placing it on his lips, causing his eyes to flutter closed.

He looked back down at her. "I've completely fallen for you," he said, taking in a breath as if he could breathe her in. "How long are you going to make me wait to send you the letter? I'll do it tomorrow."

She smiled. "Two months. Send a letter in two months and I'll wait an eternity."

"Will you be attending that girls' school in the fall?"

She shook her head. "No. I've decided not to go."

He gazed into her eyes. "Not because of me, I hope. I'll wait if that's what you want to do. I'll wait forever."

She put her hand on his face, his eyes closing. "It's my own decision, I promise."

"If I'd only known I'd meet you," he said, shaking his head in frustration, "I would never have signed up for this tour in California. I can hardly stand being across the country from you."

"Love always finds its way home," she said.

He kissed her forehead. They sat back down together on the bench as the sun went down, casting an orange and pink glow in the sky, and talked about everything and nothing until he had to say goodbye. And when she had to let him go, she didn't know how she'd ever manage those two whole months without him.

"Promise me you'll wait for me," he said, clearly biting back his emotions, his square jaw tightening.

She put her hands on the arms of his crisp uniform. "Promise you'll come back."

And Miss Andrews knew in that instant, that when he boarded the ship, he was taking her heart with him.

*

"Is there anything for me?" the woman asked Gabby, their house-maid, as she flipped through the mail she'd retrieved from the letterbox.

"No, ma'am," Gabby replied, fumbling with the stack of mail, wobbling the duster and cleaning rag in her hand. "All of it is addressed to your daddy, Miss Andrews."

It had been four months and she had gotten no word from Alfred. She'd given him double the time. While she didn't want to believe that their time together had been only a fling, he'd left her with no other explanation. She wanted to kick herself for falling so hard for him. Now she had to deal with the emptiness and pain swallowing her whole.

Their summer together went through her mind on a loop as she tried to analyze it to find some indication that he hadn't really felt anything for her, but every time, she came up blank. She closed her eyes to recall the way he'd laughed at something funny she'd said, his arm around her as they sat together above the world on the Ferris wheel at the town fair. She could still feel the movement of his hands on her body as they'd danced on the old wood floor at Barney's in town, the way his gaze followed her as if he needed the view to breathe. And then there was that ice cream shop in a neighboring village where he'd named that brand new flavor for her. They'd had vanilla with blackberry crumble over it, and he'd called it the Lovebird Special. *Love.* Had she misread it all?

She'd never met anyone like Alfred before. He'd made her laugh, he'd challenged her, and yet he was tender and one of the kindest people she'd ever known. Even though she'd only known him for six months, it felt as if she'd known him for years. *Stupid woman*, she told herself, realizing that she was no different than the girls her mother had told her about. She'd seen them—all standing at the dock, crying and waving as the sailors steamed away in their ships. Meanwhile, the men aboard went back to life as usual, clapping each other on the back for another successful off-duty jaunt.

"That boy Samuel was here today looking for you again, Miss Andrews," Gabby said, still fiddling with the mail, getting it into some sort of order.

She tried to smile through her heartbreak. She would've married Alfred if he'd asked her, there was no doubt about it. She was torn between complete sadness and frustration.

"I think he's smitten with you, miss," Gabby said, pulling her back into the present.

"Do you think so?" she asked absentmindedly.

"Mm hm." Gabby set the letters down on the hall table. "He's been by three times this week. He wanted to take you to the picture show."

"He's a very nice man," she said, but her mind was still on Alfred.

"Yes, he is. And he's from a good family too."

She considered the idea that poor Samuel was popping by to see her and she wasn't emotionally available because of some sailor who hadn't thought twice about her. She'd never considered Alfred as *just some sailor* before now. The idea filled her eyes with tears. Her lip wobbled as she blinked them away. Well, he'd taught her a hard lesson, and she was glad that her mother had warned her about men like him.

"If Samuel stops by again, would you come and get me?" she asked, still feeling hollow. She needed to move on even if she didn't feel like she could right now. It wasn't healthy to keep obsessing over someone who clearly wasn't the person she thought he was. "I'm going to go to my room for a while."

As she made her way up the large staircase leading to her room, her mother bustled in, chatting to Gabby. "Oh my goodness, Gabby, look," her mother said when the young woman had rounded the hallway upstairs. "You accidentally dropped an envelope. It almost went down into the draining vent."

Miss Andrews stopped, her hearing perking up, her heart racing.

"Good thing I caught it," her mother continued, "it's from the electric company. Can you imagine if we were late on our remittance?"

"Oh, I'm terribly sorry, Mrs. Andrews…"

Her daughter came rushing down the stairs and dropped to the floor, lifting the slatted vent plate out of the hardwood that had been put in to drain floodwater from the house in the event of a storm.

"Good Lord, child, what are you doing?" her mother asked.

The young woman peered into the dark hole in the floor and then plunged her hand down into it, feeling around to see if perhaps her own letter had fallen in. Her fingers reached out as far as they could go, her right pointer finger stretching until it hurt.

"What are you doing?" her mother asked again, disapprovingly.

"Just making sure no other letters have fallen," she said, pulling her hand out.

"You're going to get your dress all dirty. I'm sure there's nothing down there."

She reached in again, but she came up empty. Had she gone mad? An envelope wouldn't have traveled that far into the draining vent…

Suddenly, she felt a hand around her arm, pulling her up. Her mother's consoling eyes were on her, giving light to the girl's desperation. "There's nothing in there. Perhaps you should wash up and make yourself look more respectable. You're so pretty," she said, brushing a curl out of her daughter's face. "You wouldn't want Samuel to come by when you're not at your best."

Gabby replaced the vent cover, closing the chapter on Alfred and the summer that she would no longer allow to haunt her.

"Yes, Mama." She straightened her dress and went upstairs, feeling foolish for being so frantic. She closed her bedroom door, dropped onto her bed, and cried herself to sleep.

Chapter Two

Present Day

The old Victorian-style house at the end of Sandpiper Lane stood like a ghostly gray mammoth, poised between the road and the dazzling turquoise waters of the Gulf of Mexico. Its faded white paint had peeled and cracked from years of exposure to the beating coastal sun and unrelenting winds. A pair of lace curtains still hung in the dark upstairs window. Melanie stared at it, praying she wouldn't see an apparition floating by. Just the idea gave her a shudder.

"Are you sure about this?" Kathryn asked, as they lugged Melanie's suitcases past the mounds of moving boxes and over the wild overgrowth that had crawled across the battered front walk.

Melanie shielded her eyes from the sun, peering up at the structure. "Not really," she said.

"If you're doing this for Gram, she's not here to enjoy it," Kathryn said gently. "This is a big project, Mel."

"It's not like I had any other options," she replied. "Gram was right in her letter—I don't have anything left for me in Tennessee. I haven't worked in three years, except for taking care of Gram."

When Gram had to start chemotherapy, it was a logical solution for Melanie to step in. Kathryn was married with a child, and her mother was too busy with the farm to stay with her. Melanie was single and could easily drive into the city to work if she had to.

She'd been able to juggle it all for a little while, but as Gram got weaker, spending long hours getting ill from the chemo and needing someone to help her move around the house, Melanie found herself with less and less time to spend at her apartment with her fiancé, and many late nights opting for Gram's sofa. When the apartment's lease was up, to her surprise, Adam suggested they live separately. But she understood. It wasn't sensible to spend such an incredible amount on a home that she never lived in. But none of it felt permanent, until Adam sat her down about two years ago and told her they were going in different directions. What he'd meant was that *he* was going in a different direction. She hadn't gone anywhere but Gram's. She wondered if she'd ever be able to go back to her old life again.

"You don't want to just rent a nice new apartment somewhere and get your feet wet in corporate America again?" asked Kathryn now, tearing Melanie away from the past. "Get those marketing guns firing once more…"

"My last interview—the *third* one I've gone on now—was a no. My skills are outdated." She rubbed the pinch that was forming in her shoulder, her attention fluttering back to that dark window upstairs, the eerie blackness of it chipping away at her resolve.

Her sister's gaze swept across the front porch with uncertainty and she grimaced as she jiggled the railing.

With a sense of purpose, Melanie headed toward the door. When she stepped onto the porch, her foot suddenly plunged through the rotted step to the sandy ground below and she reached out for her big sister.

"Oh!" Kathryn blurted, grabbing Melanie's arm. Her sister held her hand while Melanie attempted to free herself, her balance wavering.

"I mean, your inheritance is better than what *I* got, which is nothing," Kathryn said, helping Melanie to right herself. "But I totally get it. You were always the closest to her. You were there with her until the very end…"

"You sure it's better?" Melanie teased with a bewildered chuckle, pointing down at the gaping hole in the steps.

Kathryn shared in her amusement as they slipped the key into the lock and opened the door. When they got inside, the house smelled of rotting wood and age. Melanie's bag fell with an airy smack onto the old floor and sent a plume of dust into the air, making them both cough. The old floral wallpaper had yellowed and peeled off the wall in the humidity.

Melanie clicked on the light switch and the old chandelier in the parlor lit up like a neglected piece of costume jewelry, sections of it missing. "So, they've gotten the lights on," she said. "At least there's that."

"Don't you want to stay in the hotel with me?" Kathryn asked.

Melanie shook her head, opening the old lace curtains at the window, stirring up more dust. "I have the air mattress I packed, and I want to plan the redesign right away if I'm going to transform this place into a bed and breakfast. I need to start turning a profit."

Kathryn sent a tentative look up the stairs. "You're not worried about ghosts?"

Melanie laughed. "Not at all."

But she was putting on a brave face for her sister. She knew all the stories about the man who'd lived there alone ever since he'd built it, and while she hadn't ever had proof the house was haunted, there was definitely a thick sadness that penetrated the air.

Kathryn pulled the rest of the bags through the front door and then the two women set about bringing in Melanie's moving boxes.

"All right," Kathryn said, clapping the dust off her hands once they'd finished. "I'm heading back to the hotel so I can work. I've got three investment portfolios to draw up for clients and Ryan wants me to read him a story on video call—I promised." She slid a box out of the way and opened the front door, letting in a salty breeze. "But swear that we'll do some beachy things together before I head home tomorrow morning. It will have been just Ryan alone with Toby for twenty-four hours, so you know what a mess I'm going back to."

Melanie laughed. Kathryn might be going home to crayon murals all over the white walls. Toby was a big kid himself, the most fun brother-in-law she could have asked for. She'd often thought about how great an uncle he'd have been for her own children. The only emotion left from her breakup with Adam was the emptiness at the loss of her plans for a family. It had always been an anticipated step, but with no one in her life now, it seemed an impossible one.

"And I know you want to get started on this," Kathryn continued, waving a hand through the air, "but you've had a lot to deal with. You could use a little me-time. We're at the *beach*!"

"I promise to take a break, and we'll go out," Melanie assured her.

"Call me if you need me."

"Okay," she said, before Kathryn closed her into the gloomy air of the house.

In the silence after her sister left, the space was unnerving and lonesome, making her feel as if she couldn't catch a breath. "Gram, what am I supposed to do with this?" she asked, her voice echoing through the entryway. She remembered Gram's words about ghosts being there if they had something to say, and she listened with every bit of her focus, but all she heard was the buzz of the chandelier in the parlor.

The weight of the job ahead of her settled on her shoulders, and she wondered if she'd done the right thing taking the inheritance money. She paced to the back of the house and opened the door with a creak, the briny air filling her lungs. White sands and turquoise water glistening in the sun stretched as far as she could see. The rhythmic shushing of the gulf as it lapped onto the shore instantly relaxed her. At least she had this view to calm her spirit. Melanie sat down on the back step, thinking about the last time she'd talked with Gram about this house, the breeze blowing her hair and momentarily relieving the sticky heat that had enveloped her.

"I've always loved this house," Gram said as they strolled by it. That vacation had been the last time Melanie remembered her being well. Every morning that they were at the beach, her grandmother got up with the sun, did her makeup, styled her hair, and put on her favorite vacation attire: a flowing tank top and a pair of shorts with her braided sea-grass sun visor. They would spend their days taking a walk together, collecting shells and talking.

"It's a mess," Melanie had said to Gram as she took in the rundown house. "It's a wonder someone doesn't just tear it down."

Gram stopped in front of it, putting her hands on her hips as a seagull squawked overhead. "It is definitely a mess." She turned to Melanie. "But I don't think it should be torn down."

"You're right," Melanie agreed. "Maybe someone could buy it and fix it up, return it to its original glory."

Gram's eyes lit up. "That would be something, wouldn't it?"

Allowing herself to fall into the dream they were spinning, Melanie stared at the house, and in her mind, the peeled siding healed itself to a bright white, the sagging front porch straightened, pots of red begonias appeared next to white rocking chairs that sat under whirring paddle fans. The crumbling brick chimney became new again, pulling the roof up with it, and the shingles began popping back to their glorious slate gray. The dark space inside the windows lightened, the bright interior paint showing through them. The stone path leading to the house began to fill with moss, the bright green tucking in around each stepping-stone. The sea grass out back blew to the side, revealing the foaming cobalt water just behind it.

"It definitely would be something," Melanie said, breathless. "Alfred Ellis spent his whole life in this house all alone. It's so big… As if he'd planned to fill it with a family but never did."

"Mm," Gram said.

"Something in my gut makes me wonder if he haunts the house because he doesn't want to be alone."

"So you believe he haunts it?" Gram asked.

"Only if he has something to say." She repeated Gram's words with a grin.

Gram smiled back at her, her eyebrows lifting.

"If I owned it," Melanie carried on, "I'd make it into a bed and breakfast, every space occupied by people, their laughter and chatter keeping him company. He'd never have to haunt it. He could just be."

"That's a lovely idea," Gram told her.

Now, Melanie sat on the broken back porch, digging her feet into the sand, wondering if she shouldn't have let the romantic idea of the house affect her that day. Look at her—Gram thought she'd been serious! Before taking care of her grandmother full time, she'd worked for a marketing company, after all. What did she know about restoring a historical house or running a bed and breakfast?

Her grandmother had spent her childhood in this village before she'd met Melanie's grandfather and moved to the small town of Spring Hill, Tennessee. Rosemary Bay was one of Melanie's favorite places to visit. Once a year, she and the family would all come back, and Melanie's fondest memories were of the village. She and Gram had played checkers at the counter of the old drug store, and they'd visit with the owner of the local bookshop who always threw in a free book if they bought two. And one of Melanie's favorite memories was riding bikes with Gram down the old wooden boardwalks, bumping along, the little baskets on the front of their bicycles bouncing in time with the *clack clack* of the wheels on the boards.

Rosemary Bay was a safe place where she could come to get away from it all, but Melanie had never considered living here. She'd grown up in Spring Hill and the only other place she'd lived was in Nashville with Adam. She had never considered trading in her wedge heels for flip-flops. Yet here she was. It was as if she were still on autopilot, just trying to find some relief from the loss of Gram. But even the calming waters couldn't give her that.

Melanie let herself back inside and had to lean against the door to make the latch match up with the frame so it would stay closed. With a sigh, she stared at the narrow hallway wall, thinking how she couldn't wait for it to come out to make the galley kitchen that sat behind it bigger. Hoping it wasn't a bearing wall, she knocked on it and the plaster gave way, crumbling under her fist and fluttering down to the floor, settling like powder on the dark wood.

"Awesome," she said flatly, kicking the debris over toward the wall with her foot.

The bathrooms were awful—there were even old toiletries in the cabinets still, giving her a shudder as she pushed the old combs and a dirty toothbrush out of the way. The kitchen wasn't in any better shape. The appliances were long gone, many of the cabinet doors either missing or hanging by one hinge. A long, wide, yellowish-brown stain ran down one wall. Melanie tapped it with her finger, the surface mushy from the elements. She went over to the sink and turned on the tap to see if the water worked. The spigot coughed and gurgled, spitting out a brown sludge with a splat. The rusty smell of it turned her stomach and she twisted the knob back to off.

Tears filled her eyes and she'd never felt more alone and lost in her life. "Gram, you've got to help me here. I helped *you* for three years! It's your turn," she said in a whisper. One of the pipes whined, startling her.

Needing to keep going to keep the grief at bay, she pushed her way through the sea of boxes and rounded the staircase, holding on to the loose railing, and slowly climbed the steps of the grand staircase. Something moving caused her to jump, her heart slamming in her chest, but she realized it was only a flapping piece of wallpaper, a draft from down the hall pushing it back and forth. She surveyed the hallway, holding her breath, thinking about the ghost that everyone in the village talked about.

The old wooden boards creaked under her feet, and she dragged her fingers along the wall in a feeble attempt to keep her balance if the floor gave way. She checked all the rooms, delighted that none of them had felt extra cold or off in any way. "And *you*, Mr. Ellis, just stay where you are and don't come out," she murmured to Alfred. "You'll give me a heart attack."

She stood there in the silence and waited, testing the house, praying she wouldn't hear anything from the owner. Gram's voice filtered back into her mind: *If he has something to say.* She was aware of the rising and falling of her chest with her breathing, the grittiness on her fingers from the dust in the house, and the perspiration trickling down her neck. But to her relief, there was nothing more. The quiet was bittersweet because, while she didn't want the home to be haunted, she felt more isolated than she ever had before. It was just her and this house.

With a deep breath, she went downstairs to start unpacking boxes.

"I don't think I'd ever felt so grimy in my life," Melanie said, as she applied lip-gloss in the visor mirror of her sister's car. After spending the entire afternoon unpacking and cleaning the house, she'd barely scratched the surface. She'd called the air-conditioning guys, ordered her appliances, and scheduled to have someone knock out the wall in the kitchen to open up the space. Then she'd showered at Kathryn's hotel when she'd realized that even the water in the bathroom pipes at the house was the color of apple cider, like it had been in the kitchen.

"Were you able to get a plumber?" Kathryn asked, making the turn to the main road leading to the beachside bar they'd chosen for drinks and dinner.

"Yes, thank goodness. I've got someone coming first thing tomorrow morning." She leaned her elbow on the open car window, the coastal wind blowing her dark hair back as she took in the view. The long stretch of pristine beach was the color of a fresh pearl, peeking from behind the mounds of sea grass that lined the road. "But as I was cleaning, I kept finding more and more that needs to be repaired inside, and I know I've got a lot more to do."

"Oh, I wish I could stay, but I've got to get back to work."

"I know. Thanks for bringing in all the boxes with me. That was a big help."

They pulled into the lot of Buster's Beachside Bar, a little thatched-roof structure that was plopped right in the sand, brightly colored surfboards flanking the teal door, all the oversized windows open to the street on one side and the beach on the other.

"Think we could join them?" Kathryn asked, pointing to a game of volleyball going on in the back.

"I'm not lifting a finger," Melanie replied with a grin. "Unless it's to lift a cocktail to my lips."

She opened the door and the sound of beach music filled her ears, the laughter at the tables instantly elevating her mood. This was why she'd moved here, and she'd keep reminding herself that once the renovation was finished, she'd spend every day in paradise.

The hostess showed them to a table that overlooked the gulf and handed them their menus. "Are you on vacation?" she asked as they got settled.

"She is," Melanie answered, nodding to Kathryn. "I'm a new resident."

"Oh, wonderful," the hostess said with a smile. "Whereabouts do you live?"

"I just bought the old house on Sandpiper Lane."

The hostess's eyes widened. "Seen any ghosts?"

Kathryn gave her a knowing look.

"Not yet," Melanie replied. "So far there's just a lot of renovating to do."

"See that guy over there," she said, pointing to a tall man in the back corner, playing darts with a group of friends. He had broad shoulders and an easy smile. "He's amazing at renovations. And one of the greatest people in town." The hostess called over to him to get his attention. "Hey, Josh!"

The man turned around, his piercing blue eyes looking their way and then sliding over to Melanie, his chiseled jaw setting.

"This is the owner of the old Ellis house. Think she could use your contracting services?"

He laughed.

"I'm serious," she said with shared amusement.

He shook his head. "I'm not available." He turned back around toward his friends. One of them clapped him on the back, making him laugh again, and his wide smile lifting all the way to his eyes nearly took Melanie's breath away.

"Wait, *contracting*?" Melanie asked, trying to concentrate on the matter in hand. "What kind of contracting?"

"Josh Claiborne is a builder. The best in the village."

"He's probably too expensive for me then…"

"He works for himself, so his prices aren't bad. He did a kitchen remodel for my mom, and she was really happy with it. But he's leaving us, so if you want him, better grab him now. He's moving in a week or so. We're all gonna miss him so much."

"Oh," Melanie said, looking back over at him. He'd thrown a dart, just missing the bull's eye.

"We're so sad to see him go. Josh is a great guy—grown up here all his life…"

The manager called the hostess, pulling her attention in another direction.

"Well, I've got guests to seat," the woman said, gesturing to the group of people that had gathered at the front of the bar. "Your waiter will be with you shortly."

"Maybe you could get him to give you a quote," Kathryn suggested once the hostess had walked off.

"On what—the whole house?" Melanie let out a desperate laugh. "I don't even know where to begin articulating what I need done yet," she said, shaking her head, deflated. "Even if he was staying in town, he didn't seem interested anyway."

Just then a waiter came over. "Hello," he said with a polite smile. "I heard you all talking about Josh. He gonna do some work for you?"

"I don't think so," Melanie said. "He's moving, I hear."

"Ah, yeah. Mickey, the owner, swears Josh can't leave or the revenue from bar tabs will be cut by fifty percent."

"I heard that, Alex," Josh called over to the waiter, without looking around.

"I'm just the messenger," he teased.

"I don't drink *that* much." Josh turned now, his gaze flitting over to Melanie again before settling on the waiter. "Half the beers he gives me are on the house."

"Yeah, he's just gonna miss ya, that's all."

Something crossed Josh's face and he waved a hand. "Better get their orders. Mickey needs his bar tabs."

The waiter grinned, turning back to Melanie and Kathryn.

Melanie ordered a Rosemary Bay Smash, a concoction of three different rums and island fruit with wedges of pineapple in the shapes of different sea creatures, and Kathryn got an Island Banger, with rum, lemon, mint, and lime soda. The waiter set down two paper napkins on their table before heading to the bar.

"If I can teach you something as your big sister," Kathryn said, standing up, "it's that you have to be assertive if you want things done. I'm going to go ask the contractor if he'll give you a quote."

"Wait," Melanie said, scooting her chair out with a screech. "I need to get my ducks in a row before I start taking bids."

"Seize the moment," her sister said over her shoulder.

Melanie scrambled to follow Kathryn. He was leaving anyway; what was the point?

"My name is Kathryn Woodward and this is my sister, Melanie Simpson. Would you mind if we joined you for a game of darts?" Kathryn asked, as Melanie came to a skidding halt behind her.

"Definitely not," one of his friends said, handing Kathryn a dart. "I'm Steven." The rest of them paired off, Josh's attention falling on Melanie who seemed to be his new partner. He took in an annoyed breath, and at the sight of it, she instantly regretted following her sister over.

The waiter, who'd come from the bar with their drinks, followed them to the corner of the restaurant and set the glasses on a barrel that doubled as a table. Josh eyed Melanie's curving glass with the pineapple dolphin, subtly shaking his head.

Kathryn tossed a dart toward the board, hitting the very rim on the outside.

"Let's practice." Steven leaned in, clearly flirting, and took her hand to show her how to aim it. Kathryn pulled back and wriggled her ring finger in the air, her wedding ring glimmering in the light. Melanie rolled her eyes at Steven's behavior and the corner of Josh's mouth rose just slightly in amusement.

"He's a good guy," Josh said into her ear, his voice low and deep, surprising her.

She picked up her drink and took a sip, the bite of the rum tickling her taste buds through the fruity nectar.

"So, what made you buy the Ellis house?" Steven asked Melanie, giving a glance to Josh. Josh turned away, the breeze coming through the windows blowing his sandy blond hair across his forehead. He ran his fingers through it, pushing it back into place. He was effortlessly attractive but clearly put out that Melanie and Kathryn had imposed on his group.

"I needed a challenge," Melanie replied, not wanting to get into it.

That condescending smirk she'd seen on Josh's face showed up again. "Well, you definitely got one," he muttered over his shoulder.

"Melanie actually needs someone to help her fix it up," Kathryn said, leaning in between them.

"I'm sure she does," Josh replied, handing Melanie another dart.

Melanie tossed the dart, but it hit the edge of the board and tumbled to the floor.

Josh went over and picked it up. Then he threw it at the board, the dart sailing through the air. It only missed the bull's eye by a millimeter. He offered an annoyed shake of his head at the dartboard.

"Can't quite hit the mark tonight," Steven said to him, slugging him playfully in the arm. "Your focus is off."

In defiance, he sent another dart toward the board. It hit just beside the center. "Damn it," he said under his breath, making Steven laugh.

"We heard you're the best person for the job," Kathryn continued, while Josh plucked the dart from the board.

"Well, I'm not." Josh threw his last dart, hitting the mark. With a look of satisfaction, he pointed to Steven and then took a swig from his bottle of beer. "My focus is just fine," he said.

"Sooo…" Kathryn continued, waggling her eyebrows at him. "Know anyone interested in renovating Mel's house?"

"Is that what you go by—Mel?" he asked, avoiding the question.

"Melanie, actually," she replied, finally making eye contact. The intensity in his eyes was so strong, however, that she quickly glanced back toward her drink.

"Well, Melanie. I don't have a clue who could take that project on, but it's definitely not me." He took another drink from his beer, draining it and pitching the bottle into the trashcan in the corner, sinking it like a three-point shot.

"Did you all want to order some dinner?" the waiter asked, appearing beside Melanie and offering her a menu.

"Yes," she replied. Distracted, only then did she realize that Josh was telling his friends goodbye and leaving the bar. "Wait!" she heard herself call over to him. Holding up a finger to the waiter, she ran over to Josh. He definitely didn't seem like the right person for the job, but she didn't have a clue where else to turn.

"Could you maybe just come over and show me what repairs might be the best investment for my money?" she asked.

He pursed his lips, his chest puffing up with air slowly before he let it out. "I don't think so."

"Why?"

"He's heading for those big city lights next week," Steven said from the other side of the dining area.

"Just a few minutes of your time?" she wondered aloud, hoping he could at least give her the number of another contractor. He was the best in the business, the hostess had told her. Surely, he'd know someone who could help her.

"I just don't have time," he replied. "I took a job in New York. Those guys over there—this was my farewell party." He pushed the glass door open, the orange sky making it difficult to see. "I hope you enjoy the house." Those sapphire eyes landed on her for just a tick before one of the guys called his name, beckoning him back over to them.

"Come on, Josh," the guy called from where Kathryn was standing. "It's still early. Mickey hasn't even come in. You know he's gonna want to buy us all beers."

"And I haven't had a chance to beat you yet," another one said, waving a dart.

Despite clearly wanting to leave, Josh relented and returned to his friends.

"You've definitely got time for one more game," Steven said when they'd reached the group. "And this pretty little lady just put a bet down on the table." He gestured to Kathryn. "I figured you might want to be aware of it before I accept."

"What's that then?" Josh asked, his body language screaming that he'd rather be anywhere but this game.

"The girls play you and me. We win, and they buy us all a beer. You don't have to be home just yet, do you?"

He eyed the group cautiously. "And if they win?"

Out of respect for the women, Steven didn't flinch, but Melanie knew what he was probably thinking: after hers and her sister's attempts at dart throwing, their wallets would be empty by the end of the night.

"If we win," Kathryn replied, "you spend your last week helping Melanie with the house."

"I'm not working on that house," Josh said.

"Are you afraid we'll actually win?" Melanie asked, the rum giving her courage.

He stared at her, a tiny spark of interest in his eyes.

"Free beer is a good way to end the night, my friend," Steven said, giving him a clap on the back. "We'll play one to twenty."

"Fine," Josh said, flagging the bartender and ordering himself another drink.

"I'm a quick learner," Melanie said to the group of guys, although she'd surprised even herself. Josh's jaw tightened. He hadn't spoken in the last ten minutes, his irritation steadily growing.

She and Kathryn had hung in there, and two more cocktails later, they'd managed to make it to the final number. With one dart left, all Melanie had to do was hit the twenty, and then if Josh missed, they'd win.

Melanie aimed, steadying herself, and sent the dart off, squeezing her eyes shut.

"What?" Josh whispered in complete shock, causing her to open her eyes.

She'd hit the mark. Kathryn's eyes bulged, as she looked over at her sister in complete shock. Melanie clapped a hand to her mouth.

"Wait," Steven said, coming between them, addressing Josh. "What happens if you hit twenty and there's a tie?"

"Then we go our separate ways," Josh replied, looking at his watch. "I really need to go soon."

"Why don't we do sudden death so we can get our beers?"

"How did I let you talk me into this?" Josh asked, swinging the dart between his fingers. "If I miss this, I'm spending my last week working on the Ellis house, my mother will literally stop speaking to me, and I still have to pack and get my house ready."

"Sorry," Steven said. "Just hit the twenty and it'll all be fine."

"No pressure," Josh said with a derisive chuckle.

Josh squinted, his gaze laser-focused, his breathing steady. Shoulders relaxed, he aimed the dart and let it go. Melanie held her breath, the dart seeming to take a painful amount of time to reach its target. It was headed directly for the bull's eye and then suddenly, it curved just slightly, and then, *thump*, it stuck in the dartboard. Kathryn and Melanie shared a moment of hushed silence.

"You've got to be kidding me," Josh said under his breath.

Instead of twenty, the dart had hit the unlucky number thirteen.

Chapter Three

"Morning," Josh said, unsmiling, from his vintage red and white Ford truck, a ladder sticking out of it. His tone was even more sobering than it had been last night, the festive air of his going away party no longer surrounding them, the set of his lips letting Melanie know he had no desire to be there. He scratched his stubble as he neared her in jeans and a wrinkled T-shirt, looking like he'd just rolled out of bed.

"Morning," she returned from the front porch.

Melanie had gotten up with the sun. The plumber had been by, and while he'd fixed the kitchen sink and the downstairs bathroom, he'd told her that a lot of the pipes would have to be replaced, which wasn't surprising, given the yellow and brown liquid they all spewed. She'd had to brush her teeth with a bottle of water, and without a shower, she'd pulled her long hair into a ponytail to keep the tangles at bay.

Josh's gaze roamed her face for a moment before he turned his attention warily to the house, leaning over and tugging on an old piece of wood siding that was loose.

"Not much to shield you from the elements," he noted, pulling the plank off the house with his bare hands.

She folded her arms and peered up at the thick gray cloud cover, praying it wouldn't rain before she could repair the broken window she'd found in the back room upstairs.

He climbed the steps, joining her on the porch. "Better be careful with your bare feet. You could get hurt." He tapped the edges of the wood around the hole she'd made yesterday when she'd stepped onto the porch. The old board crumbled under his boot. "Where do you want to start," he said, his lips set in a straight line.

"I thought I'd let you look around and see what stands out the most so I can begin to make a plan," she replied, opening the front door to let him in.

He blew air through his lips, the disapproval in his expression causing her to question her sister's decision to make last night's bet.

Even though he was less than friendly, she tried to make light conversation as they walked through the rooms. "It's nice having someone in the house with me. Last night, it felt so cold and spooky being here all by myself." It had taken her ages to fall asleep on her air mattress, the emptiness of the giant house having its way with her imagination. Every creak and pop as the old house settled in its spot caused her to see things in the dark, her heart racing. Twice, she'd turned the lights on just to make sure she was alone. The rest of the time, she'd squeezed her eyes shut and willed herself to go to sleep by conjuring up what Gram had told her when she was a girl: *There's nothing to be afraid of. The night is just the day, tucked in tight and fast asleep.*

Melanie tried to get a read on Josh when he didn't say anything, noticing the curiosity that flickered in his eyes as he took in the space. He tipped his head up at the dusty chandelier, studying it as he clicked on the light switch, the timeworn glass fixture coming to life with a gentle buzzing sound. He clicked it off.

"I've heard about the guy who lived here," she said. "How he was some sort of recluse." She hoped to have a friendly exchange, but he didn't respond, instead answering his phone which was ringing in his back pocket.

"Hello?" He turned away from her without even a glance. "I told you before, I'm not interested in selling." He paced back and forth, the phone pressed against his ear. "Not. Interested. If you want any further information as to the legalities of the situation, you can call my lawyer. The land is private." He hung up on the caller.

Melanie smiled uneasily in an attempt to defuse the tension.

He went into the kitchen and looked around as if the call had never come in, making her even more curious about it. But as she watched him more closely, she could see the thoughts swimming around in his eyes even though he was working to hide them. He pressed on the floor by the sink with his foot, the surface bending with his movement.

"The floors are all rotted," he said.

"I'd noticed that when I was mopping yesterday. How bad is it?"

"Well…" He stomped his foot down with all his might, the boards giving way, a cloud of dust and a foul earthy stench pluming up, making them both duck away, covering their mouths and noses.

"So the floors should *all* be replaced?" she asked once it had settled, holding her breath between her words.

"Definitely. Have you had the house tested for asbestos?"

She nodded. "It's had certified asbestos removal—I had it done before I moved in."

"Good," he said. "But with the debris floating around this place, you'll want to protect yourself. Do you have a face mask and a pair of work boots?"

"No," she replied, worry settling over her.

"You should definitely have a mask, gloves, and boots." He frowned, obviously displeased by what was in front of him. "I've got a couple of face masks in the truck we can wear."

She shuffled up beside him as he made his way back to the front door and followed him outside, tiptoeing carefully across the path.

"You do understand that a renovation of this size could take years with the wrong contractors," he said, handing her a mask and shutting the door of his truck while assessing her bare feet. He looked back up at her face. "You need to know what you're doing."

She felt short of breath. She understood that this would be an undertaking to say the least, but now it was clear that she was in well and truly over her head. "I don't have years. I'm hoping to open a bed and breakfast to bring in some income. I need to get up and running as soon as possible."

He looked past her at the house. Then he laughed disbelievingly, causing her to bristle. "Somehow, while trying to get free beers for my friends, I've managed to get wrapped up in *this*." He laughed again. "Unbelievable."

Melanie snapped into business mode to keep the tears from pricking her eyes. "All I need is to get your professional opinion on the best course of action, and then I'd like to get the repairs completed as soon as possible." She already wanted to get rid of this guy. She had enough concern over the house without him making her feel worse.

His laughter faded. "I'm a contractor; you need an inspector first to make a list of immediate potential problems. Have you had a full inspection done?"

"I had a general one with the sale of the house."

"All right, let me take a look at that one, and I'll start there."

They spent the next hour sitting on the broken-down porch out back, going over the inspection on her laptop, the wind picking up speed and blowing wildly around them. Dark skies had provided some much-needed relief from the intense heat, but the humidity wrapped around them with a menacing thickness.

Melanie wrote notes madly, scratching down any comment Josh made. But she felt even more dejected after he explained what the repairs on the list would probably cost her. It would use almost all the money she'd inherited from her grandmother, plus what she guessed she'd get from the sale of Gram's house back in Spring Hill.

When they'd finished going through the document, Josh stood up and stretched his back. "Well, I'll guess I'll try to see you tomorrow."

"You're leaving already?" Melanie asked. He hadn't even looked through the house properly.

"We can't just sit around. I've gotta run to the hardware store if I want to get plywood before it sells out," he said. "I wasn't exactly planning to do this job, and I have a laundry list of things to get done."

"You need plywood?" she asked, wondering if he had another job he was doing or if it was for her floors and, if so, how much it would cost her.

He stared at her strangely for a second before exhaling slowly. "I suppose you have no plan in place to get this heap of wood ready for the hurricane that's coming through in about thirty hours?"

Her blood ran cold. "A hurricane?" Her head began to pound as panic set in. She'd been without a television or a radio since she'd gotten there, and she'd been so concerned with the state of the house that she hadn't even considered what might be going on around her. "I've never prepared for a hurricane before. What should I do to get the house ready?" she asked feebly.

His expression was blank, that all-too-familiar frustration lurking under his features. He got out his tape measure and left her, trudging over the yard toward the end of the house. He stretched the tape across a window and then fed it up to the top of the frame. When he'd finished, he walked around the back, checking a few more measurements.

Peering at his watch, he jogged back over to her. "Go get some shoes and I'll show you what you need."

When Melanie got to the truck with her flip-flops and her handbag which she'd grabbed inside, Josh was already in the driver's seat with the engine running. He seemed pensive. Without a word he pulled away, the peeling, rundown house looking defiant in her side-view mirror as they drove down the sandy beach road toward town. The sea grass along the edge of the road danced in the breeze, the gulf ebbing and flowing as if it were in a hurry. When they reached the main road, the line of fleeing vacationers in their cars headed out of town was miles long in the other direction.

"You might want to take a look at your insurance policy," he said with that same laugh he'd had earlier, and she wished he'd stayed quiet. "If the storm knocks the house down, they might pay to build you a new one. That's your best-case-scenario."

"I want the house that I have," she said defensively. "It's important to me."

He looked over at her curiously. "Why?" His indifference rubbed her the wrong way.

"Because my gram and I always loved the house. She grew up here, and we used to drive by it every summer when we came for our vacation. We had long talks about how we'd bring it back to life. When she passed, she left me the money to buy it."

He made a turn down a side street, his silence making her feel like he disagreed with her decision. "I can board up your windows," he finally said, "but we haven't checked the condition of the roof. I'm willing to bet there's a whole lot more to secure than what we know... Do you have flood insurance?"

She nodded.

"Good." He pulled into the parking lot. "I wonder if I can access the roof through the attic—do you know?"

"I haven't gotten that far," she admitted.

"This evening, I can try to add some roof straps inside the attic that will attach the roof to the walls and keep it from blowing off the top of the house. We'll need to seal the windows, secure that broken one at the back, and make sure the porches are firmly anchored in the ground."

"Okay," she said, feeling overwhelmed by it all. *When it rains, it pours*, she thought. *Literally.*

Chapter Four

The narrow village streets were littered with cars as vacationers tried to escape the upcoming storm, heading inland. Horns honked and people were yelling out their windows, frustrated at the traffic jam that stretched in every direction. The sky grumbled in protest, the gray clouds so thick it felt like they were pinning everyone down.

Josh had gotten the plywood for her house and the materials he needed to secure the roof, but it didn't help Melanie's confidence that the house could withstand a storm which, according to Josh, could literally rip the roof off the place. Melanie wasn't sure what other supplies she'd need to weather the hurricane, but she didn't want to sit around waiting for it. So she ventured into the village to see if she could get some nonperishables and a flashlight. Bewildered by the manic scene, she didn't even know where to go. Stores were boarding up, closing their doors, the local supermarket dark, the hardware store a ghost town. She pulled into the next strip mall and got out of the car, aimlessly walking toward the shops, hoping something was open. The wind pushed against her, the palm trees arching precariously to the side in the gusts.

"Oh my Lord, child," a woman said when she got inside the small beach shop. "What are you doing out in this mess? You need to go home!" She was buzzing around, moving glassware to the center of the store. "I can't help you right now," she said, as she strained to pull a table away from the window. Melanie grabbed the other side to help her.

"I don't know what I'm supposed to do," Melanie told her, tears forming in her eyes, with no idea where to go now all the stores were shut. "Let me help you get this shop ready for the storm. Show me what to do."

It was clear that the woman had no earthly idea why Melanie had come in, but she wasn't asking questions. "Grab those displays over there," she said, pointing to a glass jewelry display case of handmade necklaces. "Let's get that stuff into the back room and up on the shelves in case it floods."

"Okay," Melanie said urgently. Rushing over and opening the case, she started emptying it, threading necklaces onto her arm to keep them from tangling. A small sign beside them read that they were all Maryann Originals.

"This your first storm?" the woman asked, an understanding look washing over her.

"Yes," Melanie said as they went into the back room.

The lady delicately removed the first necklace from Melanie's arm. "I'm Maryann Bowman," she said.

"Melanie Simpson. I bought the old Ellis house."

Maryann's eyes grew to the size of saucers. "Oh my… Did you bring an army of carpenters to assist you with that?"

Melanie shook her head. "Josh Claiborne is helping a little."

Maryann broke out into a fond expression. "Well. Then you're in great hands."

"You know him?" she asked.

"Everyone around here knows Josh." She returned to the front room, gathering the coffee mugs from a table display in the center. "Hand me that box over there, would you?"

Melanie grabbed the empty cardboard box by the register and passed it to Maryann.

"Yep, we all know him," she said, pulling a piece of bubble wrap from the box and covering the mug, working efficiently. "But none of us can figure out why he's leaving us. Things just won't be the same without him."

As Melanie helped with the mugs, she wondered why the woman's perception of Josh was so different from her own.

"What do you mean, things won't be the same without him?" she asked.

"He's such a light to everyone he meets. There's not a bad bone in his body." She lifted the full box and carried it over to the counter on the back wall, quickly grabbing a second box and moving in on the table of sand sculptures. "Did you know that the school bus broke down one day along the side of the main road? The kids were so scared with all the traffic going by. Josh saw them and stopped to help. While they waited for another bus, he went next door to the ice cream shop, gave them his credit card, and took the ice cream orders of every child on the bus."

"That's so… kind of him," Melanie said, now wondering if it was just her who made him so standoffish.

"He does stuff like that all the time."

"He's going to board up my windows for me," she said.

Maryann smiled. "That's real sweet of him. He must really like you. Especially since not a soul in his family would ever dare set foot in the Ellis house."

She wondered why that was. But as she went to ask, a clap of thunder silenced her. If he did like her, he had a funny way of showing it.

"Hey," Melanie said to Josh from behind her mask when he came through the door at sunset, the sky a deep shade of gray, carrying a bag of supplies. She was on the floor, taping a tarp she'd gotten from Maryann over the hole he'd made in the kitchen.

When he got closer to her, she could see beads of perspiration at his temples and redness on his skin from the heat. With a bang, he dropped the bag down on the kitchen counter. All business, he tuned a portable radio to the weather report and set it next to the bag. "*If you are remaining in the area,*" the announcer chirped, "*please use extreme caution. Find shelter and prepare. The national weather service has predicted seventy-five-mile-an-hour winds, and landfall is expected within hours rather than days. We're tracking the storm and will bring you the latest every half-hour.*"

"The storm's picked up speed. We need to hurry," he said without even a hello. So much for Maryann's version of Josh.

"What's in there?" she asked, pointing to the bag.

"Three days' worth of food and extra batteries for the radio. I figured if you haven't prepped a house for a hurricane, you probably haven't ridden one out either. It's a wild ride."

She stood up and brushed her hands off on her shorts, worry consuming her.

"I've got bottled water in the truck. I'll bring it in, in a minute. Is the plywood still stacked out back where we put it?" he asked.

"Yes," she said, pulling down her mask. "How can I help?"

"Try not to get in my way," he snapped. "I'll get the windows covered and then work on the roof. We don't have time for chitchat."

She narrowed her eyes at him. His tone was still irritated, and Melanie had enough to manage with the house and her grief over the death of her grandmother. She didn't need him coming in and barking orders. Frustration bubbled up inside her.

"Please don't speak to me like I'm some sort of incapable sidekick," she blurted, marching after him as he made his way to the door.

He turned around, his expression unbothered, only infuriating her more. "A category-four hurricane is headed straight for us, arriving well before we were all warned, the town is in literal chaos as everyone scrambles to prepare, and I'm trying to secure the house that I'm selling so that I can pay my rent in New York. Yet here I stand, wasting valuable time, trying to hold down this pile of junk."

Melanie squared her shoulders defiantly to hide the total fear that now consumed her. A blast of wind blew outside. The back door latch gave way and sent the door flying open, slamming into the wall behind it, causing her to yelp.

Josh laughed. "You ain't seen nothin' yet."

She walked over and shut the door. "I didn't ask for this," she said, swallowing her emotion. "If you want to go, then go. I'll board up my own windows."

"It won't do much good when the roof blows off this place," he said. "You gonna secure that too?"

"I will if I have to," she retorted, overwhelmed, her hands starting to shake, silently pleading with Gram to tell her why in the world she thought this was a good idea. She shoved her trembling hands into the pockets of her shorts, blinking as tears started to fill her eyes. One escaped down her cheek and she brushed it away.

Josh's intensity withered, and he softened a little bit. "Come outside with me a second?" he asked.

Melanie followed him through the back door, leaving it open. The gulf water was rough, crashing on the beach in angry white foam under a hazy, dark sky while the wind lashed at them.

"Look," he said. "I know I lost that bet, and I know you need help, but I can't work on this project. I'll get you ready for the storm, and then you'll need to find someone else."

She nodded, sitting down on the sand, oblivious to the gales coming off the gulf, completely dazed by everything. It didn't matter to her that Josh was standing there or that she probably seemed like she had no idea what she was doing. The truth was, she didn't. She shouldn't have bought this house. It was too much to take on. Unable to cope with the absolute anxiety of it all, Melanie put her face in her hands and started to cry.

Josh hovered over her, seemingly hesitating as if he were going to say something. She felt his movement toward her, and for a second, she anticipated his arms encircling her and him telling her it would be okay. But then, without warning, he went inside, the door clapping shut behind him. She hadn't been looking for sympathy, but she would've welcomed even a little compassion.

Melanie took a gulp of briny air and dragged her fingers under her eyes, trying to get herself together. She went in after him and found him hunched over the radio. With a newfound focus, he went out the front door, returning with jugs of water and more food.

"We're not ready," he said, his eyes intense.

"What?" she asked, her lip still quivering.

"We've got to get to work. We're looking at mere hours before the storm makes landfall." That was the first time she'd seen panic on Josh's face.

*

"I can't hold it!" Melanie yelled from her ladder, the rain slamming her as she pressed her soaking hands against the plywood to keep it in place while Josh hammered, his hands moving at warp speed.

"You can do it!" he called back. "Just a bit more!" He pounded again, every bang muffled by the howling wind.

Another large gust rattled the ladder, causing her to wobble, her muscles aching from the weight of the wood as she tried to hold it steady. She knew that at any minute the wind could whip her right off and send her crashing into the angry gulf behind her, but she had to press on. They'd gotten the roof as secure as possible, and all the windows were done except this one, but the storm was worsening and they still hadn't secured the porches.

"Done!" Josh bellowed over the wailing storm, climbing down.

Just then a gust yanked the ladder out from under Melanie and she felt herself falling, the ladder tumbling to the sand below. Her arms flailed as she scrambled for anything to break her fall. She braced for the smack of the hard ground, all her muscles tensed, only to land in a heap on top of Josh as he attempted to catch her. She lay on top of him, his scent of cedar and orange blossom tickling her nose. He'd broken her fall but her body still shook from the shock of it. He stood up and grabbed her hands, pulling her to a standing position. Dizziness made her legs give out under her and Josh threw an arm around her to keep her steady. He helped her walk as quickly as possible, every stride making her wince, the pain in her leg making it difficult to move.

"We have to get inside," he roared, pulling her through the sand as they made a run for the back door. He threw it open and shoved her into the house, straining against the wind to shut the door behind them. "The latch isn't strong. We're going to need to do something to keep this door shut," he said, his wet hair falling across his forehead as he swiveled back and forth, looking for something to keep the door from flying open.

He opened the door again, the rain soaking him and the floor just inside, and grabbed another piece of plywood from the pile at the back of the house. This time, when he shut the door, with the light switch out of reach, it plunged them into darkness. He clicked on a flashlight from his tool belt and handed it to her.

"Hold this steady and aim it toward the door," he said, grabbing nails and the hammer from his belt and nailing the plywood over it.

Melanie stood, aching and trembling as she gripped the flashlight, the beam of light illuminating the darkness, her clothes soaking wet, while Josh nailed furiously to keep the door shut. The wind was too much for him at one point, forcing the door open and ripping the plywood free. In the slip of light outside, she could see that the gulf's furious waves had already gobbled up the shore and were now grabbing at the sand precariously close to the back porch. The house groaned in protest, the wind howling. There was a loud snap outside, but with the windows boarded up, she had no idea what had broken. She focused on the beam of light shining from her flashlight and tried to calm her thumping heart.

When the door was finally secure, Josh started moving the cases of water to the dining room and then he snatched the radio from the counter. "Looks like I have no choice but to ride this thing out with you. Grab the food," he said. "We need to stay in the middle of the house." He clicked on the chandelier, sending beads of yellow light onto the dusty hardwood floor.

"We could bring my air mattress down from upstairs," she said, breathless.

"Great. I'll go get it. Start moving any boxes of things you want to keep safe into the dining room. Is your cell phone charged? If not, you might want to plug it in right now. We probably won't have power very long."

With no ventilation, the temperature in the house was climbing. Melanie wiped the perspiration off her forehead with the back of her arm as she limped into the kitchen and got her cell phone and charger. The screen was alight with a text from Kathryn, asking if she was okay. Melanie fired off a message that she was with Josh, that they were riding out the storm together, and not to worry if she didn't respond. She wasn't sure how long her phone would have service. Then she started frantically digging through her boxes of things to see what needed to go into the dining room.

While the radio blasted updates, Josh returned with her air mattress and dropped it onto the dirty floor, lumping her linens and the pillows she'd brought on top. Another loud crack and a slight movement of the house sent her eyes to the ceiling, but there was no evidence of damage.

"This is a good spot," he said, assessing their location. "It's away from most of the windows and it's close to the stairs in case we flood and need higher ground."

Melanie's breath left her at the thought of fleeing to an upper floor to escape rushing water below. It was as if some sort of cosmic force was protesting everything about her intrusion on this house. Was Alfred trying to tell her she didn't belong here?

The radio barked, *"The worst of the storm is headed toward the Gulf Coast within the next few hours. Please take cover."* The house sounded like it was being torn apart piece by piece from the outside with long squeals and moans, the whole place as unsteady as a deck of cards.

"Are you sure we're safe in here?" she asked.

"Safer than we are outside," he replied, his gaze roaming the ceiling with uncertainty.

The rain pelted the house, the sound of it like a wild fizz as it dropped from the heavens.

"I'm scared," she whispered.

Josh dropped down onto the mattress and patted the space beside him. "We'll get through it," he assured her.

Something crashed against the back of the house, making Melanie scream. She eyed the wall through the open doorway, convinced there could be a boat or a small car sticking through it, but there wasn't anything. She swallowed, gripping her chest.

"The wind might have uprooted a palm tree," Josh said, grabbing his phone and tapping the screen. "The phone tower must be gone. We're on our own."

A muffled howl circled them as if the house itself were whipping around in the storm. Her equilibrium was off from the rocking as it swayed in the wind. "We're gonna blow away," she worried.

"Hopefully not," he said.

Something else hit the house outside and Melanie ducked instinctively. "*Hopefully not?*" she repeated. "You mean there's a chance?"

"The house has stood through years of storms," he told her. "We just have to hope that it makes it through one more."

She glanced around at the crumbling surroundings, suddenly not terribly assured it would.

The rain came down so hard that it sounded like shattering glass now, striking everything in its path. A transformer blew outside and she caught the sight of sparks through the gap in the plywood.

"Are you hungry?" he asked, getting off the mattress and digging around in one of the food bags.

"I don't have an appetite." She felt as if she had a cinderblock on her chest and her body was shaking so much that she could hardly sit up on the air mattress. "I'm terrified," she admitted.

Josh's hands stilled and he came over to her, sitting down so close that their arms were touching. "I don't remember my first hurricane," he said. "I've dealt with them my whole life, living here."

"My grandmother grew up here too, and she said that her family would evacuate whenever a storm came. You don't evacuate?"

He shook his head. "We've been here for five generations. For us, it's just a part of life."

"So I'm going to deal with this alone year after year," she said absentmindedly, expressing the thoughts that she had meant to stay in her head, the weight of her decision to buy the house settling even more heavily upon her shoulders. What was Gram thinking?

"Hey," he said, his tone gentle, the surprise of it snapping her out of her thoughts. "My grandfather used to tell me that a hurricane is just a couple of crazy hours and then you pick up all the pieces and keep going."

Melanie tried to smile. She knew it wasn't as simple as that—people lost their possessions, some even their lives, but she was glad that Josh had tried to soothe her a little. Despite his earlier mood, it was good to have him here.

Melanie was truly rattled, her whole body trembling by the time the eye of the storm reached them. It had been the oddest thing: the tormenting wind and rain, the flying objects hitting the house, one of the boards unstitching from the window, shattering the glass, the pieces falling to the floor in the kitchen—and then it had all just stopped.

Josh opened the front door to view the damage and tears welled up in Melanie's eyes. The yard was nonexistent, littered with large tree trunks, furniture, and a car upended at the edge of the property. She swallowed to keep the sobs from exploding out of her.

"It's a mess," he said. "But it can all be removed. That's part of living on the coast, Melanie. It's terrifying, but then the sun comes out, the gulf waters rush back to where they should be, and the plants begin to bloom again."

She nodded, one of her tears spilling down her cheek. She wiped it away with a jittery finger.

"We're halfway," he said, offering her a little of his strength with the first genuine smile she'd seen on his lips since she'd met him. "We can do it. Let me just fix that window. We've got some extra plywood stacked inside."

She took a step nearer to him, his proximity making her feel safer than she had just a second ago. "I'm glad you're here," she admitted.

"I'm glad *you* are," he said. "I'm certain my mother would give me a solid piece of her mind over the fact that I'm working on the Ellis house," he teased, despite the serious atmosphere. His laugh was different this time. His humor was almost like a peace offering after what they'd just been through.

"Why would your mom be upset?" she asked, allowing the conversation to move away from the sheer mayhem that surrounded them.

"Well, when I was growing up, my mom asked me specifically to never come onto this property if I was invited. She said if I did, my grandmother would roll over in her grave."

"What did your grandmother have to do with this house?"

"My family stayed clear of the owner Alfred Ellis the entire time he was alive. I saw him around town from time to time, but he never looked anyone in the eye. He just took care of his business and went back home. My grandmother couldn't stand the sight of him. I remember once when I was about eight, she was behind him in line at the grocery store. He dropped a bar of soap and I picked it up for him. He smiled at me, but it was forced, almost like the act of smiling was uncomfortable for him. My grandmother set her things down, took my hand, and walked out of the store without buying anything."

"What did she not like about him?"

"She'd never say exactly. We asked her outright once, but she refused to speak of him at all. He must've been a terrible person for her to hate him like that. She loved everyone. He was generally a grumpy man, so people tended to steer clear of him."

"What about your grandfather? Did you ever ask him why your grandmother disliked Alfred?"

Josh shook his head. "He would never talk about anything that would upset my grandmother." He stepped onto the porch and tested the strength of one of the railings, pushing on it. When it didn't budge, Melanie was hit by a wave of relief. She'd half expected it to topple over, given the state of the rest of the house. "It was always just sort of understood that we didn't have any contact with Alfred Ellis or this house, so it didn't come up in conversation. We kept quiet about it so as not to trouble my grandmother."

"I wonder what he did to make her so upset," Melanie wondered aloud.

"All I know is that he wasn't a very nice man. That was all my grandmother ever said about him." Josh brushed away the wet leaves that had blown onto the porch during the first part of the storm, and sat down on the step.

Their clothes still damp from the humidity and running for shelter in the rainstorm, Melanie sat down beside him, indifferent to the fact that she'd sat in a puddle of water. She leaned back on her hands, tipping her head up to allow the sunshine to warm her face, the bright blue sky above her a stark contrast to what had just been over them.

"How long do we have before the eye passes?" she asked.

"By the speed of the storm, I'm guessing we have an hour or so."

"I'm not sure I can take that again," she admitted, looking over at Josh, but he didn't say anything. He seemed to be lost in thought, a sense of calm settling in his expression. The curve of his face was familiar to her now—the first person she'd met as a resident of Rosemary Bay and now the one she knew the best. "I wonder if your house is okay."

He ran his fingers through his wet hair, his pleasant smile falling. "There's no way to know. But there's no use in risking leaving shelter when we've got the other half of the storm to endure."

"Even though the hurricane sort of forced you to, thank you for staying with me," she said. "I truly couldn't have managed this without you."

His chest filled with air, more thoughts surfacing on his face. "You're welcome."

Josh had been her saving grace today, and she knew there was a whole lot more headed their way. She'd never imagined she'd be on the front porch of this battered house with him. But she was glad she was.

Melanie's heart hammered as she lay curled in a ball on the air mattress and tried to sleep, Gram's voice playing over and over in her mind: *Every storm comes to an end.* Josh was next to her, facing the wall. The house swayed so badly in the wind that Melanie was convinced they were going to blow away. A loud creak sounding as though the building was being torn in half moaned from upstairs, and then something crashed, causing her to scream.

"It's all right," Josh said, turning over and facing her.

"It's not all right!" she replied, tears spilling over. "None of this is all right!"

He fixed his gaze on her face in the dim glow of the hallway light he had left lit so that they could assess any damage if something threatened their safety. Hesitantly, he put his arms over her while the house rocked in the high winds. His own heart was pounding against her arm, giving away his own fear. They'd lost another two windows after the plywood had been torn off the house, and the entire back porch was ripped off and floating somewhere in the Gulf of Mexico. The angry waters battered the sand precariously close to the back door, the walls crying out in protest with cracks, booms, and the grinding sound of siding being ripped, nail by nail, from its surface. The second half of the storm was proving to be far worse on the house than the first half, after the storm had taken a turn, moving further inland.

"We might have to make a run for it up the stairs if the back door doesn't hold," Josh said into her ear, causing a shiver to run up her spine, his arms wrapped around her so tightly that she felt like they were holding her together.

A loud pop sent them into darkness, the lights going out. She held Josh's shirt in her fists so tightly that she couldn't feel her fingers anymore.

"It's okay," he said. "A tree probably knocked down the power line or something. I'm surprised we had power as long as we did."

His voice was reassuring despite everything. But she was so scared that she couldn't tell anymore if his shirt was still wet from the rain earlier, or from her perspiration and tears as she squinted her eyes shut with the freight train of sound circling them.

The radio continued to filter into her consciousness, giving her a play-by-play of the storm and where it was moving. While the weather service center said they were through the worst of it, it certainly didn't feel like they were.

"We should move to higher ground," Josh said, letting go of her and then pulling her up quickly. He lumped the bags of food into her arms, the weight of them making her shake, fear turning her muscles to jelly. He set the radio on top and grabbed the air mattress and pillows, hauling them out of the room. The wind wailed outside, the plywood straining against the elements in such a way that she wondered if they'd lost the back door along with the porch.

The stairs creaked loudly with every step, her legs barely able to carry her up.

"What if the roof is taken off the house when we're up there?" she asked, wishing she were still inside his protective embrace.

"I secured it, so we have to hope for the best, but what we *do* know is that the water is right at our back door, and if that plywood gives way, we'll be in a world of trouble if we're down there."

Melanie hadn't spent much time upstairs before tonight, and now, in the dark, the bedroom's striped, peeling wallpaper gave her the same feeling she'd had when she'd gone through a Halloween fun house aged thirteen. It was eerie and unsettling, mocking her with its dilapidated pageantry. The storm rattled right above her up there, as if it were knocking at her door.

Josh dropped the mattress down, sending dust into the air. She set the food and radio on the floor next to it and lowered herself down. She felt grimy, sweaty, and completely exhausted, her body pleading for a moment's rest. As she collapsed onto the air mattress, Josh did the same, enveloping her with his arms as the storm raged on around them.

Chapter Five

The first thing Melanie was aware of was the loud squawk of seagulls, and she wondered if she'd been washed out of the house and dumped onto the sand. She took in a thick breath of humid air and licked her dry lips, but they didn't taste salty. She tried to swallow, her mouth parched. Then suddenly, she noticed the weight of Josh's arms around her, his body turned to the side and draped partially over her. She opened her eyes to the white light of morning sun breaking through a crack in the ceiling, part of the roof gone. The radio beside them was buzzing with accounts of the area's destruction: "*There is currently no travel in and out of the villages, and six hundred people are displaced…*"

Josh stirred, his sleepy eyes landing on her. Clearly realizing how close he was to her, he pulled away and sat up. "I wonder what time it is," he said, his voice hoarse.

Melanie felt for her phone in the back pocket of her shorts and was relieved it was still there. She checked the time, her eyes stinging from dehydration, lack of rest, and emotion, her head throbbing as she tried to focus. "It's 7 a.m."

He reached into the food bag and grabbed a couple of breakfast bars and two bottles of water, handing one of each to her.

"We made it through," he said, the corner of his mouth turning upward just slightly as he unwrapped his bar.

Melanie followed suit and took a bite before answering, "Yes." She allowed her relief and utter happiness to show. But then reality filtered in. "I wonder how much more damage was done to the house," she said, peering up at the hole in the ceiling.

"There's only one way to find out." He stood up, threw the wrapper into the food bag, and held the bar in his teeth, tightening the laces on the work boots he'd worn all night, before heading to the door. It creaked loudly when he opened it and peeked out. "There's no water at the bottom of the steps," he said, now pinching his breakfast between his fingers and opening the door wider.

Melanie stepped into the hallway, the brackish, sticky air filling her lungs. They walked together down the stairs to the bottom level. The wide entryway was totally dry, and she'd never been so relieved to see the dust still covering the floor.

"The wood on the window frames was so soft from previous water damage that the boards didn't hold," he said. "I wondered when I was putting them up, but I didn't want to alarm you any more than I already had." Shards of glass were all over the floor, with an enormous hole where the window used to be. Josh gently kicked the broken pieces against the wall. "But the good news is that replacing windows and framing is relatively straightforward."

They moved through the house, and it didn't look like the storm had done much more than they'd already seen, although Melanie was dreading taking the plywood off the back door and seeing the gaping area where the porch had once been. She peered through the broken glass to the gulf out back. Planks of wood and debris littered the powder-white shore, causing dismay to settle upon her.

"Looks like high water got under the house," Josh said, pulling her attention toward him. He stomped his foot along the soft wood planks, following the leak to the closet in the hallway. "It seems as though this might be the lowest point on the property. The floor's wet, so you'll definitely want to check the subfloor underneath. I hope you don't have anything in this closet."

"No," she said, dropping her head in bewilderment.

He opened the door and peered inside. "It's empty."

"How much damage?"

"Let me see how far it goes. Hopefully it isn't pooling somewhere." Josh went inside the closet, the light illuminated on his phone, searching for further rot and water damage. He got down on his knees and began feeling around the floor. "This closet goes way back," he said with a muffled voice.

Something rattled from inside it.

"What's that?" she asked, almost afraid to know by this point.

Another rattle—-it sounded like metal.

Moments later, Josh emerged holding a rusted tin box. "I'm guessing this isn't yours," he said, setting it on the kitchen counter.

"Nope," she confirmed.

He fiddled with the rusted latch, but it wouldn't budge.

"I wonder what's inside it." Melanie tried her hand at the latch with no luck.

Josh went into the dining room and grabbed the tool belt he'd abandoned last night, pulling a flathead screwdriver from it and prying the box's latch, wedging the tool underneath it. With a pop, it came loose and he lifted the lid.

"Oh my goodness," she said, thumbing through the box's contents.

She picked up a wind-up pocket watch that told the time in every country, twisting the dial to find that it still worked. It ticked quietly as she set it aside, grabbing two books that were in the box: one was a bible and the other a book of poetry. She opened the yellow pages to a folded corner and read the single verse.

I stand beneath the stars,
That gleam with whispered purpose,
Mocking the loss of innocence,
As I wait for you.

"That seems like such a sad poem," she said, stacking the two books neatly on the counter.

Josh reached in and grabbed a military medal, holding it up. "U.S. Navy," he said, reading the inscription. "I'd heard that Alfred Ellis was in the navy."

"What else do you know about him?" she asked, pulling a tattered, formal black-and-white photograph of a man in uniform from the box, wondering if the dashing young soldier in front of her was Mr. Ellis. She flipped it over, hoping for an inscription, but there was nothing, leaving her mind to wander. Then, she pulled out a small key with the number 0113 engraved on it.

"Not much," Josh replied, pulling her focus from the key.

She slipped it into her pocket.

"He kept to himself and hardly came out of the house at all. Like I said, he was only seen getting groceries from the market. From the little small talk he made, people in town have pieced together stories that he was originally in the navy, spent some time here on military leave, and then built this massive house later on, only to cut himself off from the world, eventually letting the place fall into disrepair."

"That's so strange…" Melanie wondered what would make someone draw into himself like that.

At the bottom of the box was a stack of letters, tied with a ribbon. She ran her finger over the embossed return address on the flap. There was no outgoing recipient or stamp. "These are all addressed from here," she said, noting the house number and street. But they've never been stamped and sent."

"I'll leave you to look at those later," Josh said. "We have to assess what work you'll need to contract, and then I have to get home."

"Uh, yes," she said, setting the letters aside, trying to curb her curiosity and turn her attention to the issues at hand. She grabbed a pad of paper and a pencil and followed Josh to the back door.

Using his tools to unfasten the plywood over the frame, Josh lifted it, setting it against the wall. As expected, the door itself was gone, so without the plywood, there was nothing between them and the glittering gulf.

"Do you know where I can order a new door?" she asked. "I can't sleep here if there's nothing to secure it. I need to get it fixed as soon as possible."

"You and every other person along the coast," he said, inspecting the bent hinges and then measuring the space with the tape he had in his pocket. "You might want to pull that tarp off the floor in the kitchen and put it over the doorway for now. It's going to be tough to find help."

"I shouldn't have bought this house," she blurted. She pressed her fingers against her burning eyes in frustration, anger over her situation bubbling up. "What was I thinking?" She stomped through the room. "I can't believe I let Gram talk me into this in her letter! I thought I could invest in this and have a future, but I have nothing..." She took in the space in disgust. But then the metal box on the counter came into focus, and softened her anger. Once upon a time this place had been shelter for someone else who was alone in the world. Someone who clearly had a love of poems and saved unsent letters… She blew air through her frustrated lips.

"Calm down," he said, reaching for her arm, but she pulled away, even more infuriated.

"Easy for you to say," she snapped. "You aren't stuck with this place."

"I can replace the door and repair the roof and windows for you," he said, following her with his eyes. "I've got a connection in town, but we need to hurry before everyone else has the same idea." From the look on his face, doing more work on the Ellis house was the last thing he wanted to do, but her sudden burst of anger seemed to have affected him. "I want to stop by my house to see what I'll need to fix there too."

"Okay," she said, her emotion now pushing to the surface in the form of tears. She blinked them away and swallowed the lump in her throat.

Josh gathered up his things and they headed out the front door. Seconds later both of them stopped, and Melanie gasped at what was in front of them. Josh's truck was bent in the shape of a V with an enormous palm tree lying across the bed of it. He stared at it, his lips in a straight line, his jaw tightening.

"I'm so sorry," she said, not knowing what else to say. The bad luck of this house seemed to settle on anything in its path.

"Do you mind driving?" he asked, his tone flat.

"No, but how will we get the supplies back to the house?" She considered the small trunk of her Honda, knowing there was no way a door and windows would fit.

"I've got another truck back at mine. I just hope it starts."

Chapter Six

As they drove, the sun beamed down from above, the gentle breeze returning as if nothing had happened at all.

"Pull over here," Josh said, motioning for Melanie to stop the car at the end of the dirt road in front of her.

He jumped out and got right to work, pulling his toolbox from the trunk of her car. The only indication that anything had happened in this wooded area was the For Sale sign that lay abandoned at the edge of the road, a far cry from the devastation of her home.

Josh carried the large wood sign back to its original location, dropping it down into the holes in the ground. It read: *For Sale, 15 Acres.*

"So this is where you live?" Melanie asked through the open car door.

"Mm hm." Josh grabbed the mallet from his box and whacked the post, using his foot to push the dirt back into place.

"You're selling fifteen acres?"

"Yep." He banged the top of the post. It shook with the force of his frustrated blow.

"So why exactly are you moving to New York?"

"I'm expanding my horizons," he said, putting his things back into the trunk and getting in.

"Meaning?" she pressed.

"Head down this road," he told her before giving her an answer. "I'm taking a better job."

"Better how?"

"Well, for starters, I won't have any hurricanes to deal with. Or friends who get me mixed up in ridiculous bets. No more surprise projects on the Ellis house."

She eyed him, making her way down the dirt track.

"It's a good move," he said. "It's at a company called Crosby and Mills. A college friend of mine works there and suggested I interview for the operations manager position. It was competitive—I was one of twenty call-backs—so I wasn't holding my breath. But with my friend's recommendation and the experience I've had working with other companies around here, I got it. I couldn't believe it."

"That's amazing."

"Yeah. I finally feel like I have a direction."

They came to a stop at his residence.

Josh's house was a cabin set in a patch of pine trees. The windows were boarded, and the wide front porch was tied down and empty. Nothing at all looked out of place.

"This is beautiful," Melanie said. She could just imagine the porch all done up with rocking chairs and ferns, potted flowers flanking the door.

"Thanks," he said, letting himself out of the passenger side of her car. "Wanna buy it?" He cracked a smile.

"After looking at mine, it's a possibility," she teased back, enjoying the lighter atmosphere between them.

But the moment vanished when he started assessing the safety measures he'd put in place.

Walking over to the front porch, she took a seat on the step. The property was so secluded at the edge of town that it felt like they were worlds away from everything that had gone on.

"Looks like it all held up in the storm," he said.

"That's a relief," she said.

"I'm sure I'll have repairs with the inspection when we get a buyer, and the less I have to coordinate from New York, the better."

"You never really answered my question. Honestly, why are you moving?"

He sat down next to her, his shoulder grazing hers. "I grew up here my whole life, and I have nothing to show for it. I woke up one morning and realized that I'd become my father—working all day, having beers with the same guys, and coming home to an empty house. I needed to break the cycle."

"Your parents aren't together?" she asked.

He shook his head. "Divorced when I was five. He was hard to live with, or so my mother says." He turned his attention to the line of pine trees at the edge of the woods separating the front of his home from the street, unsaid thoughts lingering on his lips. "I just want more, you know?"

"I do know," she said. "I absolutely know." She didn't have a plan yet, but she knew, without a doubt, that she did want more than being alone. "That's why I opted for a crumbling house," she teased.

He looked at her and their eyes locked. That hard exterior melted away for a second, giving her an unexpected flutter. Then, with a vengeance, it returned. He got up and went inside.

Ready to call him out for just leaving her on the porch, she let herself in but was immediately distracted. The interior of his home was nothing like the mess she'd been living in. Even though there were boxes everywhere, they were stacked neatly. The wood floors were in perfect shape, the masculine surfaces—all stained wood in dark hues—new and coordinated. A stone fireplace sat at one end of the room, with the most inviting leather sofa at the other. Suddenly, she wanted a shower and a fresh change of clothes, followed by a hearty meal at the rustic dinette that sat in the open area between the living room and kitchen.

"Everything's secure here," he said, breezing past her with a set of keys dangling from his fingers. "Now I need to see if the old truck will run."

She shuffled behind him, trying to squash her growing frustration with his mood, as he made his way to the back door.

He opened the door with a set of keys in his hand.

"Wait, stop," she finally said.

He turned around.

"Can't we be friends? I mean, we've gone through so much together, and sometimes I think you're finally being friendly, and then—"

"I don't need any new friends. This is business, and we've got a lot of work ahead of us if we want to get that house even remotely secure before I leave." The words were coming out, but there was a glimmer of something else in his eyes that told her he wasn't allowing her in for some reason.

Her shoulders slumped in defeat. "Look, my sister's back at her house in Tennessee," she said, putting her hand out to stop him again as he started walking. She hoped to make him understand how much she appreciated his help no matter how she'd gotten it, and at the end of the day, it was nice to see a friendly face. "I don't know anyone in town…"

She held her breath as he looked at her. Did she see his stare soften just a little at her admission?

"Not my problem," he clipped, turning away and walking up the gravel drive, a very different person from the one who had held her last night.

She balled her hands into fists at her sides to keep herself from completely falling apart. "I don't want anything from you," she said through gritted teeth.

"Yes, you do," he replied. "You want three new windows and a back door."

"I didn't mean the work… Never mind."

He stopped. "No, what did you mean then?"

"I don't need a new best friend either. I just thought we could be sociable, that's all."

"For what reason?"

"Because it's nice!"

He hesitated as if wrestling with his own thoughts. "It's a waste of time."

She stared at him in utter disbelief and snapped her gaping mouth shut. "You know, the people in town who tell me how great you are—they're wrong. You're not a very nice person," she said once she'd finally gotten her words back. It was almost as if he wanted her to be angry with him, but why?

"It's not about being nice or not," he said. "It's about me fixing your house before I leave when I have plenty of better things to do besides standing in my driveway and arguing over whether or not we should be friends. In a week, we'll never see each other again."

She'd never met anyone as infuriating as the man standing opposite her now. And yet, she could see in his gaze that there was more to him than this. She didn't want him to leave on these terms. Truthfully, she didn't want him to leave at all. But that wasn't an option. And when he did go, would she be up to the task of taking care of her house on her own?

"We'd better get a move on."

A timeworn, faded blue farm truck sat at the back of the house next to the barn. Josh lifted the hood, fiddling with something. Then he put the key in the old truck, the engine protesting and then falling silent, sending him back under the hood. The relentless summer heat wrapped around Melanie, heightening the stickiness on her skin as Josh tinkered with the engine.

"We're lucky I've still got this," he said. "A friend of mine was coming to tow it away next Tuesday. Now we just have to hope it starts." He tightened a nut, wiping the grease on his T-shirt, streaking charcoal gray across it, and she looked away, trying not to stare at the muscles under that stripe he'd just made. "Hop in and hit the gas when I tell you to."

Melanie got into the vehicle, sliding along the ripped vinyl bench seat and lumping her handbag beside her, a mixture of hay and dust filling her nose.

"Got it in park?" he called, leaning out from under the hood.

She peered down at the stick shift. "Yes."

"All right. Step on the gas."

She couldn't see what he was doing and, even if he was a jerk, she didn't love the idea of pumping an engine full of gasoline while his head was mere inches from it, but she did what she was told and pressed her foot against the pedal, the engine revving. Hope swelled in her chest, but then it clicked loudly over and over until it finally came to a stop.

Josh walked off to the garage, returning moments later with a wrench. He took something off the engine and rearranged a few things before putting it back. "Okay, try it now."

Her head started to pound, the exhaustion of the whole ordeal overwhelming her. She felt dirty and hot, and while she knew she had to press on if she wanted to have a back door, she suddenly didn't know if she could. With her last ounce of energy, she hit the gas, the engine revving. But this time, it didn't stop. It kept on purring.

"You did it!" she called out the open truck window.

Josh shut the hood and threw his wrench into the back. "Yes, ma'am. Looks like we've got ourselves a truck. Scoot over." He got in behind the wheel and set off down the drive, passing her Honda and heading down the long, quiet road toward town.

"So where are you getting the door?" she asked, the salty air from the open window a welcome break from the humidity. "You said you had connections?"

"My friend Roscoe is a supplier for my larger jobs. He sells wholesale, so the public won't think to find him, but all the builders will. Hopefully we'll get to him before the others since we got such an early start this morning."

"Okay," she said, looking over at him. "How far is Roscoe's?"

"About two hours."

"*Two hours?*" She didn't want to sound ungrateful, but two hours both ways with a grump at the wheel who wouldn't even throw her a smile was an incredibly long time. "I'm starving. And I could use a shower. I'd like to grab a good meal before we make a drive like that."

"All my stuff is packed back at the house," he said, clearly thinking as he took the winding road into town. Then something appeared to occur to him. "Do you have a credit card?"

"Yes," she said, double-checking her handbag.

"Okay. I've got an idea… But you have to be up for something a little crazy," he told her with a challenge in his eyes. "And judging by what I've seen of you so far, I'm guessing it might be the craziest thing you've ever done. You game?"

"I'm going to try not to be offended by that statement," she said with a laugh. While everything in her being was screaming to tell him no, she didn't want to be outdone by Josh Claiborne. "Of course I'm game."

Chapter Seven

One of the few shops in Rosemary Bay with minimal damage was the souvenir store on the way out of town. Melanie took the receipt from the cashier for the items she'd bought: an orange pair of shorts and a white T-shirt with matching orange lettering that said, "I Heart Rosemary Bay" in cursive script across the front. She'd also gotten herself a new pair of woven flip-flops, and a Rosemary Bay visor.

Josh eyed her items, standing next to her at the register.

"What?" she asked, stacking them near the salesperson. "You're just jealous that they don't have these flip-flops in your size," she teased.

Josh only shook his head.

"Are we going to change somewhere?" she asked, stepping outside with Josh.

He swung his own shopping bag over his shoulder. "Yes. But we need to stop in here." He pointed to the market next door. They had a few broken pots of flowers outside, but clearly this side of the street had been spared.

Inside, Josh grabbed two toothbrushes, a tube of toothpaste, a stick of deodorant, travel bottles of shampoo and conditioner, a bar of soap, and a pack of peanuts, setting them on the counter. The store clerk rang him up and he tossed her the bag of nuts. She fumbled to catch them, bobbling the bag before securing it in her arms. He dropped the remaining items into his bag.

"Can you hang in there a little longer if I promise that literally the best breakfast spot in the Panhandle is on the way to Roscoe's? It's far enough inland that I'll bet it didn't get any damage at all."

"Okay," she said.

They got back into the truck and held their breath, both of them exhaling in relief when the engine started with a clacking rumble. As they drove further out of town, away from the blue tones of the gulf, the sun beat down as the road stretched out before them.

"Where are we going?" Melanie asked, carrying her bag as they left the truck behind and plodded through the deep woods, thick with inland trees of pine and oak. They'd stopped about an hour into the trip and gotten breakfast at a little diner as Josh had promised, then parked along the side of a dirt road.

"You want a shower, right?" he asked, holding his bag from the store and the food they'd just picked up. The warm comforting smell of buttermilk biscuits and the savory aroma of eggs and bacon were giving her hunger cramps.

"Well, yes, but there's nothing here," she said, pointing to the expanse of forest. "Are we headed to some sort of campground or something?"

"Better."

"There's a five-star hotel in the middle of no man's land that you have to hike to?"

He allowed a tiny grin, but then straightened it out, not playing into her banter.

Twigs snapped under her feet as they moved through the dense woods, full of evergreens, on some sort of invisible path up and down hills that only Josh knew about. She wiped the perspiration off her forehead, the humidity and exercise causing her to flush. She looked around for any indication of where they could be walking, but there was nothing except trees. They were the only two people for miles.

"We can get back to the truck, right?" she asked, realizing that she'd lost sight of the vehicle completely.

He turned around to look at her like she shouldn't have even asked. "Why would I drag us into the woods if I couldn't get us back?"

She shrugged, wondering how in the world she'd gotten herself into this situation.

"I've been hiking these woods since I was a kid." He held a young tree limb out of the way so they could get by.

They continued a little further and then suddenly the trees cleared, revealing large slabs of rock framing the most stunning waterfall, which cascaded into a pool the color of sea glass, so clear she could see all the way to the bottom. The shushing of the water and the singing of the birds around them was like music. "What is this?" she asked, breathless at the spectacular sight.

"It's our shower."

"What?"

"Ladies first." He set their breakfast down and opened his bag, tossing her a brand-new beach towel. Then he put the toiletries he'd bought on the rock nearest to him, and turned his back to her.

"No way." She walked around to face him. "I'm not stripping down right here in the middle of the woods. What if someone sees me?"

"No one will see you," he replied. "Look around. We're the only ones here."

"What if someone comes?"

"They won't. The land is private."

"Whose is it?"

"Mine." He sat down on the rock and put his hands over his eyes. "Now hurry up. I'd like to have breakfast."

"There's no chance I'm doing this," she said, crossing her arms, the thought of being naked making her cheeks burn with unease.

"How gross do you feel right now?" he asked.

"Pretty gross," she admitted.

"The only thing standing in the way of making that better is you."

"Absolutely not." She shook her head.

"Suit yourself. I'm getting in and washing up before my breakfast gets cold." He grabbed the bottom of his shirt and began to pull it up.

"Wait!" she said, his bare, chiseled torso making it difficult to get a thought out.

"I'm not waiting indefinitely," he said, dropping his shirt. "Either you get in or I do." He closed his eyes again. "I promise not to look."

She stared at him, deciding.

"You're not moving, and my food's getting cold," he said with his eyes still squeezed shut.

The waterfall gurgled softly, the pool at the bottom so inviting that it sent a prickle across her skin. Giving in, she opened her bag and set her new clothes on the rock. Then she grabbed the soap, shampoo, and conditioner and made her way to the water.

Not taking her eyes from Josh, her heart pounding, she nervously slipped her shirt over her head and then wriggled out of her shorts, the key from the old box they'd found dropping from the pocket and rattling onto the rock. She caught it just before it slipped into the water and set it next to her clothes. Josh's back was to her now, his breathing steady, his body still. Holding her breath, she took her undergarments off and jumped in with a splash, the cool water instantly refreshing her.

"It's about time," he called, causing her to squeal and cover herself even though his back was still facing her.

She swam over and grabbed the soap, lathering up. As she ran the lavender-scented bar down her arms, up her neck, and onto her face, it felt as though she were washing the whole ordeal off of her. "How do you know all this land so well?" she asked, looking around at the jagged rock jutting out of the hillside across from her. "It's a huge piece of property."

"It was my grandfather's. I used to camp out here as a kid," he replied, his back still turned. "If you want to wash your underwear, it'll dry pretty quickly in the sun, so I'd do that first and put it on the hot rock to dry."

She wrapped her arms across her body to shield as much of her as possible and grabbed her undergarments from the rock, running the bar of soap over them and plunging them into the water. Even though it was just the two of them, she felt exposed out in the wild like that. She placed her unmentionables on the rock like she'd been told. Then she went underwater and ran her fingers through her hair before soaping her scalp with the shampoo. With every minute she spent in the refreshing water, she felt more reinvigorated.

Once she'd finished conditioning her hair and getting clean, she got out and wrapped the oversized beach towel around her, deciding to stay in it until her undergarments were nearly dry. Then she ran the brush through her wet hair. "Okay," she said. "You can turn around now."

His gaze swept across her bare legs and then up to her face, causing the warmth to return to her cheeks.

Still feeling exposed despite the fact that she was in a towel which covered more of her than her favorite sundress, she swiped on some deodorant and grabbed a water bottle he'd placed by the toiletries to brush her teeth.

"I'll be quick," he said, his gaze fluttering over her before he cleared his throat and turned his attention to the waterfall.

She twisted around and faced the edge of the woods, the forest floor covered in tall, leafy ferns and sweeping vines.

There was a splash and her breath caught.

"As a kid, did you come out here all by yourself?" she asked, trying to distract herself from the fact he was naked just feet away.

"Nope. In high school I used to bring my girlfriend here." He let out a little chuckle.

"She trusted you out here alone?" she teased him, hoping to lighten things between them.

"I was a perfect gentleman."

She had to admit that he had been nothing but a gentleman since they'd gotten there, despite his mood. "I believe you," she said, and she meant it.

After a few minutes, she heard the ripples of him getting out of the water. "Breakfast time," he said, walking in front of her, wearing nothing but a towel.

She had to remind herself to breathe. Water trickled down his muscular chest to his waist where he gripped the towel in his fist. With his free hand, he ran his fingers through his hair, wet strands falling across his forehead, looking like he'd jumped straight out of a magazine ad.

Tucking his towel into itself to keep it from slipping, Josh pulled another one from the bag and laid it across one of the larger rocks. Then he got out their food, opening the boxes. "Maxine's has the best grits in the south," he said, spooning some of the buttery mixture onto her plate, next to two huge buttermilk biscuits, a pile of scrambled eggs and two crispy pieces of bacon.

As the savory smell wafted toward Melanie, her mouth watered and she suddenly felt like she hadn't eaten in weeks. He set a small orange juice next to her, and she dug into the food, taking a bite. "This might be the most delicious breakfast I've tasted in my life," she said, barely taking a breath from the rich saltiness of the biscuits slathered in warm butter.

"I've got a container full of pancakes too," he said, "and Maxine's homemade blueberry syrup."

"I'm not going to be able to move after this." She took in another mouthful and leaned back on the rock, peering up at the beam of sunlight that filtered through the trees, the tumbling of the water behind them lulling her into a state of calm.

He offered a curious smile as she tightened the towel around her, tucking the corner into the top of it to keep it in place. When that wall he'd built crumbled every so often, she couldn't take her eyes off him.

In that moment, as they sat in their brightly colored beach towels, she didn't want to think about all the work ahead of them, the grief that overwhelmed her, or the collapsing, empty house that sat miles away from them on the shore. She just wanted to see that smile a little longer.

Chapter Eight

"That sure ain't Janie." A man with a white scraggly beard that dangled just above the front pocket of his overalls came toward Josh and Melanie as they got out of the truck at the old warehouse.

"Hey, Roscoe," Josh said, clapping the old man on the back. "This is Melanie."

"Got ya a cute one," he said, causing Melanie to look away, her eyes falling to the pebbled parking area. "Janie know about this?"

Who's Janie? she wondered.

Josh laughed good-naturedly. "Nope. But I doubt she'd care anyway. I haven't seen her in quite a while."

Roscoe's bushy eyebrows rose in interest. "You didn't say nothin' about this."

Josh shrugged. "It never came up in conversation. And it didn't end well so it wasn't something I really wanted to discuss."

Roscoe's belly bounced with his laugh. "You never been one for talkin'. Janie still live in town?"

"Yeah," he said, clearly not wanting to spend too much time on the subject.

Then Roscoe turned to Melanie. "You know what you're gettin' into with this one, Miss Melanie?" he teased.

"Don't worry, Roscoe. She's safe. She's just a friend."

"Aren't they all…?" Roscoe offered Melanie a playfully suspicious smirk, and she smiled back as his gaze darted between them before refocusing on the task at hand. "I heard that hurricane got y'all good. Y'all here lookin' for supplies?"

"We need a back door and some windows," Josh replied.

Roscoe stroked his beard. "Dang. That bad?"

"Yep."

"Everything I've got's out back," the old man said. "Y'all help yourself and then text me what you got. I'll add it to your bill."

"No, I'm paying," Melanie said, cutting in. "It's for my house."

"It's fine." Josh brushed away her offer. "It's easier to just throw it on my tab, and Melanie and I will settle it later."

Roscoe chuckled. "You're the boss."

Before Melanie could protest further, Josh led her to a barn at the back of the property. They walked in and made their way across the concrete floor where an entire wall was full of stacked doors.

"I have one in mind that I was considering for another job," Josh said. "I hope it's still here." He looked through the doors along the bottom of the wall, stopping at one and lifting it out of the stack carefully. It was clearly antique, with beveled panes of glass and ornamental work at the top.

"Oh, that's gorgeous," she said, running her hand over the curling woodwork. "It would go perfectly with the period features of the house."

"I think so too," he said, peering down at it. "With a thick coat of white lacquer, it could be incredible."

"What if we moved away from traditional just a little bit to make it more current, and painted it seafoam green?" she ventured. "With the porch widened when it's redone and painted bright white, the old shutters replaced with wider ones coated in a dark navy blue, and a seafoam-green door with a seashell wreath, the house would be incredible."

He stared at her.

"What?" she asked.

"That sounds amazing. Have you ever worked in interior design?"

"No. I was in marketing."

"Looks like you might have talent in design."

"Thanks," she said, happiness bubbling up. If she wasn't mistaken, that was the first time he'd said something nice to her.

"So, who's Janie? An ex-girlfriend?" Melanie asked Josh when they'd gotten out of their vehicles at the Ellis house. She'd been curious the whole way home from Roscoe's, but hadn't gotten the courage to ask until now for fear that his good mood, which she'd been enjoying so much, would dissipate.

Josh shut the old truck door and walked around to her Honda to meet her in the small area of the drive that was clear of debris. "Janie's my wife."

A thud of disappointment hit her in the chest, surprising her. "Oh?" She held her hand over her eyes to shield them from the bright sunlight as she struggled to hide her interest. Josh seemed so closed off that she couldn't imagine him ever getting down on one knee to profess his love to someone.

"Actually, my ex-wife," he clarified.

Divorced. That didn't totally surprise her. He could definitely be difficult; she'd known him for a grand total of two days, which was long enough to figure that out.

"What?" he asked, startling her.

She hadn't said anything, had she? "What do you mean, 'What?'" she asked.

"That look you just had. What were you thinking?"

Her cheeks got hot and she prayed that they hadn't actually flushed. What could she say? She certainly wasn't going to tell him that she was having trouble imagining him in any sort of long-term relationship.

"Nothing," she replied. "I don't know what you're talking about."

Gravel crunched under his boots as he stepped toward her. "No, you had a strange look on your face when I said Janie was my ex-wife," he pressed.

She took in a deep breath. "I was just surprised by it, that's all," she replied.

That frustrated scowl had already penetrated his features once more. "I can't wait to get out of this town," he muttered under his breath, as he walked with purpose back to the truck and threw open the tailgate, sliding one of the windows out of the back and setting it against the house.

"I'll head inside and start sweeping up the glass from the broken windows," she said awkwardly, but Josh just continued to unload the truck without anther word.

As she let herself inside, she took in the surroundings: the smashed glass, the missing back door, the darkness of the boarded-up windows. Once again, the familiar lonesome gloom of the house washed over her.

"Gram, you're killin' me here," she said quietly before looking around the room, hoping her grandmother would give her some indication that she was there. But all she was met with was silence. Gram's words came back to her: *Find that life that's floating around the universe just waiting for you to grab it and never let go. And if I have any say in heaven, I'll be right there, pushing it toward you the whole way.* "Well, push it toward me then," Mel called quietly, irritated that she couldn't hear anything.

Refocusing and thinking back to her dream of that seafoam-green door on a bright back porch overlooking the water, she wondered if it would ever be possible. With a disheartened sigh, she went to get the broom and dustpan.

But as she passed the kitchen counter, she stopped at the old metal box and its contents, which were still stacked beside it. She ran her fingers over the letters, jumping with a start as the loud buzz of Josh's power tool blasted its way into the room. Suddenly, the board against the kitchen window fell away, the sunlight piercing her eyes. Josh's gaze met hers through the broken glass, but a second later he stepped down off his ladder, leaving her in silence.

Trying to ignore her disappointment, Melanie grabbed the broom and dustpan. With every swipe across the old hardwoods, the glass shards clinking together, she felt an overwhelming feeling that she was just spinning her wheels. She yearned to make this house what Gram would've wanted her to make it, but it was all just a shot in the dark.

Another sheet of plywood came off a window outside, sending a sunbeam onto the hallway floor just outside the kitchen, a cloud of dust circling in its light. And then there was the earsplitting whine of a saw, making her head pound. Melanie squeezed her eyes shut and kept sweeping, dumping the pieces of broken glass into the trashcan. When she was done, she eyed the letters again, wondering what was in them and if they would take her mind off all this for a little while. Clapping her hands together, she grabbed the envelopes and went upstairs, settling in the room at the end of the hall where they'd slept during the storm. With a deep breath, she sat down in the middle of the empty, dusty floor, leaning toward the light from the hallway to read.

She opened the first letter in the stack, gently unfolded the yellow page between her fingers, and took in the slanted, scratched-out handwriting.

April 23, 1959

My love,

I sit here in the approaching darkness of evening, still wondering after two years why you didn't keep our promise. I was away longer than I wanted to be, but every minute that I was out at sea, I thought of you. Without warning, every day you fluttered into my mind like a warm summer breeze, a brief reprieve from my daily work. Just as you asked, I painfully waited two months and then sent a letter to you vowing to come home and promising to make you my wife. I kept my side of the bargain. I waited for you. And I'm still waiting.

Forever yours,
Alfred

Melanie stared at the letter in her hand, stunned. Alfred Ellis wasn't a loner like everyone in Rosemary Bay said he was; he was *heartbroken.* She turned the envelope over to find out the name of his love interest, but Mr. Ellis had never addressed it, nor stamped it. A thud against the wall sent her heart racing. Then, suddenly, the plywood fell away and Josh was on the other side of the window. His attention flickered to the pile of letters before he ignored her completely and fired up his drill, the machine whining against the window frame. When he'd lifted the old window out of the space, leaving an open hole between them, she walked over to him.

"Is there anything I can do to help you?" she asked, peering through the window at the scaffolding.

"Nope," he said. "I work most efficiently alone."

"Hey, I started reading these." She waved the letters. "Want to take a quick break and read some of them?"

With a short breath, he brushed her off. "I need to work on this right now." His eyes lingered on her longer than she'd have expected them to, but he didn't budge.

"Okay. Let me know if you get thirsty or anything. I'll bring you some water."

He nodded, getting back to work.

Melanie turned away and busied herself by straightening the air mattress from last night, pulling off the sheets and balling them up to take to the laundromat later. She understood Alfred Ellis a little more after reading his first letter, and the loneliness of the house took on a different frequency. It seemed to be crying out with unfinished business. Suddenly what Gram had told her about ghosts returning only if they had something to say flooded her mind. She glanced back down at the letter, then looked up and took in the peeling feminine wallpaper, wondering if Alfred had chosen it for the woman he loved. Had she ever gotten a chance to see it?

The idea that he'd waited in this house night in and night out for the woman he loved gave her an unexpected lump in her throat. She understood what it felt like to be alone. For so many years, she'd defined herself by being Gram's caretaker, but now she didn't have anyone. A tear slipped down her cheek and she wiped it away, surprised. Quickly, she looked over at the window to see if Josh had noticed. His eyes were already on her, an unspoken sympathy in his gaze.

Chapter Nine

"I told you it's too much to take on," Kathryn said on the other end of the phone as Melanie turned her face to the warm sunshine. "You don't need all this, Mel. Just sell that place and find yourself a nice townhouse where you can relax every night with a good book and a glass of wine."

Melanie ran her hands through the fine sand where she was sitting, the waves quietly foaming over her toes. "I think I need to stay," she said, looking back at the house where Josh was working on the last window before fixing the door. The plumber had also surfaced and fixed the bathroom and kitchen plumbing, which she was thrilled about. After he'd left, she'd tried several times to help Josh, but he'd told her he had it under control. It was pretty clear to her that he wanted to be left alone.

"Why?" her sister asked.

"I don't know," she replied honestly. "I feel like there's unfinished business here. The house has a story to tell. Did you know that Josh and I found some letters from the owner in one of the closets?"

"I'm more interested in the fact that you and Josh were in a closet together," Kathryn teased.

"Funny," she said. The memory of Josh's bare chest at the waterfall came into her head and she turned her focus to pushing her toes into the sand to clear the thought. "But seriously, from the first letter I read, the man who owned this house spent years waiting for the love of his life."

"Oh, wow," Kathryn said. "Did he ever find her?"

"I don't know. I'll let you know when I read the rest of the letters."

"I haven't ever thought of you as a dreamer—but I like it," Kathryn said. "But whether there's an interesting love story behind the house or not, I'm not sure you'll ever get out of it what you're going to have to put into it."

"I'm scared," Melanie admitted. "I don't know how to get it where it needs to be, on my budget, but I kind of have to make it work at this point. And I *want* to make it work."

"I've accrued some vacation time. Why don't I come down there and help you with the house for a week or so? Toby can watch Ryan."

"You'd have to clear it with Toby that he's okay to have Ryan for an entire week," Melanie pointed out with a chuckle.

"But having a sister in peril counts as an emergency, and he'll be fine. Plus the nanny comes twice a week."

"You've got it all together," Melanie noted, feeling more frazzled suddenly.

"On the outside," Kathryn said. "But not really. None of us do."

"Thanks for trying to make me feel better."

The sound of Kathryn's voice lifted Melanie's spirits. "I'm not just trying to make you feel better. I'm serious."

"Even more reason for you to stay where you are, then," Melanie said. "Thank you for offering, but I'll figure this out on my own."

"All right," Kathryn said, clearly unconvinced. "Don't try to be a hero though, Mel. If you need me, I can be there in a few hours."

"Thank you," she said, turning around again and seeing that Josh's scaffolding was down. "I should probably get back up to the house."

"Okay. Call me later."

Melanie ended the call and stood up, brushing the sand off her bottom. She walked down into the waves, stepping in the surf with her bare feet, the cool gurgle of it instantly refreshing. The bright blue water was so clear that she could see tiny schools of fish jetting past her. The small waves danced onto the shore, foaming happily and retreating, the rhythmic sound like music. *Was this what you wanted for me, Gram?* she thought. As if Gram were right there, she could almost hear her answer: *It's beautiful, isn't it?* Melanie took in a breath of the fresh air and promised herself that, in the coming weeks, she'd spend more time out here to keep her centered.

"It's nice out there," Josh's voice came from behind her.

She turned around to find his attention on the horizon. "Yes," she agreed.

He stepped up beside her.

"You look worn out," she said.

"Yeah. But it's done. The windows are in and the doors all work."

"Thank you." She turned into the wind to look at him. "I'm hungry," she admitted, hoping they could have a little more time together over drinks and dinner. "Want to get some dinner?" Her fear of being alone again outweighed any worry about how he'd take the question.

Josh stared at her.

"We both need to eat."

Contemplative, he nodded. "Sure."

Had he just agreed to go to dinner with her? Working to hide her delight, she asked calmly, "Where should we go?"

"I know where to get a good fish dinner."

"You do?" While there was no shortage of seafood restaurants in the area, she was intrigued to hear which one he liked the best. "I'm excited," she said. "My tummy's already rumbling."

He allowed a tiny smile, the corner of his mouth twitching upward. "Maybe have a little snack, then. I'll pick you up at seven thirty."

Was Josh Claiborne suddenly being sociable? She couldn't wait to find out.

Melanie ran her hands through her wet hair and dried them on the towel that hung in her very own *working* bathroom. Thank goodness the plumber had come. It felt great to finally be able to get clean in her own house.

She smoothed the wrinkles out of the shorts and ruffled tank top she'd pulled from her suitcase and tried unsuccessfully to see her reflection in the new window that Josh had installed. She'd attempted to put on makeup, and she'd curled her hair and put on her dangly earrings. After everything she'd been through in the last day, she almost felt decent.

"Gram?" she called into the air on her way to the front door. "If you're here, can you work a little magic? Nothing big, just a nice night. I need a break."

"Hi," Josh said, meeting her in the yard. As he took in her appearance, so different to Hurricane-Melanie, a hint of a smile played on his lips. She suddenly felt like her knees wouldn't hold her up. He had on a handsomely rugged T-shirt, worn in all the right places and showing the perfect amount of muscle, and a pair of shorts. "Ready?"

"Yes," she said, pulling her handbag up on her shoulder and climbing into the old truck. Its unique scent, a mixture of salt and hay, hit her when she closed the passenger door.

"Some guys I know are coming to tow my other vehicle tomorrow," he said, pointing to the red and white truck with the palm tree still pinning it down. He cranked the engine. "They'll take care of the tree too, and while they're here they're going to remove the rest of the debris out of your yard."

"They are?" she asked, shocked by his generosity.

"Yeah. They want to chip it all up. Free mulch."

"Ah," she said, not wanting to admit she was disappointed that he hadn't done it from the goodness of his own heart. Friendliness seemed to lurk just below his surface, but something was keeping him from letting his guard down. Or at least that was what she wanted to think. The alternative was that he was only helping her out of pity.

"I had fun at the waterfall today," she said, the memory of his smile and the ease of their conversation bubbling to the surface.

He gave her one quick nod, putting the truck in gear, but then blew air through his lips when the engine cut off. "Hang on," he said, getting out. He threw up the hood and fiddled with the engine. "Put it in park and rev the gas," he said from outside.

Melanie scooted over on the old bench seat and hit the gas pedal, the engine roaring.

"One more time."

She did what she was told and he hopped back in, reaching across her bare legs to open the glove box, pulling out a rag. His spicy clean scent filled her lungs, and she turned toward the open window to calm the pattering of her heart that happened with his proximity. He wiped the grease off his hands and placed the rag back in the glove box.

"This truck should be fun to drive to New York next week," he said dryly.

"You're driving *this* from Florida to New York?"

"It's all I've got. My work truck is now a very large lawn ornament, remember?"

"Is there any way you can postpone your move, given the circumstances?" she asked, holding her hair back as the warm air blew in from her open window.

"Probably not," he said, putting the old truck in gear and hitting the gas.

Silence settled between them as the sea grass slipped past her view. The shoreline opened up, the teal and sapphire water showing off like a rare jewel on the coastline. The only evidence on the beach that there'd been any kind of storm was the debris that occasionally littered the sand.

Not very far down the road, they pulled into a marina.

"I didn't know there was a restaurant here," she said, as they both hopped out of the truck.

Josh pursed his lips in thought. "There isn't," he said. Then he went around to the back of the truck and pulled out two fishing rods, handing her one. "I said I know where to get a good fish dinner... The boat's around back." He grabbed a tackle box and a large backpack, saying, "Follow me."

She should've known better than to think that Josh was planning to take her out for a nice meal. She wanted to kick herself for spending the extra time on her makeup and hair. In the humidity, it would all be for nothing. Instead of holding a nice glass of rosé, she was going to be snatching slimy, wriggling fish off the end of her line.

"I figured after the storm, we needed to kick back and relax," he said, turning to walk up the dock. "I've been living on my friend's boat while he's in Australia so I could pack up my house."

She nodded, barely able to speak due to her disappointment. She didn't want to seem ungrateful, but fishing off the end of some old boat wasn't really her idea of relaxing. She followed him along the dock, past white, gleaming boats, while holding her fishing rod, the bobber swinging back and forth on the line.

"I was so glad to hear the dock made it through the storm," he continued, shifting the bag on his shoulder. "The harbor around it actually protects it most of the time, but it can take a lashing if the storm hits it just right."

"Oh," she said, her eyes wide, shocked and delighted by what was in front of her, when they came to a stop at the last boat on the dock. "A houseboat?" The question came out with a quiet laugh of complete relief. She held her hand over her eyes to shield them from the setting sun so she could view the beautiful light blue clapboard houseboat. It had two stories, with window boxes overflowing with cascading pink periwinkles and decks full of wicker furniture, rocking chairs and potted plants, looking like something out of a magazine.

Josh stepped from the dock onto the wide rectangular base of the boat and unlatched the white picket fence that went all the way around it, securing the outdoor table with a lime-green umbrella and matching printed chair cushions. He held his hand out to her from the bobbing structure.

"My friend owns a surfboard company. His wife designed this for when they're in Florida. He had it brought inland and secured during the storm, thank goodness," Josh said, helping her onto the boat.

Melanie gripped his strong hand, noticing how he could keep her steady while maintaining a gentle hold on her, electricity zinging through her at his touch despite her attempts to keep the feeling at bay. When she got both feet onto the boat, he let her go and shut the fence.

Josh took the rod from her, leaning it against the house, slipped the key in the lock, and allowed her to enter. The space was temperature controlled, the cool air immediately hitting her skin. It had a full kitchen with four gray barstools tucked under a white quartz bar. A driftwood chandelier hung above it. She looked up at it, thinking how sparkling and new it looked compared to hers at the Ellis house. She'd work in shining hers up when she got back home.

Josh went over to the fridge, retrieving a platter of grapes, cheese, and crackers, along with a bottle of white wine. He set the tray between them before he pulled out a container filled with gorgeous filets of fresh snapper.

"I thought we were going to fish for our dinner," she said.

"The rods are for later. You'll be amazed how relaxing fishing is when the sun goes down and you've had a few glasses of this." He held up the bottle of wine and then rooted around in the drawers for a corkscrew.

"You surprised me," Melanie said.

He didn't respond to her admission, keeping his attention on the corkscrew, but Melanie noticed that he seemed calm tonight, like the water outside, the storm having passed for the moment. With a pop, the cork came loose in his hand and he poured them each a glass of wine. He handed her a glass and she held it up.

"A toast to new friendships," she said.

Reluctantly, he tentatively tapped his glass to hers, his shoulders tensing, making her feel like she'd crossed some sort of invisible line. He gathered up their dinner and wrapped the filets in foil, covering them with butter and slices of lemon.

"I'll just throw these on the grill outside," he said, picking up the pouches of fish and the cheese tray.

She followed him to the deck outside and settled on a cushioned bench at the back of the boat. The coastal breeze blew across the deck, the overhang above them creating a shadow and shielding them from the sun.

"This is amazing," she said, leaning over to look at the pot of flowers next to her as they rocked softly on the water. She took in his rugged charm, the way his stubble complemented the laughter lines at the corners of his eyes. He just didn't seem like he'd fit in the city. "Aren't you going to miss it here?"

Josh looked over at her, thoughtful. His lips slackened just slightly as if he were considering her question, but then he shrugged, turning back to the grill. He set the foiled fish on the grates, the flame lightly licking the bottom of them as the charcoal smell of the coals wafted up toward them.

Once he'd closed the lid of the grill, he lifted the top off the outdoor coffee table in front of her, and flipped a switch on the side of the table. A bright blue and orange flame flickered up.

"Oh, that's wonderful," Melanie said, leaning back and taking a cool, crisp sip of wine. She wiped the beads of condensation off the glass with her finger and peered out at the cobalt-blue water in front of her.

When he flipped another switch, suddenly the entire canopy above them was twinkling in white lights. With the water under the boat and the lighting surrounding them, it felt like magic. Josh sat down beside her on the bench and took a drink from his glass.

"New York is really different from here," she said, making conversation.

"Mm hm," he returned, gazing at the water.

"How do you know you're going to like the Big Apple?"

"I don't," he said. "But I won't know until I try."

"I know what you mean," she said. "That's how I feel with the Ellis house."

He nodded, pensive.

"Does your move have anything to do with getting away from your ex-wife?" she asked, guessing at his motive for leaving since he wasn't being forthcoming on his own.

His jaw clenched with the mention of Janie, his shoulders shifting a little higher. "It's *my* choice to leave," he said abruptly. "It has nothing to do with her."

"I'm sorry. I didn't mean to bring up a sore spot," she said. "I just wondered if you were trying to get away. She still lives here, right?"

"Yes." He had that closed-off look on his face. He took a long drink of his wine. "Can we talk about something that doesn't make me want to tear my hair out? What's next on your to-do list for the Ellis house?"

"You like talking about your work," she noted.

"There's no controversy in construction," he said vaguely.

"That's not true."

"What do you mean?" he asked, the tension from mentioning Janie dissolving.

"Well, have you told your mother you're working on my house?"

He huffed out a little chuckle at the connection she'd made. "Not yet," he replied. "But in this town, it's only a matter of time before she knows."

"What do you think she'll say?"

"She'll probably warn me about the tongue lashing I'll get when I see my nana again."

"I read one of the letters that was in the box, and from the sound of it, Alfred Ellis was in love."

He puffed out a breath of indifference.

"He promised someone he'd come back for her and propose, but it never happened because the girl didn't keep her end of the bargain, the letter said." She leaned back, propping her arm on the top of the bench. "It wasn't your grandmother, was it?" she mused.

"I seriously doubt it, the way she hated him."

"He only addressed the woman as 'Love,' so I don't know who she is. I have the letters in my purse though. We could see if any of them say her name."

He shrugged it off. "We're nearly out of wine. Let me grab the bottle and refill our glasses."

"The story is so mysterious," she said, standing up and following him inside. "Do you think your grandmother told someone in Rosemary Bay why she didn't like Mr. Ellis?"

"I don't know," he said. "Why does it matter to you?"

"I feel like there's more there than what people know." She remembered the sadness in Alfred's words. "It's a gut feeling."

"I think he was an old miser who wasn't all there," Josh said, tapping his temple.

"Maybe. But maybe not. Does your nana have any friends in town? I'd love to see if they knew anything."

"You've got a lot of repairs you could be focusing on with that house. If I were you, I wouldn't waste my time on this."

"Just give me one name," she pressed.

He frowned. "My nana's best friend is the only one left who was around when Alfred Ellis lived here. Maybe you could ask *her*."

Melanie brightened. "What's her name?"

"Adelaide Wetherby. She goes by Addie."

"I think my gram knew her. She might have stopped by her house once or twice when we were on vacation here."

He pulled the cork from the bottle and refilled her glass, the floral and citrus scent of it mixing with the bite of alcohol. "She's super sweet—I help her get her groceries sometimes—but she's senile, though. She decorated for Christmas last month, convinced it was winter."

"Oh…" she said, disappointed.

"Don't worry about any of that right now. It's time to eat," he said, getting up. "I need to get that fish off the grill before it burns and we actually do have to catch our dinner."

Melanie sat next to Josh as the sun slipped below the blazing orange horizon, the water lapping under the houseboat, her eyes heavy from the long day, a full tummy, and several glasses of wine. She took in a long, slow breath of salty air and allowed her shoulders to relax as the fire danced in front of them.

"I'm not sure I'm up for fishing," he said sleepily, leaning his head back against the bench and peering up at the stars that had emerged like little diamonds in the darkening sky.

"Next time," she offered before realizing what she had said.

He turned his head to look at her, a question in his eyes. They stared at each other for a second, and at the indecision that slid across his face she wished she hadn't said anything, because now all she wanted was for him to stay.

"You should probably get going," he suggested warily.

"Don't you want to read the letters?" she asked, hoping to buy more time.

"Seriously. It's getting late."

"We need to know once and for all that Alfred Ellis's dream girl wasn't your grandmother," she said, smiling.

"Trust me, it's not her. But if you find the woman's name in any of those letters, my nana's maiden name was Vera Wilson."

Her own curiosity winning, she got up and took the stack from her handbag, opening the second letter. She sat back down and leaned in so Josh could view the looping, formal handwriting, their faces so close that her breathing became shallow in response.

April 23, 1960

My dearest,

I went to the farthest edge of Willow Pier and sat on our bench—

"Wait, stop," Josh said, suddenly peering down at the letter.

"What is it?" Melanie asked.

"This *is* Willow Pier." They both turned their heads toward the other end of the pier that jutted out from where they were, only now seeing the wrought-iron bench at the end of it.

"What are the odds?" she said in a whisper, breathless.

Josh threw his head back with a laugh. "In this little town, at the only working pier that's been here since the fifties, the odds are pretty good."

"Still," she said, grabbing his arm and hauling him up.

He stood for her but took a step back, pulling away from her.

"We're here, though. What are the odds that we're reading this letter on the very pier Mr. Ellis mentioned?" She tugged on Josh's bicep, pretending not to enjoy the feel of his arm under her hand. "Let's finish the letter over there." She pointed to the bench.

"It's just an old iron chair," Josh said, looking down at her. "Why would we go over there in the dark when we could sit right here on this bench—one with cushions, lights, a fire and more wine?"

Melanie huffed playfully. "You're not much of a romantic, are you?"

His mouth hung open, his eyes full of humor. "Lights, fire, wine," he repeated. "Cold bench," he said, throwing his thumb up to the Willow Pier bench.

She laughed at that one. "So you're saying that all this is you being romantic?"

Suddenly the humor left him and he seemed flustered, sitting back down. He took a gulp from his glass and swallowed. "Let's finish the letter," he said, waggling his finger at it.

Not wanting to alter his mood at this moment, she sat down and began reading again.

The weather has turned slightly warmer as the summer months creep in. I must admit that every time I sit there, I keep my eyes on the gulf with the hope that your delicate hands will fall on my shoulders from behind me unexpectedly. Sometimes I close my eyes and imagine what it would be like. I constantly wonder what I did or didn't do to cause your silence.

Last year, unable to stop myself, I knocked on the door of your house and asked for you, but your housemaid told me you'd left. She wouldn't tell me where you'd gone. My heart broke in two, wondering if you'd ended up going to the girls' school, so I waited, but every summer that you didn't return, I lost hope, until so much time had passed that it was clear you weren't coming back. While I want nothing but happiness for you, I sit here on our bench praying that one day you'll come find me.

Forever yours,
Alfred

"He didn't give us her name," Josh said, looking over at the old bench.

"No." Melanie shook her head.

"Well, at least we can rule out my grandmother," he said. "She married my grandfather Randall Claiborne here in town. They'd grown up together, so they'd had a huge celebration in the park and invited everyone. The pictures are fantastic. If it was her, Alfred Ellis would've known exactly where she was."

"Hm," Melanie said, no closer to solving this little mystery. But something in her pulled her to find out. She couldn't restore the house to a happier state until she knew, because, by the letters in her hand, she could feel that Alfred wanted to tell her.

Chapter Ten

The next morning, Melanie sat at the kitchen bar with a fresh cup of coffee, the nutty aroma filling the air. She yawned and rubbed her eyes, then stretched.

Bang, bang, bang.

What was that? It sounded like it was coming from the front door. Then a loud buzz filled the house.

Bang, bang, bang.

Melanie rushed from the back of the house and opened the door to find Josh standing in front of her, holding two to-go cups of coffee while a team of guys got to work in her yard, piling up palm trees to throw into a chipper, the pulp spewing out in an arc of fine shreds.

"I took a wild guess that you like sweet coffee…" Josh said over the noise. He held out one of the cups. "Vanilla latte."

"Thank you," she said, taking the cup, grateful for the gesture. "Where's your truck?"

"I got a ride in the chipper," he said. "The old thing wouldn't start this morning, so it's in the shop."

"Oh no."

"Looks like I've got some free time on my hands, which is good because I thought I'd knock out a few things for you before I leave for New York tomorrow."

"You're leaving tomorrow?" she asked, hearing the distress in her words and hoping he didn't.

"Yeah, I sold the house and I'm granting the buyer immediate occupancy. It's good, though. The more time I have to unpack in New York before the job starts, the better."

She nodded, at a loss for words. Abruptly, the feeling overwhelmed her that she didn't want him to go.

"We've got enough plywood to patch the roof until you can contract someone. And I'll make sure the back of the house is secure where the porch was."

"Thanks. I thought that before I get to work on the to-do list for the house, I'd go see Addie, if you want to go with me," she ventured, hoping their last day together wouldn't be spent with him on the roof.

"I'll work on the house," he said.

"We can walk to her place, you know." She pointed to the small yellow bungalow at the other end of Sandpiper Lane.

"I hope you find some answers. Now, I've got to set up that scaffolding again so I can get to the roof."

She nodded, wishing he'd said he'd go with her. "Thanks again for the coffee," she said, holding up her cup. After she closed the door, his spicy scent lingered like her thoughts of him.

"Hello," Melanie said, striding up the short path from the road, reaching the canary-yellow bungalow with its white porch stretching across the front. "Are you Addie Wetherby?"

A portly woman with gray hair pulled tightly into a bun at the back of her head sat on a rocking chair out front, her yard still full of debris from the storm. "I am," the woman said. "You the new owner of the Ellis house?"

"Yes, ma'am," Melanie replied, standing at the bottom of the three steps separating the two of them. "I'm Lou Simpson's granddaughter. Did you know her?"

The old woman gave her a friendly once-over. "I certainly did. I still remember the apple tart she made me for my birthday a few years back."

"I remember her making that," Melanie said, delighting in the shared memory. "The whole cottage smelled delicious and if we tried to dip our finger into the batter, she shooed us away, telling us it was for someone special."

The corners of Addie's eyes creased with happiness. "Did Lou know you were buying the Ellis house? She loved that place."

"It was her idea, actually. I'm planning on opening a bed and breakfast."

"Is that so?" Addie patted the rocking chair next to her.

"Yes," Melanie said, heading up the steps to the porch and sitting down in the chair, the coastal heat wrapping around her.

"Are the local legends true? Any ghosts?"

Melanie grinned at the thought. "Not yet," she said. "I did find some letters in the house, though."

Addie's eyebrows rose in interest.

"I was wondering if you knew anything about Alfred Ellis, the man who lived there."

The old lady pursed her lips and then said, "He caused quite a stir…"

"Why?" Melanie asked, leaning toward her, hanging on the old woman's every word.

"No one in Rosemary Bay wanted that house to be built by an outsider. Mr. Ellis came into town and threw that thing up right on the beach for everyone to see, and then he just let it fall into disrepair, our gorgeous coastline eaten up with an eyesore."

Melanie nodded, knowing exactly what Addie meant. It was her eyesore to deal with now, she thought. "You were friends with Vera Claiborne, is that right?"

Addie's gaze landed on her cautiously. "Mm hm."

"Is that why Vera didn't like him?"

"It was certainly one of the reasons."

"What were the others? Do you know?"

Addie tipped her head up toward the clear blue sky as if she were speaking to someone up there. "Sometimes our secrets are better off buried," she replied.

"What about this?" Melanie pulled the old key with 0113 engraved on it. "Do you, by any chance, know what this is?"

Addie took the key and held it out to get a good focus on it. "I have no idea, dear. What does it have to do with the Ellis house?"

"I'm not sure," Melanie said, disappointed. "I found it in the house so I wondered if it had any significance. It's probably just an old key."

The woman pushed herself to a standing position, her hands wobbling against the arms of her chair as she attempted to steady herself. "I'm tired, dear. I'm going to head inside. It was lovely to meet you."

"I can see if the people cleaning up my yard will come do yours if you need some help," Melanie offered, changing the subject quickly in an effort to make Addie stay a little longer. She hadn't meant to run her off.

"That would be very much appreciated, thank you," Addie said, opening the door.

"Maybe we can chat again sometime?" Melanie asked.

"Maybe," Addie replied, her back to Melanie as she made her way inside. "Have a nice day." The door swung shut, leaving Melanie on the porch, wondering what secrets Addie was holding on to and why she wouldn't dare tell them.

"How's it going?" Melanie asked Josh, walking up to the ladder back at the Ellis house.

He stepped down the last few rungs and wiped the sweat from his forehead with his wrist. "The roof is patched for now," he said. "But you'll want to get a roofer on it soon, or rain might leak between the shingles and damage the interior further."

Her shoulders slumped at yet another thing that could go wrong. "Okay."

"Any luck with Addie?" he asked.

"I passed a farmer's market just down the road. I figured I'd drop the laundry off at the laundromat, since it's close, and then stop by to see what they have. Why don't you take a break and we'll get something to eat while we chat about it?" she asked.

"I'm busy."

"You should take a break every now and again."

He closed up the ladder and hoisted it onto his shoulder. "Breaks won't get this house fixed."

"Starving carpenters won't get this house fixed either. Come on."

"All right," he said, shaking his head, unfastening his tool belt and setting it down.

On the way out, Melanie mentioned Addie's yard to the guys, who said they'd be happy to do it. Then she and Josh headed down the street with her bag of laundry and a roll of quarters, dropping in and filling the machines with her dirty linens. While it was all washing, they headed over to the market.

The market's A-line tin roof was a welcome reprieve from the relentless summer sun, the paddle fans underneath it whirring against the salty breeze. The sweet aroma of home-baked goods filled the air as they walked past tables full of jars of fresh honey, local produce, and homemade pies. They stopped next to a booth offering freshly squeezed lemonade slushies.

"Two, please," Josh said, handing the attendant a few bills.

"Thank you," Melanie said with a smile.

"How do you know they're not both for me?"

"Fine," she kidded back. "Then when I get two slices of pecan pie over there"—she pointed to the table down the aisle—"I'm eating them both."

"Two slices of pecan pie would make you very thirsty," he said, taking the two lemonade slushies from the woman and handing one to Melanie. "Good thing they're not both for me."

She grinned at him and then took a sip of the icy, tart drink, his banter making her stomach do a little flip. "Maybe I won't start with pie," she said as they started walking again. "I haven't eaten at all yet. I'm so hungry."

"While we're here, we should pick up some groceries for you to take back to the house. You can't go on eating restaurant food indefinitely."

"True, but my new appliances don't come until tomorrow, and with the storm, I'm not sure if they'll still be delivered on time."

He nodded, clearly thinking.

"Thank you for being here," she suddenly said, pulling him out of whatever it was that was on his mind. "My gram wanted me to redo the Ellis house, and I thought maybe I'd enjoy opening a bed and breakfast there. But I had no idea what I was getting into. Thank you for helping me."

"Why did your gram want you to buy that house?" he asked.

She fiddled with a basket of strawberries for sale on the table next to her, drawing her thoughts together. "She felt like I'd lost myself in the three years I'd taken care of her."

"Did you?"

She looked up at him. "Yeah," she said, those early days before caring for Gram feeling like an ancient memory—like someone else entirely. "I devoted my whole life to her for those three years, but it changed me too. I can't go back to who I was."

"You don't have to go back," he said. "That's the great thing about life: it's always moving forward. You just have to know how to pick up the pace to run with it. After my divorce, I wasn't the same either. It opened my eyes to the realization that the life I'd been building wasn't for me. Now, I'm changed but still the same in a way... Moving forward." He offered a smile.

As she took in Josh's statements, she realized that the two of them weren't all that different. His breakup was traumatic like losing Gram, and the loss of the life he'd had sat behind him in his past. Now he was trudging through this new reality just like she was, trying to figure out who he wanted to be.

"You'll figure it out," he said, pulling her from her thoughts. "From what I know of you already, I can tell that much." He offered her his arm. "But we won't get anything straight if we fall out from lack of food."

She laughed, grabbing his arm and directing him down the row to a small chalkboard menu. "Look," she said, pulling him over to a stall a few booths over. "Breakfast sandwiches! Local farm-fresh eggs, bacon, and melted gouda on bread with a salted pumpkin seed crust."

"Two, please," they both said at the same time.

Then suddenly, the smile fell from Josh's face.

"Hey," a young woman with pretty green eyes and blonde hair said. Her shoulders were squared and she had a smile that was equal to someone putting lipstick on a tiger.

Josh didn't return her greeting.

"Typical," she spat under her breath.

A rage in his eyes burned like fire. "You want me to tell you hello like we're two old friends, Janie?" he asked, his voice level as still waters on a calm day, but Melanie could tell it was taking all his strength to do it.

"I think we can both be civil about this," she said, flashing that fake pageant smile.

Josh ground his teeth, his jaw bulging. "Civil is rooting through my documents when I wasn't home? Or how about shacking up with your boss when I *was* home?"

"You're an ass," she huffed and rolled her eyes, spinning around and heading in the other direction without a word.

Melanie watched her go, speechless.

The man behind the booth slid their sandwiches toward them, tearing Melanie from the moment. Josh cleared his throat and paid for their food.

Roscoe had been right: Melanie definitely wasn't Janie.

"That's weird," Josh said, as Melanie dug her feet into the pearly sand, her half-eaten sandwich sitting on its paper on top of her laptop as she looked out over the lulling waves of the gulf.

"I know." She was still trying to make sense of Addie's reaction. Melanie had told Josh about her conversation with the old woman while they were eating on the beach, but he, too, seemed to be at a loss.

She looked out at the water, thinking. A dark gray cloud loomed on the horizon, making her nervous. She felt as though one more rough storm might blow her house right over. She focused on the rays of sun and the gulls soaring in the electric-blue sky above them, trying not to worry about it.

"So, here's my list of repairs," she said, switching gears. She balled up her sandwich paper and put it in her pocket, opening her laptop. "Maybe you could tell me the best people to call, since you know this industry."

"Sure," he said, leaning over. "I've got some people who can knock this out in no time."

"Really?" she said, feeling a swell of hope. "I've separated the list into repairs and remodeling. The damage from the hurricane will set me back on my remodeling budget, so it's important for me to get the best prices on repairs."

"You'll want to replace the porch first," he said, tapping that item on her screen. "And then anchor the foundation."

"The water system in the house is a mess. I've still got major pipe work to take care of as well. I've gotten the kitchen and bathroom fixed so far," she said, her stomach churning. "But there's more to do and the guy I have is expensive."

"I've got a plumber you can call. He'll give you a deal if you tell him I sent you."

"That's amazing, thank you," she said, cupping her hand over the screen to view the list in the sunshine.

"No problem. And I can help you find a carpenter for the porch. You're looking at probably fifteen thousand dollars for that…"

She nodded, wondering how she'd ever get up and running. He was right; this would take years and more money than she had. Her mind floated upstairs to the pocket in her suitcase where she'd packed her old princess cut engagement ring.

"What are you thinking about?" he asked.

"Hm?" She turned toward him.

"Your face looks like that afternoon storm cloud right now. What's bothering you—is it the money?"

She nodded again, for fear that if she tried to say something she'd burst into tears.

"I get it," he told her.

"You do?" she asked, her voice cracking.

"The land that's in my family, where the waterfall is—it's left to direct male descendants only. My grandfather left it to me. It's sort of like my security because I know that no matter what happens, it'll be there for me when I need it—it's just waiting for me to settle there. A developer named Bowland Enterprises is trying to buy it from me to build retail shops, but I won't sell. It's been in our family for generations and there's no price tag for those memories."

"Do you think you'll ever come back and live on it?" Melanie asked.

"I absolutely plan to live there. I want to retire on that land, build my dream house. That's the real reason I'm moving to New York. That job is going to pay for the house I build."

"You can't just work here?" she asked, wishing he would. The thought was crazy, since she'd only just met him, but with no one else, having him there felt comforting, even if his moods were unpredictable sometimes.

"I just can't make what I need in this little town. If I want the life I dream about, I have to make the change."

"I understand. I need to shake up my own life too if I ever want to move on from Gram's death. I have to pick up the pieces and figure out who I am."

"I hear you."

She looked up at the sky. "Another storm's coming," she said, eyeing the clouds that had now shifted above the water, casting a shadow on the horizon.

"Summer storms—you'll get used to them." He locked eyes with her. "They seem to pop up just when you start to get comfortable."

Chapter Eleven

"Road crews have the main road blocked. It's the only way out of the village," Josh explained, his cell phone at his ear. After they'd returned from the laundromat and farmer's market, he'd been calling his contacts to see if any of them could help Melanie, and no one was available, all of them overloaded with work from the hurricane. The last one had given Josh the news. "It'll be three days before the road's passable again?" he asked, his focus returning to the call. "Thanks, Poncho. I'll call ya soon," he said, hanging up.

"What does that mean?" Melanie asked, leaning on her elbows, her hands at her chin, as she stood at the kitchen counter.

"Well, for you, it means that my friend Poncho can't get here to quote you on a new porch for three days. For me, it means that I can't pick up my truck." He set his phone down and ran his fingers through his hair, pursing his lips. "So much for leaving tomorrow."

"I'm sorry," she said.

"It's not your fault," he told her. "My friend with the houseboat is coming back from Australia, so now I guess I'll have to stay with my mother." He tipped his head back and took in a deep breath. "She and I don't always see eye to eye on things. I'll spend the entire time I'm there defending my reasons for moving to New York."

"Maybe she just wants you to stay," she offered.

"Yeah, but she'll drive me crazy trying to convince me. She's really upset about the whole thing and she won't listen to me at all when I try to explain why I'm going."

"Are you her only son?" Melanie asked.

Josh nodded. "She means well, I'm sure, but I can't deal with her sometimes."

"You could stay here. I have plenty of space," she suggested, but as she looked around at the dirty floor that stretched across an empty room, she knew that wasn't offering much.

"It's definitely an attractive offer, given the alternative. I could check with my friend Steven…"

"You *sure* you can't stay with your mom? How bad is it?" She thought about her own mother, and the idea of not being able to go to her when she was in need was unthinkable.

"She's constantly telling me I'm… running away from things." He rolled his eyes.

"Are you?"

"Of course not," he said a little too quickly, getting agitated. "I told you why I was leaving."

She put her hands up. "Sorry," she said, curious as to why he was getting defensive.

"Let's just drop it," he replied, that wall that he was so good at building around himself sliding right back up. Without warning, he dialed a number on his phone. "Hey, man," he said, turning away from her and explaining the situation. "Oh, okay. I'll catch up with you later."

"Everything okay?" she asked when he was finished.

"Steven's already got a full house from the storm. A couple of the guys you met playing darts the other night are staying with him."

"Seriously, you can stay here. At least until you can find something better. I've got fresh produce and eggs for breakfast from the farmer's market, remember?"

He swallowed, thoughts evident on his face, his mouth resting in a straight line. "Thank you."

"It's no problem. We spent one night on the air mattress. What's another?" A fizzle of excitement ran through her, remembering the feel of his arms around her.

"If I'm going to stay, I'll need to stop by the storage unit and pick up a few things. Could I borrow your car?"

"Sure."

"Okay. Let me run over there and I'll be right back."

She went over to her handbag and dug out her keys, tossing them to him.

"Thanks," he said as he caught them. "Need anything while I'm out?"

"Not unless you want to grab us something to drink with dinner. I've got one working burner on the stove until the new one comes, but I can still cook us something."

"Hold off for now. I'll see what restaurants I can get to. Be right back."

"Sounds good," she said.

He threw up a hand to her and left her alone in the room.

Melanie opened the cooler that she was using until the fridge came tomorrow, and pulled out a bottle of water. As she was peering out at the sparkling stretch of gulf, she heard a pop and all the lights went out, the paddle fans stopping.

"Great," she said to herself, as she walked around flipping switches to no avail.

Hoping it was just the crews doing work on the lines and not something else wrong with the house, or worse yet, Alfred Ellis getting irritated that she was still there, she grabbed his letters and headed outside for some fresh air. The sea grass swayed in the unrelenting breeze, while the seagulls dipped down over the water, in search of dinner. She felt helpless, unable to move forward with the house at the moment, literally stuck, and sat down on what was left of the porch floor. As she opened the next envelope she noticed the date and, flipping through the other letters, realized they were all dated April 23, a year apart.

April 23, 1961

My love,

For the last two years, I have considered tracking you down, but I'd never do that to you. If you've gone off and found someone you love more than me, then I want you to have that happiness at whatever cost. The cost is most certainly my heart. It is in pieces without you. I can close my eyes and still see that innocent gaze from your angelic eyes, and it floors me every time. I miss it so much it hurts. I keep telling myself that one day this will all make sense, but I fear that I'm wishing too much.

Yours truly,
Alfred

Melanie stared at the words, wondering why this woman had chosen another life, breaking Alfred's heart. But one thing she'd learned was that sometimes things just didn't make sense. They hadn't made sense when her wonderful Gram had gotten cancer. They hadn't made sense when Melanie had had to uproot her life to help Gram battle the disease as it took over her body. And they hadn't made sense when her fiancé Adam had broken things off with her, completely out of the blue—so much for "for better or worse."

With the setting sun painting red and yellow streaks in the sky, Melanie decided to go back and try the lights once more. Inside, after she flicked the switch but nothing happened, she ran over to her boxes and fished around in them, finding all the candles she could and a pack of matches. Then she searched through her linens box and grabbed a blanket. Spreading it out on the living room floor, she set the candles on the hardwoods around it, lighting them, their flames sending a warm glow across the room.

"Wow," Josh said when he returned, carrying two grocery sacks with a duffel bag thrown over his shoulder. "What's all this?" He looked almost terrified.

"The power's out," she said matter-of-factly, seeing the romantic scene through his eyes and trying to put his mind at ease. From the way his shoulders relaxed, her explanation had worked. She'd opened the windows to keep the heat at bay, the soft, salty breeze making the candles flicker. "What's in the bags?"

"Carryout from the Seafood Shack."

Her eyes grew round. "Oh, I love that place. My gram and I used to eat there the first night of vacation every time we came to visit. It was her favorite."

There was a crack of thunder outside, and she was glad he'd come back when he had. He set the bags down on the floor and retrieved a couple of cardboard containers. "I ordered us tuna dip, coconut shrimp wrapped in bacon, and crab cakes."

Melanie's tummy rumbled. "That sounds amazing."

"And I got us a bottle of Riesling to drink."

"That'll be delicious," she said, her mouth nearly watering. "I just have to see if I can unpack us two wine glasses…"

"I grabbed these, too." He held up two plastic wine glasses wrapped in cellophane.

"You've thought of everything," she said.

They both sat down on the blanket in the dim candlelight, the dishes opened between them so they could share, just as the onslaught of rain filled the silence, sending a wet coolness into the air, an avalanche of raindrops pelting the roof. Josh handed her a fork, and she stabbed a bacon-wrapped shrimp, the buttery saltiness tickling her taste buds.

"So, I've got you for three more days," she said.

He studied her, as if deciding whether that was a good thing or a bad thing. "Well, two and a half. Originally, on my way out of town, I was going to stop off to see a little boy named Cole. I promised him I'd come for a visit, and I was hoping you'd loan me your car."

"Oh?"

"He's four. He lives with his foster parents outside of town."

"Is he someone in your family?"

"No, he's living with friends of mine. After they took him in, I joined a program that matches children with adults as nurturers and mentors. His foster father Eric and I used to build houses together."

"Oh my goodness," she said, seeing him through new eyes. This was the version of him everyone in town had talked about. "How often did you see him?"

"Every day."

"I'll bet he's sad to see you go."

Josh's smile dropped, contemplation in his eyes. "I promised him I'd visit. I'm not just going to leave him and never come back."

"I hope not," she said. "So you're going to see Cole tomorrow morning?"

"Yeah."

The mood had shifted significantly, and Melanie couldn't help but feel for the little boy. As a foster child, he probably wasn't used to people sticking around, and she wondered how he would handle Josh's leaving.

"Could I go with you to meet him?" she asked, stabbing a piece of her crab cake and taking a bite.

"Sure," Josh replied.

"Maybe I could step in for you when you leave, although I have no idea what I could do with the little guy, since building certainly isn't my forte."

"He likes fishing," Josh said. "And I owe you a lesson."

She smiled. "I'd like you to teach me. I grew up with my grandmother and my mother and sister—all girls—and we didn't do much fishing. My dad died in a car crash. I was only three."

"Mm," he said, thoughtful. "I'm sorry to hear that."

"I only have fuzzy memories of him."

"And your grandfather?"

"He passed away when I was twelve." She set her fork down, the candles flickering around them.

Fondness washed over Josh's face, the corners of his lips turning upward. "After dinner, once the rain stops, I want to show you something." It was the first time she'd seen a sparkle in his eyes.

"Where are we going?" Melanie asked as they padded through the wet sand, the late evening storm having left in a hurry, leaving a sea of shimmering stars in its wake. The moon hung amidst them like a guardian, casting its white light over everything.

"What you said—it made me think of something I hadn't thought of in years." He led her off the beach and across the road, into the darkness of the woods. As he took her hand to help her through the brush, every nerve in her arm tingled. With his free hand, he turned on his cell phone light to illuminate a well-worn path as they headed further into the mass of trees.

He stopped her, shining his light on an enormous red maple. "Take a look at this."

Melanie gasped at the stunning sight. All the way up, as far as it could go, the trunk was painted with brightly colored messages. She ran her hand along the smooth bark, reading the words: "Please watch over mittens; Help my mother beat cancer; Keep my Sam safe…" She tipped her head to see all the way to the top, the messages towering over them. "What are all these?" she asked.

"Wishes." He took a step up next to her. "It started when I was young. There were just a few. And it caught on." He shined his light over to a small wooden pole with a metal box at the top. Opening it, he pulled out a couple bottles of paint, a paper plate, and two disposable paintbrushes. "The news got wind of it, and they did a local piece on the way it offered hope. People started researching paint that doesn't harm the tree, and they donate supplies, leaving them in this box for people in town." He handed her a brush. "What do you want to wish for?"

She took the paper plate from him and, squeezing out a small blob of blue paint, dipped her brush in it. Then she went over to a spot where the paint had faded and began to draw the letters of her message. Josh directed his light onto the trunk for her. She ran through ideas—she had so many wishes. She wished Gram could explain why Melanie had needed the Ellis house. She wished Alfred could've found his love. She wished she didn't have to be alone so much… All of it fell under one message. She wrote the words: *Change the story*.

"Change the story?" he asked.

"Yes. I want to alter the history of the Ellis house. It doesn't have to be the awful, sad story that it is. I'm going to try to change it."

"That's great," he said. "I hope you can." He filled his plate with a squirt of paint. "My turn," he said, handing her his cell phone so she could light the tree. He thought for a moment and then began to paint: *Start over.* "Hoping to make this a reality if I can ever get my truck back." He gave her an amused pout, but her heart plummeted down to her stomach.

They both stared at the tree, taking it all in.

Melanie sent a silent wish up to Gram. *Give me a push, Gram. Show me the direction I should go.* "Have any of these wishes come true?" she asked aloud.

"I'm not sure."

She gave the messages one last look.

As they made their way back to the house, Melanie felt a tiny spark of hope. It was the nudge she needed to find her determination. She was going to organize the budget, make all the calls she had left to make, and get to work. Melanie planned to give this everything she had.

Chapter Twelve

The old brown shingled beach house on the edge of town sat on a sandy lot without a view, between two enormous prickly pear cacti. But in the window, a freckle-faced boy with almond hair and dark eyes smiled brightly at Josh and Melanie, bouncing up and down.

Josh waved at him.

The little boy disappeared and then swung the front door open, running out and jumping into Josh's arms, sending him slightly off balance.

"Hey, buddy," he said, holding the boy with one arm while he ruffled his hair with the other.

"We goin' fishin'?" the boy asked.

"I thought we might," Josh replied. "I brought my friend Melanie along. She wants us to teach her how."

"You must be Cole," Melanie said.

Cole nodded, looking at her in wonder. "You never been fishin' 'fore?" he asked in his thick southern drawl.

"I haven't," she replied with a grin, unable to hide the fact that she found him absolutely adorable.

"Hey, Josh," a woman said from the doorway. Her blonde hair was wrapped up in a red bandana, and her smile stretched from ear to ear.

"Hey Suzie, this is Melanie. She's coming with me to hang out with Cole today."

"Hi there," Suzie said, walking toward her and holding out her hand in greeting. "It's nice to meet you."

"Suzie and her husband Eric are Cole's foster parents," Josh explained.

"We call Josh the third parent, though. He spends as much time with Cole as we do. We're certainly going to miss him."

"Do you have to go?" Cole asked. The boy's innocent eyes rounded on Josh.

"I do," Josh replied softly, his voice thick with emotion as he held the boy in his arms. "But I promise to come back all the time."

There was a hint of disbelief in Cole's expression after Josh made his promise. "My mama and daddy went away and didn't come back," he said.

Josh nodded. "But I'm not them. I promise never to do that."

"Is New York far away?"

"Yep. But there are airplanes that can get me here in a flash."

"Okay," the little boy said, but it didn't seem as though Josh's explanation had helped settle his young mind a whole lot.

"So!" Josh said, setting Cole down and clapping his hands excitedly. "You got your fishing pole?"

"Yes, sir!" Cole giggled, running into the house. Suzie followed him inside.

"How long has Cole been with Suzie and Eric?" Melanie asked once she and Josh were alone together.

"Almost a year," he replied. "Eric is a friend of mine and when he told me they were fostering Cole, I wanted to help, so while I have breaks in my day, I pop in and spend time with him. Eric's a landscaper so he has a tighter work schedule than mine in the summers. Cole's parents skipped out on him, and he hasn't had a good adult figure in his life until we stepped in."

"I'm ready!" Cole said, coming out with a pair of rainbow rubber boots on.

Suzie leaned two tall fishing rods and one smaller one against the house and then set a small bucket of shrimp next to them. "Y'all have fun!"

Josh went up onto the porch and grabbed the three rods, handing them out to Melanie and Cole. "Let's show Melanie how we catch redfish."

"Think she'll catch any?" Cole asked, looking up at him.

"If we teach her how to do it. You gonna show her?"

"Yeah!" Cole ran ahead, crossing the road and racing over the dune.

"Slow down," Josh called out with a laugh. "We won't be able to catch up." Josh grabbed Melanie's hand and took off, her legs working overtime to keep up.

Gripping her fishing rod in one hand and holding on to Josh with the other, Melanie sprinted through the sea grass, the wind blowing her hair behind her shoulders. When they got to the soft white sand, they finally slowed down. The end of Cole's rod was stuck in the sand and he stood facing them with his hands on his hips.

"Y'all comin'?" he called to them as the surf bubbled up the shore, fizzing and popping behind him.

Josh and Melanie joined him. "Let me get Melanie's bait on her hook," Josh said. "You wanna do yours?"

"Isn't that dangerous for him?" Melanie asked. "That hook is sharp."

"Josh taught me how to do it like the big guys do," Cole said. "Look." He pinched the far end of the hook away from the sharp edge.

"You just gotta know where to hold it." He threaded a small piece of shrimp on it, his little fingers working with precision. "Then you cast it out like this." His arm maneuvered the rod just so, and the shrimp sunk beneath the water.

Josh took Melanie's rod, preparing to load the shrimp.

"Hang on," she said, stopping him and taking the bait from his fingers. "Let me see if I can get it on the hook like Cole showed me. He's such a great teacher."

Cole's chest puffed up and he fiddled with his rod as if he were crafting expert tweaks to his line, making her smile. Melanie held the end of the hook between her fingers and stuck the shrimp through the middle.

"How's this?" she asked.

Josh leaned over to take a look, and she could feel his warmth next to her, making her pulse quicken. "Perfect."

Cole jammed his rod in the sand and came over to look at it, nodding approvingly. Then he balled his tiny fist up and slugged Josh playfully in the arm. "Tag, you're it!" he said, simultaneously kicking off his boots and running barefoot in the sand.

"Oh, no you don't," Josh said, racing after him.

Cole squealed with delight, dodging Josh's arms and splashing into the water, the foamy spray making the little boy's shorts wet.

"I'm going to get you!" Josh called, his large strides too much for the little boy. He scooped him up, spinning him around and plopping Cole on his shoulders.

Laughing, Cole threw his head back, his hands covering Josh's eyes as he tried to hold on.

Josh waded into the water, his clothes getting soaked. "You're goin' in!" he teased.

"Nooo!" Cole said, squeezing Josh's head and giggling uncontrollably.

"Yes, sir!" Josh peeled the boy's fingers from his eyes and waded further until he was waist deep. Then he tickled Cole's sides, causing him to wriggle around, losing grip. Skillfully, Josh flipped the little boy around and threw him high into the air, catching him just before he hit the water. "You're gonna get we-et!" Josh teased, throwing him up again.

"So are you-ou!" As Cole came down, he plunged his arms under the water and splashed Josh's shirt.

Melanie let out a yelp of laughter. She couldn't take her eyes off this playful Josh she was watching.

"Oh, that's it." Josh strode further in and threw Cole up into the air again, the boy laughing as he dove down into the water. His head popped up just as Josh grabbed him and lifted him out.

"Can we do that again?" Cole asked, the both of them sopping wet.

"Oh!" Melanie cried as her line got a pretty good tug.

Josh and Cole came over, their sodden clothes sticking to their bodies, their hair dripping with water.

"Reel it in," Josh said, as he got behind her to keep her steady. His damp arms encircled her as he put his hands over hers to help her. She swallowed, her heart pattering.

"She's got a fighter," Cole said as he looked on intently.

Melanie and Josh reeled until the fish flopped into the air, dangling from the hook.

Grabbing the line, Josh took hold of the fish. "It's a redfish," he told her. "This one's about eight pounds."

"She caught an eight-pound redfish on her first try?" Cole asked, staring at her in disbelief.

"She sure did," Josh said with a grin. "She's a natural." He took the fish off and threw it back into the gulf. "Maybe Melanie would come fish with you on the days I'm in New York," he suggested.

"I'd love that," Melanie said.

Cole looked over at Josh, the corners of his mouth turning downward before his bottom lip started to wobble. "I don't want you to go," he said.

"I know you don't." Josh kneeled down to be at his eye level. "I don't want to leave you either. And it won't be forever. But I have to go for a little while."

A tear spilled down Cole's cheek. "I'm gonna miss you so much."

"Maybe I can talk to Suzie and you can come visit me in New York," Josh said. "You could stay with me in my new apartment in the city."

Cole brightened a bit at that idea, and nodded his head.

Melanie watched the two of them, her heart breaking for the little boy, wishing she could do something to make it all okay for him.

Just then Suzie came down over the dune with Eric, both of them holding a beer in each hand. "I thought y'all could use these," she said, handing one to Melanie before reaching into her back pocket and pulling out a juice pouch for Cole.

Eric clapped Josh on the back and handed him a beer. Josh's friend was tall and thin, with sandy brown hair that was just messy enough to seem like he didn't put any effort into it, but it suited him. He had a wide smile that showed off his easygoing demeanor. "Anything good?" he asked, reaching over and tugging on Cole's line.

"A giant redfish, but I can't claim it," Cole said. "Melanie caught it."

Eric looked over at Melanie in surprise. "Wow, that's awesome."

Suzie raised her bottle. "Eric got off early today. His last landscaping client cancelled on him, so we thought we'd join y'all on the beach." She sat down in the sand, resting the bottle on her knee. "Melanie, if you get bored, feel free to give that pole to Eric and have a seat with me."

"Wait," Cole said, handing his own rod to Eric. "I want Melanie's. It's lucky today."

"Here you go," Melanie said. While the guys fished, she went over and sat down next to Suzie.

"So what do you think of our little guy?"

Melanie grinned, watching the three of them as they cast their rods into the water. "Cole is adorable."

"He's such a good boy."

There'd been a time when Melanie had imagined what it would be like to have children, when her future never included a crumbling old house and no one to share it with. Cole was exactly the type of child she'd hoped for back then. "He's so sweet, with a sense of humor beyond his years."

"Yes, that's true." Suzie took a sip of her beer. "When we took him in, we just knew that he'd have so much love around him. Eric and Josh are great friends and they both stepped in to help right away… But it's nice to have another woman around for once. All the testosterone…" She laughed, holding up her beer bottle. "I don't know what they'd do if I'd made four cocktails instead."

Melanie laughed. "Maybe we can have cocktails sometime."

Suzie stretched out her legs, digging her heels into the soft sand. "That would be wonderful."

"I'm going to miss Cole," Josh said on their way home. He took in a deep breath and let it out. "By the way, do you mind stopping off at my mother's? She asked me to come over."

"Not at all," Melanie said.

"Turn here. She's right down this road," he said. "Having you with me might defuse the situation."

They pulled into the drive of a small beach house, painted a bright teal color with a white starfish wreath on the door. A thin woman with brown curly hair got off the porch swing and put her hands on her hips.

"Well, look who the cat dragged in," the woman said with a playful grin when Josh and Melanie had gotten out of the car. "I thought you'd be halfway to the state line by now." She eyed the car, her gaze sliding over to Melanie.

"Hey, Mom," Josh said, walking up to her. "This is Melanie."

"Well, well, well," she said with an appraising stare. "So this is the new owner of the Ellis house. I'm Brenda." She pursed her lips. "How're things goin'?"

"Not great," Melanie said honestly.

"Yeah, I could've told you that. That house is cursed."

"Mom," Josh cut in, trying to stop her.

"Don't try to sweep it under the rug, son," she said. "That house brings nothing but bad luck. Remember when Mr. Ellis was still alive and that mailman broke his ankle on the step when he was delivering a package?"

"Mom—" he tried again, but she kept going.

"No, no, let me tell her." Brenda leaned in closely. "One time, a gardener was pruning the hedges—sliced his hand down to the bone."

The feeling of familiar dread about buying the house so impulsively washed over her again. "I'm not terribly superstitious," Melanie said weakly.

"That's a good thing," Brenda said, pursing her lips. "Everything about that man was bad luck. My mama used to say that Alfred Ellis was a lyin', cheatin' scoundrel. He's probably still there, pokin' pins in his voodoo doll. I cannot believe you're working on that house," she said, whacking Josh's bicep with the back of her hand.

"Ow," he said playfully.

"I don't know what Melanie's payin' you to do it, but it's the devil's money." She looked up to the sky, shaking her head as if she were apologizing to the Lord himself, and then she opened the door. "Y'all come on in."

"She's not paying me," Josh said with an I-told-you-so look to Melanie, making her have to stifle a grin. She bit her lip.

Brenda turned around. "I don't know which is worse: doin' the devil's work for free or sellin' your soul to get paid for it."

"I lost a bet," he explained. "Darts."

"How can you lose at darts when I taught you everything you needed to know about that game growin' up?"

"I don't know. We were playing Twenty-one."

"He was so close," Melanie stepped in. "His dart hit *just* beside the bull's eye."

Brenda frowned, shaking her head. "What did you get if you won?"

"A beer," he told her as they walked into the kitchen.

Brenda threw her head back and laughed. She opened the fridge, grabbed a bottle of Budweiser, and set it on the table. "Here. Next time you need a beer, you'll have one." She grabbed a mug from the cabinet and murmured, "Lord have mercy…"

Melanie gritted her teeth together to keep from smiling at Brenda.

With her back to them, Brenda said, "I'll make us some coffee. And Josh, I've got a change of clothes in your old dresser. Put on somethin' dry and I'll wash what you've got on. You look like a wet rat."

"Charming, isn't she?" he whispered, only half serious.

"I heard that," she threw over her shoulder.

While Josh changed in the other room, Melanie helped Brenda with the coffee. "So do you not want Josh to go to New York?" she asked as the coffee maker began to gurgle, the rich scent of the beans filtering into the air.

"I want him to do what makes him happy," Brenda said, "but I don't think New York is gonna to make him any happier than he is now."

"Why do you say that?"

"Josh likes to run away from things, and now is no different," his mother said, pouring them each a cup of steaming coffee and setting Josh's on the table. "When he and Janie didn't work out, right away he planned to run as far as he could go—for the last year, he's been preparin', runnin' all the way to the Big Apple, the perfect place to get lost in the crowd. But gettin' lost won't make him whole again."

"That's not why I'm going, and you know it, Mom," he said, coming into the room. "Janie and I didn't work out, and I'm okay with that. Why can't you get that into your head?"

"Look, son, I don't care if you and Janie aren't right for each other, if bein' apart is what y'all both want. But I don't think you have to move your whole life just so that you don't run into her."

Melanie thought back to their meeting with Janie, suddenly understanding why he absolutely wouldn't want to run into her.

"You refuse to listen," he said, clearly frustrated. "I'm moving because—"

"I already know. Because Janie told you that you weren't good enough, that you'd never amount to anything in this town, and that she could do better."

Josh stared at his mother, silenced.

Melanie took a seat quietly, gripping her mug, the warmth radiating through her hands. She took a deliciously creamy, sweet sip to hide that she was completely blown away that his ex-wife would say something like that.

"But the part that gets me is that you believe her."

Josh's chest filled with air as he looked down into his coffee, clearly irritated to be airing this conversation in front of Melanie.

"You've got a life here, babe. We all love ya. What's movin' to New York gonna fix?"

"I can make triple what I make here," he said. "And I can come back and build on our land. I never want to get married again. I just want to spend my days—"

"I don't believe that for one minute. You can build any house you want to right now. You don't need extra money." She shook her head. "You're runnin'. Runnin', tryin' to make something of yourself when you're enough just the way you are."

His cheeks flamed. "You asked me to come over to tell me this?"

"Pretty much," she said, with a wink toward Melanie.

Melanie was glad that Brenda had told him that, even if he didn't believe it.

"This isn't the time for this discussion," he said, evidently not amused.

His mother's face dropped. "And when is the right time, son? You're leaving every one of us behind, and none of us understand why."

"I want a different life," he said.

"What's so bad about this one?" she asked, lifting her steaming mug to her lips.

Josh didn't respond.

"Is there anything I can help you with before you go?" Brenda asked, relenting.

"Yeah," he said, taking a drink from his mug. "You can help me find an alternate route to Ferguson's Auto. I can't get my truck until the main road is clear."

"I can't help you there," she said. "But another reason I asked you over is because the sidin' was blown off the house in the storm, and I need someone to help me replace it. Looks like you've got a few days to spare," she said with dry affection.

"I'll fix it for you," he replied, fondness for his mother in his eyes.

"I won't mind havin' you around the house, that's for sure."

Melanie had to admit, she wouldn't mind having him around a little longer either.

Chapter Thirteen

Wide-eyed, Melanie held the doorknob to the front door in her hand, staring at the hole where it used to be and thinking about what Brenda had said regarding Alfred Ellis poking holes into his voodoo doll. She might have been right. With some free time on her hands while she left Josh at his mother's, Melanie had gone to the hardware store and gotten supplies to strip the old wallpaper.

She stuck her finger in the space where the knob had been and unlatched the door, heading inside, and setting the stripper and putty knife on the floor. She went into the kitchen, her head spinning. She'd been in marketing, so she had a basic understanding of what was needed to entice buyers. What would be the biggest design bang for her buck with this house? What would draw them in?

Going over to the counter to set the doorknob down, she was grabbing her notebook when she caught sight of the stack of letters. Her gaze moved around the house. "If you're upset because I'm here," she said aloud to Alfred, to ward off any more bad luck, "please know that I want to make this house what it was." Then she took the next envelope and opened it, hoping it might give her some inspiration.

April 23, 1962

Dear Eloise,

Melanie's breath caught. Gram's name was Eloise, but she went by Lou.

I received word that you are married and I am devastated. I built this house with the hope that its walls would hear your laughter, comfort your tears, and feel the patter of our children's feet. It is colossally empty now, a hollow shell of the hope that I created in my own stupidity. I hung the chandelier you'd seen in the store window, the one you told me would be perfect in our parlor. You'd said <u>our</u> parlor. I haven't forgotten the way it rolled off your tongue, the word wasted, lost in the air, meaning nothing now. One day, I will bring you here to this house. One day, we will walk through its halls hand in hand. I will believe that until my final breath.

Waiting,
Alfred

A knock at the door made Melanie jump. She took in a gulp of air to steady her thumping heart and went to the door where, on the other side, Addie was holding a plate of cookies.

"I wanted to thank you for sending the crew over to clean up my yard," she said, holding out the treats. "These are key lime coconut, and the powdered sugar on the top is addictive."

"That sounds delicious," Melanie said. "You didn't have to do that."

"What happened to the doorknob?"

"It came loose when I turned it."

"This house is bad luck, I tell you."

"It'll be fine. I just need to find a screwdriver. I've got one somewhere..." She held the door open so Addie could step inside, the old woman gazing around the space with interest. "May I ask you something?" Melanie ventured.

"Yes..." Addie replied cautiously.

"Alfred Ellis wrote letters to someone named Eloise."

Addie stared at Melanie, her lips set in a straight line.

"You were friends with Gram. It wasn't her, right?"

"Let's set those cookies down, shall we?"

"Oh, yes," Melanie said, walking into the kitchen and putting the plate on the counter, Addie following behind her slowly. "So, it's not my grandma Lou, is it?"

When Addie didn't say anything, Melanie's stomach turned. Suddenly, she thought back to the wonder in Gram's face whenever they'd stopped to look at the house, the way her eyes glistened in the sun and she swore that the light had made them water. She'd always seemed oddly quiet outside the Ellis house, which wasn't like her. Melanie had thought it was just her grandmother taking in the towering structure, imagining the way it might look one day after someone had repaired it. But maybe she'd been thinking about something else—some*one* else.

"It's her, isn't it?" Melanie asked, her voice hushed while lost in her contemplations. She turned her focus back to Addie. "Why did you say some secrets are better off buried?"

"I think you're digging around in something that you should just let be."

"If this has to do with my grandmother, then surely I have a right to know."

"You may or may not have a right to know," Addie said, "but do you really *want* to know? Because knowing could change everything. It could alter lives, Melanie; lives that may not want to be altered."

"I'd like to know for my own sake," Melanie argued gently. "Gram left me the money to buy this house specifically. She wanted *me* to have it. If Gram preferred her secrets buried, why would she push me so hard toward them?"

"Your grandmother isn't the only decision maker in this scenario. There are others at risk here." Addie shook her head. "I'm sorry, but I can't be the one to shed light on this for you. It's not something I want on my shoulders." She pushed the plate toward Melanie, the crisp lime scent of them wafting into the air. "Enjoy the cookies, and thank you for cleaning up my yard."

"You're welcome again," she said, pushing down her disappointment. "It's really Josh Claiborne who should get these, though. He's the one who called the team out to chip up all the trees."

Addie nodded thoughtfully. "You know Josh well?" she asked.

"Sort of. He's been doing a little work on the house for me to restore it, and he helped me through the storm."

Her eyes grew round, but she didn't say anything.

"What?" Melanie asked.

"I should go," she said, her gaze moving around the house again suspiciously, making her way to the door.

As Addie left, Melanie kept her eyes on the old lady's slow steps down the sidewalk toward her house, wondering what secrets Alfred still had to tell. She grabbed the stack of letters and headed out to the beach.

April 23, 1963

Dearest Eloise,

I find it inappropriate to write my musings to a married woman so I'll speak to you as only a friend now. I hear you have a child. I hope that you have everything you've ever wanted. I know you well enough to believe that you would want only the best for me as well; you'd want me to be happy, so I am going to push the pain of losing you as far down as I can push it, and I'm going to try to move on with my life. But know that every night, I turn on the chandelier in the parlor, and I keep the porch light flickering until dawn to light your path if you ever wish to come home.

Thank you for the memories you gave me. They keep me warm at night. I will be forever grateful for our time together, Lou.

Love,
Alfred

He'd called her Lou. Only her family and closest friends called her that.

"Hey," Josh's voice came from behind her. He stepped up beside her and sat down in the sand. "Mom dropped me off."

Melanie folded the letter and slipped it back into the envelope.

"Anything good in that one?" Josh asked with a grin.

"Um, nothing new," she said, deciding not to tell Josh what she'd learned. Addie had seemed adamant that she shouldn't get involved in this. Perhaps she should just keep it under wraps for now.

"He was just a lonely old man, I think. He might have even been delusional—hard to tell. No one knew him at all, and he wrote letters to himself." Josh made a face. "Just saying."

Melanie wanted to believe that Alfred Ellis was crazy because that would be easier, but Addie's reaction had assured her that was wishful thinking. He was the holder of some enormous secret, and Melanie was going to do everything she could to find out what it was.

Chapter Fourteen

"I ordered pizza. I hope that's okay," Josh said, holding the warm box, the smell of oregano and freshly baked crust making her stomach growl. Melanie climbed down from the ladder, wiping the perspiration off her forehead. They'd been tearing the old wallpaper off the parlor walls for the last two hours.

"The walls are looking good," she said, assessing their work.

"Not bad," he agreed.

She picked up a scrap of the peeled wallpaper, setting it on the counter when they got to the kitchen. "I'd like to see if I can find a current version of it. I'm trying to keep the house as close to the original as possible but adding a beachier flair."

"Sounds good," he said, distracted by Addie's plate on the counter. "Are those coconut?" he asked, lifting the cellophane.

"Yes," she said with a laugh, batting his hand away. "Maybe I can bribe you."

"Bribe me?" he asked, his eyebrow rising suspiciously.

"If you put my doorknob back on for me, I might give you one."

"One? Your security is only worth one cookie?" he teased, reaching for the plate again. She swatted him once more, grinning.

"Fine. Two."

"I'd better wash up right now then." He reached around her to get to the sink, but she jumped in front of him, turning on the tap. "The first cookie goes to me, though. Ladies first," she said, running her hands under the water and filling them with soap.

"Says who?" Josh pumped soap into his palm and placed his hands into the stream over hers, lathering madly.

"Your dirt is coming down onto my clean hands!"

"Soap is soap," he said, running his sudsy fingers over hers as she turned around to block him playfully.

When she did, she found herself holding his hands, the white foam from the soap dripping down onto her bare feet. He looked into her eyes, a small smile forming at the corners of his mouth, the water still flowing behind her. Slowly, he reached around her, his arms encircling her, her soapy hands pressing against his chest, his face so close to hers that all she had to do was look up and she'd bump right into him. Her breathing became shallow with his strong embrace, and she found it difficult to think of anything to say.

Without warning, as if rethinking the moment, he pulled back, and it felt like he'd sucked the air from between them.

"All clean," he said, holding up his wet hands, an unreadable expression on his face.

She smiled, still trying to catch her breath.

Josh grabbed two drinks from the cooler just as his phone rang. "Hello?" he answered, setting the bottles of lemonade onto the counter. "You're kidding..." He turned away, rubbing the back of his neck.

As Melanie got things ready for their dinner, setting the napkins down and dishing out the pizza, Josh finished the call and squeezed his eyes shut for a second. "My old truck's engine is faulty and they have to totally tear it apart and rebuild it. It could be two weeks. I don't have two weeks," he said.

"I'm sorry," she told him, feeling like this was her fault. She couldn't help but think that if he hadn't been over here during the storm, his truck would've been fine. He'd probably be in New York already.

"I'm closing on the house tomorrow morning. What am I going to do for two weeks?"

"Stay here?" she offered.

He shook his head, as through their moment just now was a mistake. "Thanks for the offer, but I need to get to New York. I'll call the rental truck company and see if they're up and running after the storm. I can drive up in one of their vehicles and then drop it at one of their New York locations."

"Are the roads clear enough to get out of town?"

"I think it's down to one lane, but that's all I need."

"But once you return the rental, how will you get around the city?" she asked, handing him his plate of pizza.

"My regular truck's totaled. I'll use the insurance settlement to buy something when I get there."

"Or you could stay," she suggested again with a smile.

"The faster I get to New York, the faster I can put everything behind me, build on my own land, and have the life I've always wanted," he replied. "Then I can spend my days shooting hoops with Cole, raise horses, maybe get a couple dogs…"

"That sounds amazing," she forced herself to say, knowing already that she'd miss him.

*

To say it was weird to sleep next to Josh after just meeting him was an understatement. She didn't really sleep much when he'd stayed during the storm—rather she'd passed out from sheer exhaustion—but tonight was different. They'd taken their time, making small talk as she dressed the air mattress with the clean sheets from the laundromat. He'd washed up in her bathroom and brushed his teeth in her sink. And now, his fresh, minty scent lingered as he lay beside her, his limbs resting peacefully in a manner that would make it so easy to curl up beside him and spoon.

As the moonlight filtered in around them, she considered how much she'd been through with Josh since she'd gotten to Rosemary Bay. So much that she felt close to him. She recalled his smile when he was holding Cole, the way the corners of his eyes creased when amusement crossed his face. The thought of watching him walk away made her stomach feel heavy with worry. The more she lay next to him, the more restless she became, the heat beginning to feel as though its tentacles were wrapping around her so tightly that it would squeeze the life out of her. Finally giving up, she threw off her sheet and padded quietly out the room.

The boards creaked under her bare feet as she made her way downstairs, feeling as though she needed to get outside before the walls closed in on her. It made no sense, but the idea of him walking out of her life for years made her feel like she was losing something great. She needed to catch her breath, so she grabbed her phone and the stack of letters, pulled open the back door, and gulped in the coastal air. Surrounded by an inky darkness, the moon just a slip in the sky, the waves lapping against the shore like a quiet lullaby, she sat down on what was left of the porch, turned on the light on her phone and opened the next note from Alfred.

April 23, 1964

Eloise,

This will be my final letter. I've proposed to a woman. My proposal doesn't diminish the love I hold for you, but it's time I move on, which, given the circumstances, I feel you would agree with. She's lovely, Lou. She's nurturing, kind, and bright-spirited, and she seems to love me. You'd approve of her, I'm certain. I think I can move on with her and over time, I hope to fall as deeply in love with her as I did with you.

You may even know her, as she's from Rosemary Bay, although I'd never ask her for fear of what she may see in my face when your name comes off my lips. Her name is Vera Wilson...

Melanie's mouth fell open as she scanned the end of the letter. Vera Wilson? Wasn't that what Josh had said his grandmother's name was? She folded the letter quickly and slipped it back into the envelope, looking up at the window of the room upstairs where Josh was sleeping, her heart pounding. The room was still dark.

In the morning, she needed to talk to Addie about this, but the old woman's mention of secrets gave her pause. Alfred had died alone, with Vera despising him. What had happened between Vera and Alfred? Had her own grandmother known the answers? She'd never mentioned Vera to Melanie. She noticed that despite Alfred's assertion that this was his final letter, he clearly had more to say since she held more envelopes. She opened the next one, eager to find out what was on the page.

April 23, 1965

My dearest Eloise,

Someday I hope to share these letters with you. You see, I've made a mess of things, and what I've learned is that in everything, we must be honest with ourselves. I've ruined someone's life by not being true to my own feelings. Vera and I ran off and got married. No one knows about it—her family will be devastated if they find out. We're quietly getting an annulment. And for the sake of Vera's reputation, I'll never mention again what I'm telling you.

On our wedding night, as she looked up at me with trusting eyes, I froze. She thought I was nervous, and she talked softly to me, urging me to hold her. The next morning, guilt swarmed me like a nest of bees. I couldn't live with her and not tell her about the woman whose eyes still haunted me—you. It makes no sense. I should've gotten over you. God knows I've tried, but something pulls me back into the undertow of grief and longing for what could've been, and I can't get past it. I've decided that I'd rather live alone than with someone who could only receive part of my heart.

Silently here,
Alfred

"Everything all right?" Josh's voice came from behind Melanie, causing her to nearly ball up the letter trying to get it into the envelope, her heart hammering.

"What's wrong?" he asked as he joined her, his eyes on the envelope in her hand.

"Nothing," she replied, the word coming out as a squeak. "You startled me. What are you doing up in the middle of the night?" The white light of the moon fell on his nose and square stubbled jaw.

"Shouldn't I ask *you* that?"

"I couldn't sleep," she said. "It was... too hot in there."

"What's in the letter?" He reached toward the envelope, the little lines between his eyes creasing when she jerked it away instinctively. Then a tiny smirk formed at the corners of his mouth, barely visible in the low light.

He tried to grasp it again, and she held it away from him.

"If I really want that letter, I can get it from you," he said, swiping a hand, and she stood to move out of his reach.

"It's not a joke," she warned when he got up. "These are antiques."

"I'm a history buff," he said. "Did you know that about me?"

She shook her head, keeping her distance.

"But I think Alfred Ellis was a wacko old man who talked to himself and dreamed about women who probably didn't even know he existed."

"That's not true," she said in defense of the man, biting her tongue as soon as the words came out of her mouth.

"Oh, really? What makes you think I'm wrong?" He swung a hand in her direction, causing her to take a step back. When she did, her foot slipped off the side of the porch and she found herself falling backward. Josh dove toward her, and she writhed around to keep him from getting the letters, the two of them falling at the same time. He threw his hand toward her but to her surprise, it went behind her neck to catch her just as she hit the soft sand. She lay on her back, the letters in her grip above her head, her fist resting against the sand, with Josh hovering over her.

"You okay?" he asked, his fingers still cushioning her neck.

"Yes, I'm fine," she replied, still worried.

He stared at her a moment as if he were wrestling with his own thoughts. "I didn't mean to make you fall. I was just kidding around." As he explained, his face was so close that she caught the scent of him, the lingering mixture of spice and cedar from the cologne he'd probably put on this morning. He looked down at her, hesitating, as if he was deciding something.

Slowly, he moved toward her, surrender in his eyes, his lips brushing hers as if to test the waters. Melanie could hardly breathe, oblivious to the salty air between them as she struggled to keep her composure. He reached slowly above her head, moving his fingers delicately along her wrist. Then, as he found her hand with the letters, she pushed him off of her.

"That was a low move," she snapped, before turning away from him just in case he could see the pink in her cheeks. She got up, walking toward the water and trying to slow her thumping heart. She couldn't deny the disappointment that his near-kiss was nothing more than a ploy to get the letters.

"Hang on," he said, closing the gap between them. "I wasn't trying to get your useless letters. I was… reaching for *you*."

His fingers found her empty hand, stopping her and pulling her gently in his direction. "I swear," he said, his voice serious.

His thumb caressed the back of her hand as he stepped into her personal space. Then his other hand went behind her neck, the warmth of it a shock against the cool wind, and before she could process anything more, his lips were on hers in the most perfect way, moving like silk, their breath mixing, the salty taste on his lips intoxicating.

She closed her eyes and let go of his hand, reaching around him and pulling him closer, the letters flapping in her grip behind his neck.

His mouth moved from her lips, up her cheek to her ear. "I don't know why I did that," he whispered, giving her a shiver. "It just felt right."

"I didn't mind," she told him, and his lips were on her mouth again, more urgent this time, as if he'd been holding back since the moment they'd met. Other kisses she'd shared with people she'd dated—even Alex—none of them felt like this. It was as if they'd been made to fit together, their movements in perfect sync, the shape of their lips fitting together flawlessly.

When they finally slowed, he pulled away, looking down at her. "Well, that was unexpected," he said, obviously just as surprised as she felt.

"You sure it wasn't a ploy to get my letters?" she asked. She waved the envelopes in the air. "Because you had me pretty close to handing them over."

He raised an eyebrow. "Did I?"

"Nope," she said with a laugh, wrapped up in the moment and trying to ignore the flicker of guilt that she knew his family secret.

"Oh, you're in for it now," he said, lunging toward her and making her squeal. "If I want those wacko-Ellis letters, I can get them!"

She took off down the beach in the dark, holding them over her head as her feet splashed in the salty foam of the waves. "Never!" she called to him, dodging him with a yelp as he got close to her. "You said they're useless!" she panted, out of breath from running. "You don't even want them!"

"Yes, I do!" he said, closing in on her.

"Why?" She had to stop to catch her breath, but screamed when he scooped her up in his arms.

"Because they're attached to *you*." He spun her around, their laughter causing an outdoor light to come on in one of the cottages down the beach. "Come on," he said, setting her back down, "let's go back before we get the police called on us for disorderly conduct."

They walked back down the beach under the glistening stars, the seaweed washing up onto the driftwood at the edge of the sand. Every now and again, Josh would swipe at the letters, both of them laughing when she pulled them out of his reach, trying to ignore the prickle of her conscience, wondering how and when she'd tell him, or if she should at all.

Chapter Fifteen

The musty smell of the house filled Melanie's lungs as she took her first coherent breath the next morning. She kept her eyes closed, the recollection of last night settling upon her. When they'd finally gotten settled on the air mattress, he'd pulled her in, holding her close to him before they both drifted off to dreamland. What had seemed like a romantic surprise last night felt a lot more weighty in the morning. What had she been thinking, allowing this to happen when Josh was leaving in two weeks, or less if he could help it?

She cracked one eye and turned her head just slightly, but all she could see were covers. She felt around, stretching out her fingers, but she couldn't feel a thing. She listened for breathing, snoring—something. But all was silent. She opened her eyes all the way and turned her head. Then she sat up, confirming that she was the only one on the air mattress.

The sun came in at a slant, drawing wide golden triangles on the floor. Melanie stepped into a warm spot and stretched, before heading downstairs to find Josh.

The kitchen was empty, as were the other rooms in the house, so Melanie opened the back door and walked outside, shielding her eyes from the sun to peer out to the white expanse of beach. It was empty too. Where had he gone? Going around to the front, she noticed her car was missing.

She threw her hands up in the air. "Great," she said to no one. "I've got no way into town, I'm starving, and Josh has decided to go MIA." She had two choices: she could start stripping the rest of the wallpaper, or she could pour herself some orange juice and settle in with the next letter from Alfred. The latter won out, so she did just that.

With her juice poured and the stack of letters under her arm, she sat down on one of the barstools in the kitchen. She took in the turquoise view through the window and opened the next letter.

April 23, 1966

Dearest Eloise,

I said I wouldn't write, but telling you seems to make me feel whole. It's been a year since Vera and I parted ways. She came by my house today unexpectedly, which was a huge surprise, given that she'd moved on right after our annulment and found someone else, marrying and having a child. She asked me, "Did you really love her?" I could only assume that by "her" she meant you. And my answer was yes. She nodded, and her anger faded just a bit when she told me that she understood because she'd found that kind of love with her new husband. She and I shared that single moment where we'd both become wiser, both of us realizing that the world isn't black and white; there are so many shades of gray.

I still love you and I always will. Life with you is an unfinished journey that I wanted more than anything I'd ever wanted before, but one I didn't get to take. You have this way about you that makes me feel like pieces of me are missing when you aren't here. It's as if I walk around with gaping holes that can never be filled because they are uniquely you-shaped. I've adapted to the missing pieces, but I will never be whole.

Yours truly,
Alfred

Stunned, she looked out the window at the water. It all made sense now why, in this small town, when Gram would visit her friends, Melanie had never heard of Vera. Their interactions would be awkward to say the least… She closed her eyes, going back to her last trip here with Gram. The memory was still so vivid that Melanie could almost reach out and touch her grandmother.

The bells on the door of the coffee shop had jingled that day long ago, as Melanie walked in. Gram was hugging her friends, telling them goodbye when she saw Melanie, a smile stretched across her face from ear to ear.

"I'm glad you're here! I've got your vanilla brûlée latte." Gram tapped the lid of the paper cup on the table. "Ready to go window shopping?" she asked Melanie, as her friends threw up a wave before they left.

It was their last day before heading home, and Melanie had been packing all morning. After a week at the beach, packing took hours of cleaning up the rental house and rearranging everything in her suitcase to fit the new wares she'd acquired over the days—sun lotions, straw hats, beach reads. But Gram was never concerned with it. The last day was when she always met up with her friends, had coffee and a nice chat, and went shopping one final time. She usually had something specific in mind that she wanted. Today, she was looking for a paperweight for her desk.

The sun cast its white light onto the sidewalk, which was bustling with tourists. "I remember when this sleepy little town only got busy about twice a year when the navy boats docked. It was electric, like some unspecified holiday—we all prepared for it, excitement buzzing."

"Things have changed since then?" Melanie asked.

"They definitely have. Hey, why don't we walk away from town instead? Let's go have a look at that amazing house by the beach. The Ellis house."

"Don't you want to get your paperweight before we leave?"

Gram smiled. "Memories are better than some old trinket. Let's walk."

That was certainly true. Melanie wiped a tear as it fell down her cheek, the empty feeling that had taken over when Gram died screaming to be filled. She needed answers. She had to know why her grandmother hadn't responded to Alfred's love letters. It was time for Addie to tell her.

Melanie stood on her broken front porch with her hands on her hips as Josh drove up in her car and got out. After walking down to Addie's and finding no one was home, she'd paced back and forth with nervous energy, wanting to jump in the car and drive around in a feeble attempt to find some answers to the mystery she was unraveling. But with no car, she'd waited, stuck.

"I've been wanting to go somewhere," she said. "You can't just go taking someone else's car without permission."

"Good morning," he returned, jogging up the walkway and tossing her the keys, a bag in his hand.

She stared at him as he turned the doorknob, only registering then that it had been fixed. "Thank you," she said, pointing to it before following him inside.

"I brought food." He held up the bag. "And it took me so long because I stopped off at Mason's Appliances on the off chance that you'd ordered your stove and refrigerator from them. I know Mason personally from work, and he's going to make sure your appliances are delivered today."

"Oh," she said, feeling terrible for having gotten upset with him.

"I'd have woken you up, but you were sleeping so soundly," he told her, his voice soft, his eyes sweeping over her.

"You watched me sleep?" she asked, meeting his gaze. "What else did you do while I was in dreamland?"

"Well, for one, I read those letters—starting with the crumpled ones."

She literally felt the blood drain from her face. "What?" she asked, bracing herself for his questions over why she didn't tell him about the mention of Vera in the letters, but instead, she was met with a perplexing question. "Do you happen to know what Alfred Ellis did for a living when he wasn't in the navy?" he asked.

She shook her head.

"He was an author." Josh handed her a paper bundle with a warm breakfast sandwich inside. "His only published work was widely criticized for using real people and manipulating the events of their actual lives to tell a fictional story. A few navy buddies threatened to sue him for slander, and his publisher pulled the novel."

"Where did you find this out?"

"My mother. Of course, I called her first thing when I read what he'd written about my grandmother."

"Does she know the name of the novel?" Melanie asked, interested.

"No, but it doesn't matter anyway. It's out of print and the copies were all pulled from the shelves after the allegations." He unwrapped his sandwich and set it on the counter. "He's a liar, Melanie. I don't know how much more I need to do to convince you those letters were the writings of a loner with no life at all. My mother thinks that that's probably why my grandmother hated him. Somehow, she must have found out about his letters and she was terrified he'd publish them and ruin her reputation. The very last thing she'd want people to think was that she wasn't pure when she married my grandfather."

Melanie was silent, holding her buttery croissant with eggs and sausage in her hand.

"It's creepy if you ask me," Josh continued.

"So he didn't really know Gram either?" She tried to let this idea sink in. When she thought about it, Gram had never said she'd known him at all. She'd even told Melanie that she and her grandfather had already left town when he moved here. "Gram really just willed me the money for this house because she thought it was pretty?" she asked herself. "Nothing more?"

"Sounds like it."

"I wonder if she knew he'd written about *her*."

Josh shrugged. "No idea."

But as she tried to piece together the truth, something occurred to her. "Wait. When I talked to Addie, she seemed to know something that she wasn't telling me. She said some secrets were better left unsaid. What did she mean by that?"

"I told you, she's not all there, Melanie."

Melanie turned her attention to the walls, their shabby paper, the dusty chandelier above her, and suddenly felt like there was no purpose in all this. "You know, when this house literally fell apart around me during the storm, in a weird way, it was Alfred's story that was giving me the energy. Strangely, it solidified my purpose. Now it feels like I've had the wind taken out of my sails somehow."

"You're a romantic," Josh said.

"What?" His response surprised her.

"You wanted to give him a happy ending," he said.

She looked around at the dilapidated house. "You might be onto something."

"One thing I've learned is that life isn't all happy endings. This house is *yours* now. You have to create your own happy ending."

"Mm," she said. But even as she agreed, she struggled to come to terms with the fact that the letters had been fictional. "Alfred was a wonderful writer," she said. "I believed every word."

Something crossed Josh's face as he picked the stack of letters up off the counter and flipped through them.

"Or maybe Alfred was just a dreamer," she suggested, taking them from him gently, peering down at the old script. "Since they aren't real, do you think your mother would approve if I were to frame them? They'd make a wonderful conversation piece when I open the bed and breakfast."

"No way. My mother would never agree to it."

Melanie fanned the letters, thinking about the love story that Alfred had created. "It seems like such a loss for no one to read these."

"Lies? The last thing you want is for your guests to read a bunch of untruths about our families."

"I guess you're right. It would be amazing if I could get my hands on more of his writing. I could convert the parlor to a writing room."

"We should probably get all the wallpaper ripped off first."

"True," she said grabbing a scrap from the wall and yanking it down, sending dust over the both of them. Coughing and laughing at the same time, Melanie brushed the white powder from her shirt. "We've got a long way to go."

Chapter Sixteen

"That feels amazing," Melanie said, as she stood in the open doors of her brand-new refrigerator, the cool air kissing her skin. "Thank you for making this happen," she told Josh.

"No problem," he said, unpacking the cooler, grabbing a can of soda in one hand, the bottle of ketchup in the other, and loading them in the fridge for her. He'd been pensive as they'd stripped wallpaper all morning, and now he seemed to have pulled away from her completely, the barrier she thought she'd knocked down sliding back into place yet again.

"And we have a stove!" she sang as she twirled around, hoping to make him laugh, but he offered a half-smile instead. "I can do some serious cooking on this. We've got a few ingredients from the market. Why don't we go shopping and get some real food? Do you know any local places where we can get fresh seafood?"

"There's one, but it's tough to get to. It's a ways away."

"That's all right. I don't mind."

"Give me just a second." He pulled out his phone, tapping on the screen. Moments later his phone pinged with a notification. "Perfect," he said. "Can I drive your car?"

"As long as I'm in it," she teased, but that seriousness lingered on his face. Well, she didn't have time for his up and downs. She had enough to deal with, trying to get on with her life and restore this house as her legacy.

"Grab your sunglasses. You're gonna need them."

They drove the familiar route to the local marina, past the beach shops with their wares on the sidewalk displaying an explosion of nautical loveliness.

"What are we doing here?" she asked, getting out of the car once they'd pulled to a stop in the marina's parking lot.

"We're going shopping." He nodded toward the pier. "It's quicker to go by boat, and because I've sold mine, I borrowed one."

Part of the dock was being repaired and it was nearly empty of boats, most of the owners having secured their crafts inland prior to the storm. But sitting at the end was a gleaming sailboat—white with a bright red and white striped sail that was bunched and puckered, tied down along its mast. The gulf water lapped up on its sides as it swayed in the movement of the tide.

"This belongs to one of my clients, Paul Goldman. I did a full home remodel for him and he gave me an open invitation to use it."

"You're kidding."

"Nope," he said, climbing on and offering his hand to keep her steady as she stepped onto the gleaming vessel. A man emerged from behind the sail and shook hands with Josh, clapping him on the back. "This is Paul," Josh said, introducing Melanie. "He sails every day, giving lessons, and he said we could hop on and he'd give us a ride to the market."

"It's nice to meet you, Paul," she said, shaking his hand. "I'm Melanie."

"Y'all head back to the seating," he told them. "I'll have us off in just a second."

Paul untied the line and maneuvered the boat away from the dock, releasing the sail, the large canvas ballooning in the wind, sending them gliding through the water. The salty wind blew Melanie's hair behind her shoulder and she held her locks in her fist, runaway strands tickling her cheeks. The water stretched out before them, the blue sky meeting the edge of it in a perfect line. Josh put his arm on the back of the seat, behind her, and as the boat bobbed, she felt herself sliding closer to him. He put his hand on her shoulder to keep her steady.

"After we get back, I need to figure out what to do with the back porch. I think that's the first thing I'd like to fix," she said.

Josh seemed to have so much on his mind. "I'll see if I can round up some wood."

"You'd do that?"

"Yeah," he said. "We just have to figure out how to get the wood to your house."

"Why are you helping me?" she asked, his mixed signals confusing her. "I mean, I'm glad to have your help but I just wondered why…"

He shrugged, simply shaking his head.

She wanted to know more but she didn't press him on it. Because, no matter what, that moment on the beach had made her wonder what the real Josh was like if she could just get past that hardened outer layer of his.

When they docked again, the boat swayed in the waves, the breeze causing the water to peak as it rushed toward the shore under the pier. This marina was a small clapboard structure with an array of fishing hooks lining the entrance and a sign for fresh coffee at the open window. Josh helped Melanie from the boat and thanked Paul as she stepped onto the pier.

"How will we get back?" she asked.

"Paul's picking us up in two hours," he said. "So we've got some time to kill. I thought I'd grab a couple of cookies for Cole at this ice cream shop in town."

"Ooh, I'd love some ice cream."

"If you do, that's the spot. The shop has been here since the turn of the last century. It has a two-hundred-year-old family vanilla ice cream recipe, and they mix it with all kinds of amazing flavors like maple bourbon and honey lavender."

"That sounds incredible," she said, mouth watering, as they paced together down the boardwalk that led to a small strip of shops.

Josh stopped under a pink and turquoise awning and opened the door, the glass twinkling in the sunlight as he pulled it. Melanie walked past a mint-green bicycle with a basket and headed into the cool shop, the air sweet with the scent of sugar. The menu was artfully done in bright pink script. A woman behind the counter smiled, her gray hair pulled back in a yellow bandana.

"Hello," she said. "First time in?"

"Yes," Melanie answered, taking in the rainbow of ice cream colors in fuchsia, yellow, green, and blue, while Josh browsed the basket of cookies on the counter. "What's your most popular flavor?"

"Well, that would be our white chocolate tiramisu vanilla. Would you two like to sample it?" She grabbed two little wooden spoons and filled them with ice cream, dusting them with white chocolate flakes and then adding a drizzle of chocolate.

Melanie tasted it; the ice cream flavor was like an explosion of summer in her mouth. "That's amazing," she said.

"Thank you." The woman leaned on the counter. "We've had many years to perfect our flavors. And we very rarely change our menu. We haven't made a single change since the fifties, when we added the blackberry vanilla, which we top with a reduced blackberry sauce, and sugared blackberry crumbles. It's served in a stemmed glass."

"I'll have that," Melanie said, excited to try it. "Want one?" she asked Josh.

"Maybe just these." He held up two cookies.

"Go on, get one," Melanie urged. "Once you're in New York, you won't be able to have it."

"All right. You've convinced me. Make that two," Josh said. "And these." He slid the cookies onto the counter.

"Good choice," the woman said, pointing to the menu before bagging up the cookies. "We call that our Lovebird Special—two blackberry crumbles."

"Lovebird Special?" Josh said, eyeing Melanie uncomfortably.

"Yes, rumor has it that it was originally created for two lovebirds who spent their last week here together before the officer went into the navy. It was over their ice creams that they enjoyed their last full day together."

"The navy?" Melanie asked, her interest piqued. "Do you know their names?"

"I don't, sadly." The server grabbed two frozen wine glasses from a small freezer below the counter and began scooping vanilla ice cream.

"It could be anyone," Josh said, clearly reading her thoughts. "Do you know how many navy people came through here in the fifties? Literally hundreds."

Melanie nodded, but she couldn't help wondering. "What if it *was* my grandmother and Alfred? That would be crazy…"

"Yes, it would. Especially since the letters aren't even true, Melanie."

"Addie seemed insistent that there were secrets."

"Sure, and two weeks ago, I heard she had the entire fire department at her house, claiming that she'd set fire to her oven when there was nothing wrong at all."

"She seemed so with it when I spoke to her... Talking with her made me feel like Gram was still here, you know?"

He nodded, his eyes softening slightly.

"Your blackberry crumbles," the woman said, interrupting them.

She set down the two wide wine glasses full of vanilla ice cream, a generous serving of blackberry sauce cascading down each scoop, pooling in the bottom of the glass, with blackberry crumbles covered in grains of glistening sugar topping the sauce.

"Thank you," Melanie said. When the woman had left them alone once more, she told Josh, "I took care of my grandmother for three years and this is the first real thing I've tried to do on my own in a long time. I feel a little lost without her." She dipped her spoon into her ice cream. "I was hoping that redoing the house would give me purpose, but instead it feels like a giant weight on my shoulders. I'm wondering if I should just put it back up for sale, get what I can get out of it, and never look back."

"I don't think the house is the problem," he said. "I think the problem is bigger than the house."

"What do you mean?"

"You have to figure out what *you* want. Why did you buy it? Was it to feel closer to your grandmother? Because I don't think that motivation is enough to get you through a renovation that big. That could be why you're reconsidering—and if that's the case, maybe you should."

"You think I should sell the house?" she asked, surprised by his candor.

"It doesn't matter what I think."

"I'm out of my element, that's all."

"Right, but if this is truly your passion—if it's what you want to do—you'll figure it out. If it isn't, well..."

"Is your New York job your passion?" she asked, dipping her spoon down into her ice cream, turning her focus to the sugar crystals on the crumbles on top to keep from feeling too nervous about her question. It was worth asking, though.

When she looked back up at him, he shook his head. "Not at all. But it's a means to an end that *is* my passion: living out my life *my* way, on my land."

"What your mom said about your ex-wife telling you she could do better... Is that motivating you at all?" she asked, curious.

"It has nothing to do with Janie," he said. "That's my mother reading into things." His jaw was set, his lips taut.

"You sure?"

"Let's drop it. Besides, turning the conversation around on me isn't going to make your own questions go away."

"I wasn't trying to turn the conversation," she said, bristling. The conversation certainly had taken a turn with the mention of Janie, although she wasn't about to point that out. "I was just interested."

"Why?"

"Forget it," she replied, shaking her head. But as she looked out at the dancing shimmers on the gulf outside, the view calmed her. "I didn't mean to cause any stress," she said. "Let's enjoy our ice cream and have fun today."

He agreed, but by the slight rise in his shoulders, she wasn't so sure she believed him.

Melanie stood at the open grill outside and stirred the vegetables, the pan full of the fresh produce from the market. She couldn't wait to try the jars of local jam and a whiskey bourbon sauce that she knew would be amazing on the grilled shrimp that was cooking over the fire. Josh had been all business the whole time they'd shopped to get food for the house, and he'd barely even eaten his ice cream. While he claimed that his ex-wife's comments didn't have an impact on him, it was obvious they had. And Melanie wasn't so sure she wanted to get involved with all that, so she'd decided to stay quiet.

Paul made small talk with them on the way back to the pier in Rosemary Bay, and she was glad for it. But once they'd docked, she found herself wrapped in silence once more. The slight tension buzzed around them all the way home.

When they got to the house, an old Chevy truck was waiting outside. Josh threw up a hand. "Hey, Jerry. Thanks for coming by."

"No problem," a man with curly salt-and-pepper hair and bibbed overalls said as he leaned out the open truck window.

"I'll see ya later," Josh said to her with no further explanation. Then he walked over to the man. Leaving her standing at the car, the grocery bags dangling from her arms, Josh climbed into the truck and they drove away. She stood there, watching him leave, completely fed up with his behavior. With a sigh, she went inside the house.

While she cooked her dinner, what Josh had said about finding what she wanted was still circling her mind, taunting her, telling her she was well out of her league with this renovation. Josh was right: she wasn't committed enough to this. She plated the shrimp and veggies and took them inside.

"What am I supposed to do?" she called out, hoping her gram would hear her and send some colossal sign her way, but all she was met with was resounding silence. "I don't know who I am anymore," she said, the strength of her voice withering as she spoke the words. Bewildered, she sat at the kitchen counter with her dinner and put her head in her hands, wishing she could get some kind of answer from Gram.

Chapter Seventeen

Melanie didn't feel any better the next morning. Needing inspiration, or at the very least a lift in her mood, she stabbed a shrimp, still wishing Gram was here to help her, the silence unbearable. As she toyed with her bowl of cereal, her gaze landed on Alfred's letters. Even those had let her down. But fiction or not, she decided to indulge herself and read one more, hoping it would give her some inkling of a message.

April 23, 1967

Dearest Lou,

I wish I had the power to change our circumstances, to make this some sort of wonderful happy ending for us, but alas, I cannot. So, I will make one final plea. I told you that summer all those years ago that if anything happened and I couldn't meet you, I'd carve my initials into the wood under the bench at Willow Pier to make sure you knew I was waiting for you. If you ever came looking, you were supposed to carve yours beside mine and I'd find you. I must admit that I haven't looked to see if your initials are there in over a year. I'm afraid to, for fear that the last bit of hope will drain right out of me.

But I know that I need to get closure and finish this even if it never really feels finished at all.

I'm going to the pier at the close of this letter.

All my love,
Alfred

Even if what Josh said was true, and she was just being a romantic, the thought of the pier was a welcome distraction this morning. With renewed determination, she set the letter down, leaving her cereal, and grabbed her keys, headed straight there.

But when she got to Willow Pier, to her dismay it was being power washed, and the crews had the whole area blocked off.

"How much longer will you all be?" she called to the power washer.

The man turned off his machine and looked over at her. "Sorry?"

"How much longer will you be?"

"I'm sealing the deck. It'll be dry in a couple of hours."

Melanie stood there in the early warmth of the morning sun, wondering what else she could do to prove that Alfred Ellis wasn't lying. She paced along the edge of the pier, silently asking Gram for help, when suddenly she had another idea. She peered down at the time on her cell phone. It was probably open. With a quick turn, she headed for the library.

Melanie walked up to the librarian who was sharpening pencils under a display of book posters, as she stood behind an old paneled counter.

"I'm looking for a book that's out of print," Melanie said, when the woman peered over at her with a smile.

The woman filled the little can of pencils, brushed off her hands, and came over to Melanie. "What's the author's name, dear?"

"Alfred Ellis."

The old woman arched a brow. "The man who lived on Sandpiper Lane?"

"Yes, do you know his work?"

She shook her head, her lips forming a pout of uncertainty. "Are you sure you have the right name? I didn't know he'd written anything." She thumbed through a heavy catalogue on the desk, turning to the section beginning with the letter E. Dragging her finger down each page, she finally said, "I don't see anything by him. Could he have written under a pen name?"

"I'm not sure," Melanie said, disappointed. "Do you know how I could find out?"

"Do you have any further information, like the title or publisher?"

"No, only that the publisher pulled the book from sale in response to allegations that it was infringing on people's rights."

"Any idea what year?" the woman asked. "We could check the microfiche machine for news articles relating to such a claim."

"I don't know the year either. Perhaps 1956 or a couple of years before?"

"All right, come with me. Let's see what we can find out."

The woman led Melanie to a large machine at the back of the library, where she opened a filing cabinet and pulled out a few small boxes containing spools of microfiche. She carried them over and set them down.

"We could start with this one from 1954," she said, pulling the spool from its box, loading it onto the machine's peg and then feeding the film into the machine. "You just turn this knob to flip between articles. Let me know if you find anything. I'd be interested to hear."

When the librarian had retreated to the desk and resumed sharpening her pencils, Melanie got to work, thumbing through old articles from the *Rosemary Bay Gazette*. She spent hours combing through all the microfiche, but as she went through them, she came up empty.

Then suddenly, she saw his name. Scrolling up, she read the headline: 'Rosemary Bay Becoming More than a Tourist Destination.' She scanned the 1961 article written about the number of out-of-towners moving to the area in recent years, but it was a short interview with Alfred Ellis that made her heart hammer. "Everything I love is here in Rosemary Bay," he said, when asked why he'd moved there. "I'm building my dream home here, and I plan to live out my years with the woman of my dreams." It was as if Melanie could hear his voice, as if he were speaking directly to her. "She's a local resident. I met her at Barney's and we danced into the night. But it wasn't my idea. You see, she'd wagered a dance over a game of horseshoes and I lost. It was the best loss of my life."

Melanie grinned at the thought of Gram winning the game of horseshoes. Her grandmother had fared better than she had at winning her bet. It seemed that Alfred had been delighted about her victory. Josh was another story… When Josh came to mind, it hit her: could this be more proof that Alfred Ellis wasn't making up the story?

There was only one thing left to do: she headed out of the library and went back to Willow Pier.

*

The sun shone through the palm trees along the wood slats under her feet in streaks, as Melanie paced toward the bench at the end of the pier. There was a strong pull in her gut, telling her she'd find something there. Her heart hammered harder with every step, the waves swishing as they lapped against the timber support beams. But then she stopped still, confusion filling her.

"What are you doing here?" she asked Josh, whose back was to her while he sat on the bench facing the water.

He turned around, words on his lips, but then he seemed to reconsider and said, "What are *you* doing here?"

"I need to see something," she said, dropping down and looking under the bench, Josh's legs casting a shadow on the boards. She ran her hand along the faded wood, weathered by the water, feeling for indentations that resembled letters.

"What in the world are you doing?" he asked, standing up. When he did, the shadow moved, and there in the long plank that lay directly under the bench were the initials A.E.

"Ha!" Melanie said, standing up, but when she did, she hit her head on the bottom of the bench, the blow causing her to sway. Josh quickly reached out, grabbing her and keeping her steady.

"That was a really hard bump. You okay?" he asked, concern flooding his face.

Melanie rubbed her head, dazed. "I don't know. My vision's a little blurry."

"Sit down," he instructed her, helping her onto the bench, before sitting beside her. "Let me look at your eyes," he said, his face suddenly coming into focus so close to hers that she could feel his breath on her skin, her nerves tingling. "Do you have any ringing in your ears?"

"A little."

"You might have a concussion."

"I'm fine," she replied, leaning down to see if she could find another set of initials, but the upside-down movement of her head made her woozy and she sat straight back up. "Did you ever pick up materials with Jerry," she said, still rubbing her head.

"Yes. He's getting the last of what we need now. He's helping people rebuild after the storm and he's going to be in the area later today anyway. He said he'd just drop off the supplies. I called the hardware store to let them know he was coming and put it on my account."

She blinked at him; the length of his explanation was difficult to take in with her head throbbing. "So, why didn't you go with him?"

"I slept at my mother's," he said, thoughts in his eyes. "Then I asked him to drop me off here. I needed to think."

"What were you thinking about?"

He stared into her eyes. "You."

Despite her pulsing head, her stomach did a little flip. "Me?"

"Yeah." He turned away, looking out at the stripes of cobalt and turquoise in the gulf. "It was already difficult to leave my mom and Cole. I told myself that they both have people around them who will help them if they need anything. But then you came along and I've handled it all wrong. I... didn't mean to get involved in this." He waggled a finger between them.

Melanie stared at him, the revelation that he was finding the idea of going away difficult bittersweet.

"I'm leaving you with a total disaster of a house and I don't know if you'll be okay." He clenched his jaw. "But I keep telling myself that fixing that house for you isn't in the plan, and even if it was, I'm not available all the way in New York."

"Then stay," she urged him. "I'm sure you'll have more work than you can handle after the storm."

"It's one storm, Melanie. It's not enough to sustain my retirement."

"But there will be more storms," she said, turning her head toward the breeze, knowing she was grasping at straws.

"That's not enough. In New York there's an opportunity to be promoted to a director of operations. It's essentially an office job—I've never had one. And it pays more than anything I could get here. I'd planned to start a new life, and save what I earn so that when I finally do come back, I won't have to think about how to make ends meet. I can truly retire and enjoy the land my grandfather gave me."

She snapped her mouth shut, realizing her lips had fallen open. "I didn't know you'd be gone so long."

"Yeah..." he said, trailing off into thought, his gaze back on the gulf. They fell into a heavy silence.

"Hey, did you lose an earring or something?" he asked her.

She stared at him blankly.

"Why were you crawling around the pier on your hands and knees?"

"Oh, I almost forgot." She went to stand and Josh jumped up behind her. "I'm okay," she said, but she took his arm just to be sure. "Look." She pointed under the bench.

"What am I looking at?"

"Those are Alfred Ellis's initials."

"Okay. So what?"

"He wrote in his last letter that he'd put his initials here and if my grandmother carved hers beside his, he'd come find her." She leaned down again to see if she could find any other carvings, but she didn't see any. Her heart sank at the revelation. "She never came," she said softly.

"Because Alfred Ellis was *crazy*." Josh helped her up.

"You said the letters were all just fiction. Even if only Alfred's initials are carved into the wood, it proves that the letters were more than a fictional story he'd thought up. He wouldn't need to actually engrave his initials *or* build a house if he were just writing a book, would he?"

"I don't know what he was doing," Josh said. "But the fact that there isn't another set of initials says a whole lot."

"Unless my grandmother didn't look… Or maybe she did and for some reason, she didn't carve hers." Melanie rubbed her eyes. "If only I could talk to her." She pushed the hollow, empty feeling that crept in whenever Gram came to mind back down, focusing on the present moment.

Josh held the tops of her arms and gazed into her eyes sympathetically. "She'd tell you that it was all in his head."

"This is an incredible love story. Why don't you believe it could be true?"

"Because it's a *story*. It's not real life. There's no neat and tidy ending where everyone is happy and Alfred Ellis is some sort of hero—it's a mess because that's the *real* story."

"I think there's a bigger truth than what we know."

"Stuff like that just doesn't happen to regular people."

"I think you're wrong about that." She crossed her arms defiantly.

"Name one instance in real life when someone actually had the person they love sweep them off their feet."

She chewed on her lip, thinking.

"See?"

"Wait, I'm sure there's someone…"

"There isn't. It doesn't happen. And it definitely didn't happen for Alfred Ellis."

"Well, if you're so adamant that Alfred is a madman, why did you ask Jerry to drop you here at this bench?"

"Because no one ever comes here, so I knew it would be a good place to think. But look, enough of this Alfred nonsense. Are you going to be okay once I've gone?"

"Of course I will," she lied.

"I leave you with all my contacts," he said. "They're good people. They'll take care of you."

She nodded. "You act like you're going right now. We still have a few weeks, right?"

"After I rebuild your porch, I'm renting a truck and heading out of town. I'll be leaving as soon as I'm done."

"Oh," she said, disappointment swelling in her stomach. But then she straightened her shoulders. "I'll be just fine," she assured him once more, deciding right then and there that it was time she stood on her own two feet. She was sure that it was what Gram would have wanted for her.

"We should head back," he said, standing up. "Jerry will probably have the materials delivered soon and I need to get a move on."

Melanie got up and they walked down the pier, leaving the empty bench and the lone initials behind them.

Chapter Eighteen

Melanie was on the top of her ladder, stripping off the last remnants of wallpaper from below the crown molding, when the old buzzer rang. "Can you get that?" she called to Josh through the open back door, but the whine of his saw drowned out her request. Setting her tool aside, she made her way down and opened the door.

"Oh, hi," she said to Suzie, who was standing on the porch with Cole.

Cole brightened. "Hi, Melanie!" he said, doing a little bounce.

"Hello there," Melanie told him happily.

Suzie slipped her sunglasses up onto the top of her head. "I was looking for Josh. Is he here?"

"Yes. He's out back, building the porch for me. I can take you there—come on in."

Suzie's gaze lifted when she walked into the grand entryway. "I used to peek through the windows of this old house when it sat abandoned," she said. "I've always wanted to see inside."

"You too?" Melanie chuckled. "It's a little bit of a mess right now, but I'm working on it."

"I'm sure you'll get it fixed up in no time. I actually stopped by to see if Josh could watch Cole for me so I can take Eric to a doctor's appointment."

"I'm sure he can, but if not, I don't mind watching Cole."

"Oh, thank you," Suzie said, clearly relieved, her eyes suddenly glistening.

"Is everything all right?" Melanie asked.

Suzie eyed Cole. "I hope so," she said. "Look, I'm sorry to just drop and run, but I need to go quickly." She squatted down to address the little boy. "Are you going to be okay if I leave you with Melanie?" she asked.

Cole nodded, taking Melanie's hand. "Mm hm," he answered.

"Okay. I'll be back in just a few hours."

"Is Eric sick?" Cole asked, his voice filled with worry.

"A little bit," Suzie said. "I'm taking him to the doctor to get him some medicine now."

"Okay," he said.

"I've got Cole," Melanie told her. "Go if you need to. I'll see you when you're done."

"Okay, thank you so much, Melanie," Suzie replied, rushing back to the door. In an instant, she was gone.

"Well." Melanie grinned at Cole to keep the mood light. "Looks like you'll get to hang out with us for a little while. Wanna go see what Josh is doing?"

"Yeah!" Cole said, excited.

"Follow me."

She led him out to the back deck where Josh was measuring a piece of wood, a pencil in his mouth and his hair wet with perspiration.

"Hey there," he said, stopping when he saw Cole. "Whatcha doing here, buddy?" The measuring tape slid back into its case and Josh walked over, ruffling Cole's hair.

"Eric is sick," Cole told him.

"Oh no. What's wrong with him?"

"He was sleepy this morning. Too sleepy, Suzie said," Cole explained, his little face etched with fear.

"Suzie stopped by to see if we could watch Cole for a few hours so she could take Eric to the doctor," Melanie said.

"There's no need to worry," Josh soothed him. "I'm here with you now, and if Eric is sick, Suzie will have him better before you know it." He ruffled Cole's hair.

Cole seemed at ease after that. "Can I help you make the porch?" the boy asked.

"Of course you can!" Josh swung him up on his shoulders, making him giggle, and carried him over to the area where he'd built a platform. "Want to help me measure?" He held the tape in the air so Cole could reach it.

"Yeah!" Cole wriggled down off his shoulders.

"Okay, you stand here," Josh directed. "Hold the measuring tape tightly." He handed it to Cole and then stretched the end of it across a piece of wood, marking it off with a pencil. "We need to hammer a nail right here. Can you find me the hammer?"

"Yes!" Cole ran to the end of the porch and pulled the hammer from the toolbox. "Here you go."

"You can help me do it." Josh set the nail and then gave it a couple of good pounds to get it anchored. Then he handed Cole the hammer. "Think you can work at getting the nail in while I cut some wood on the other end of the porch?"

"Mm hm," Cole said.

"I'm going to head back in to finish the wallpaper," Melanie told them, the sight of the two of them making her feel all warm and fuzzy inside. They both waved as she went back into the house.

Melanie clicked on the radio, music filling the air from under the whir of the portable fan she'd set up in the corner of the parlor. As she climbed the ladder to finish the last of the stripping, her mind was on little Cole. With a heavy heart, she tried to focus on finishing the room.

"Whatcha doing?" Cole said from the double doorway of the parlor as he peered up at Melanie.

She dipped her sponge into the bucket of soapy water she'd placed on the top of the ladder. "I'm cleaning the chandelier." The pieces she'd wiped shone like diamonds, sending gold light dancing across the room whenever she moved the light fixture.

"Josh is gonna take me down to the beach and then get dinner."

Melanie dropped the sponge into the bucket and climbed down the ladder. "That sounds fun."

"Wanna go with us?"

"I'd love to," she said, wiping her hands on her shorts. "Let me grab us a few beach towels. Where's Josh?"

"He's finishing up outside." Cole grabbed her hand. "Come look what we did!"

Melanie followed the little boy to the back of the house and opened the door. "Oh my goodness," she said, throwing her hand over her mouth and wanting to cry with joy.

A platform of fresh wood covered the ground the length of the house, with ornate pillars supporting the roof. The railings were built out, leading to a two-step sunken porch area with built-in seating. She could just imagine the navy-blue cushions covering the benches with throw pillows in coral and pearl white. She didn't want to ever go back inside the dingy house with this beautiful space that overlooked the sparkling gulf and its porcelain-white shore.

"You're so talented," she said to Josh, breathless.

"Thanks," he said, clearly happy with her reaction, the corners of his eyes creasing and a humble grin playing at his lips. He dropped the last of his tools into his toolbox.

She twirled around on the yellow boards, eager now to paint the whole thing white and get the tables and umbrellas set up. "I can't believe you did all this!" It was the first time she'd felt real hope at the Ellis house. Before she was able to stop herself, she went over to him and threw her arms around him, making him laugh. "It's unbelievable."

"She really likes porches," Cole said with a giggle.

Melanie threw her head back and laughed. "Yes, I do."

"I'm not finished," Josh told her, a bigger smile breaking out.

"What more could you do?" she asked.

"I'm going to build you a giant porch swing at this end so that you can look out at the water." He walked to the open area where the swing would be. "It'll hang from giant ropes here," he said, stretching out his arm. "And it will be the size of a small mattress, so you can fill it with cushions and fit whole families on it at once. That was Cole's idea."

"I thought you needed to get to New York as soon as possible," she said, protecting herself from the hope that would swell up if he stayed even a day longer than he'd said he would. Why had he suddenly changed course?

"Yes," he replied, his gaze moving over to Cole. "But one more day won't hurt."

"Yay!" Cole said, wrapping his arms around Josh's waist, and Melanie felt exactly the same way.

"You wanna go down to the beach?" Josh asked him. Then he scooped the little boy up and turned him upside down, making Cole squeal with laughter. "Do ya?"

"Yes!" Cole said, wriggling around and giggling.

Josh righted the little boy and gently set his feet in the sand at the bottom of the steps. "Let's go then."

The two of them ran down to the water and, as if they'd practiced it, they both dove into the small waves side by side, disappearing beneath the glistening sea. If she didn't know better, she'd swear they were father and son, the way they acted. Even if she stepped in when Josh left, there would be no way she could fill his shoes.

Cole surfaced next to Josh. "Come in!" the boy beckoned.

"I don't have my swimsuit on," Melanie said, trudging through the soft powdery sand toward the breaking waves.

Josh leaned over and said something to Cole, but she couldn't hear it. "We'll come out," Josh said. The two of them swam to shore and began walking toward her, dripping wet. Josh's T-shirt clung to his chest muscles and Melanie had to work to focus on his face.

"How was the water?" she asked, looking between them.

Cole eyed Josh, the two of them speaking some sort of language that only they could understand, their lips turning upward in sly smiles. Then suddenly, Melanie felt her legs come out from under her, Josh's solid arms around them as he picked her up and tossed her over his shoulder to the hoots of Cole below.

"Put me down!" she laughed, squirming as hard as she could, but she was no match for Josh's strength. "I don't have my swimsuit!" she said again, although it was quite clear that neither of them cared one bit whether she was dressed for the occasion.

Josh splashed into the foamy water, the spray cooling her face.

"Throw her in!" Cole laughed.

"You're gonna be in trouble for this, mister," she said, waggling a finger at him, her view upside down from being draped over Josh's shoulder like a ragdoll.

Cole kept on giggling as he ran beside Josh.

"Should I throw her up like I do you?" Josh asked.

"Wait, throw me up?" Melanie squeaked. "No!"

"Do it!" Cole said.

Josh shifted her around until he was carrying her as if they were walking over an invisible threshold.

"Josh!" she scolded, trying not to laugh. "Don't you dare!"

He swung her back and forth in a rocking motion as he made his way deeper into the water. Melanie wrapped her arms tightly around his neck to keep him from throwing her into the air.

"Don't you dare do it," she whispered in his ear.

His smile slid down to a serious expression, their faces much too close.

Cole dove under the water.

Josh leaned in unexpectedly and softly pressed his lips to hers, the salty taste of it intoxicating, sending a bolt of electricity through her body. It was only then that she realized that for the last three years, it was as if her body had been asleep, dormant, without feeling. She held on to his neck, her hands moving toward the back of his head. Then Cole popped back up just as their lips parted, and Josh grinned before tossing her into the air and making her yelp as the motion tickled her tummy. She flew through the air, heading straight for the water. Before she went under, Josh caught her, the two of them splashing into the gulf together.

"See?" Cole said, swimming over. "It's fun!"

Josh licked his lips. "See?" he said, with affection in his eyes as he repeated Cole's words. "It's fun."

"Do I have to go?" Cole asked Suzie as she stood in the doorway.

"Melanie and Josh have a lot of work to do," Suzie said gently. "But I'll bet they'll pop by and see you again soon."

"Definitely," Melanie said. "How's Eric?"

"He's getting a few more tests," Suzie said, worry sheeting down her face like a torrential rain. "We thought he had the flu—he was throwing up... He's lost about ten pounds and we're wondering why."

"Let us know as soon as you find out what's going on," Josh said.

"I will." Suzie took Cole's hand. "Thanks for taking care of my guy," she said with a wink at Cole.

"Any time," Josh told her.

They shut the door, and Josh turned to her. "I'll be right back. I need to... use the restroom really quickly."

Melanie went into the parlor and tidied the scraps of old wallpaper, sweeping the dust from sanding and pushing it all into a pile. When Josh didn't return, she went into the kitchen and he shut a drawer quickly.

"What are you looking for?" she asked.

"Uh..." He came around to meet her, putting his hands in his pockets. "I was trying to find... a pencil and a pad of paper so I could write down some of those contacts for you."

"Oh." Melanie went into the living room and grabbed her purse, pulling out a pen and an old receipt. "Here, you can use this."

"Sorry about today," he said, taking the receipt and setting it on the counter. He uncapped the pen.

"What are you sorry for?"

His chest puffed up with the uncomfortable inhale he took. "Kissing you. I got caught up in the moment, and I should've thought it out a little more."

"Thought it out…" she repeated. Did he regret it? "This is the second time you've gotten 'caught up in the moment,'" she said. "You know me well enough at this point that I was hoping your choices would be more deliberate."

He seemed to be deciding something and then he said, "I feel alive when I'm around you. I'm leaving soon, and yet, I can't get you out of my head."

A fizzle ran through her. "You can't?"

"But I don't need anything holding me back."

After his admission, this comment took her off guard. "Well, I wouldn't want to hold you back," she snapped, suddenly frustrated.

"That came out wrong." He set the pen down and focused on her, but she didn't want to look into his eyes for fear he'd see how much his comment had stung her.

"How could it come out *right*?" she asked.

He offered a contemplative stare. "This is the best it gets," he said with resolve, pointing between them.

"What?" she asked.

"I'll be in New York learning a brand-new job and you'll be here starting a business. We'll both be busy. We also haven't known each other long enough to sustain a long-distance relationship, though both of us have the personalities to try. But even if we could get through it, I've got a failed marriage to prove that one of us could hurt the other beyond repair. So this perfect thing we have right now—*this* is as good as it gets."

"Don't compare me to Janie. I'm not anything like her."

"I know you're not, but that doesn't ensure that things will work out. We've got too much going against us." He looked at the floor and shook his head. "I should probably go," he said quietly.

She wanted to tell him not to, but she was afraid that if she didn't let him leave, she'd fall for him, and—he was right—that wasn't good for anyone. "Can I take you somewhere?" she offered.

He looked up at her, an if-only in his eyes. "I'll call my mother to come get me."

"You sure?" she asked, but he'd already pulled out his phone and hit call.

Chapter Nineteen

Melanie went out to watch the sunrise the next morning on the new back porch with her coffee, breathing in the salty air and letting the deep pinks and purples of the sky center her. After Josh had left, the house seemed too quiet, so she'd spent yesterday evening priming and sanding the walls of the kitchen and parlor to get it ready for painting and applying the new wallpaper. She'd been so busy that she only noticed now that the scraps of wood had all been collected and the yard was clean. Josh must have come back at some point and not wanted to bother her.

She wished he had, her heart sinking.

But it would only make his leaving more difficult. Best he get on with it before either of them were too committed. She had loved the way he'd made her feel, the zinging excitement that pinged through her at his touch.

As she ran her fingertips along the new wood underneath her, she took in the swaying of the waves, remembering the salty droplets on his lips just before he'd kissed her. Squeezing her eyes shut, she tried to get it out of her mind. With a deep breath, she took her coffee back inside, and decided to push the thoughts of Josh aside and get ready for the day. She needed to run to the store to pick up the wallpaper she'd ordered. And there was one more thing she needed to do. Melanie reached into her pocket and pulled out her old engagement ring. As she peered down at the sparkling solitaire on a platinum band, the night she'd received it seemed like another life. But something good would finally come of it. She was going to take it into town and see how much she could get for it at the pawnshop.

"You pawning this ring doesn't have anything to do with the carpenter I've seen hanging around your house, does it?" the pawnshop owner asked with an appraising look. "Josh is pretty well known around here and people are talkin' about all the time he's spent at your place." He held the ring up and inspected the diamond with a magnifier eyepiece.

"How do they know?" she asked.

"Well, you can't walk a block without seeing someone he's visited on your behalf. Bobby Mason said Josh called his appliance shop down there to ask about your order." He pointed out the window at the small shop. "And the tree guys who helped clear my parkin' lot did your yard," he continued. "Josh had taken care of it. There's also Benny who works at the hardware store—he tells me Josh helped you get ready for the storm. Maryann came in the other day to bring me a sandwich like she does sometimes. She went on and on about the little treasure box you two were makin'. Want me to keep goin'?"

"The ring has nothing to do with Josh. He's just helping me out." She couldn't deny the little buzz of happiness the mention of Josh had caused.

"It's a mighty nice ring…" He slipped it onto his pinky to admire it.

"Yes. It's going to help pay for some of the repairs on my house."

The man punched in a few numbers on his calculator and offered her a price.

With a couple thousand dollars in her handbag from the ring, Melanie headed down the winding beach road toward the wallpaper shop across town. The wind rushed in through her open windows as Melanie drove, feeling as if a weight had been lifted, like the rest of her life started right now. As she got to the pier, she slowed, catching sight of the length of wood as it stretched out over the glistening gulf, the solitary bench at the end. It seemed lonesome out there on its own. If she squinted, she could almost see the memory of Josh sitting there when she'd walked up behind him. Thoughts of him were popping up without warning, and she needed to focus on something else.

She pulled the car over and drove into the parking lot, getting out and walking to the bench. Josh had distracted her last time she was there and something in her heart longed for a sign that this was all meant to be. When she got to the bench, she leaned down, careful of her head this time, and felt for the initials, finding them easily. She lay on her belly and looked at the crooked cursive letters: A.E. Then she moved the tips of her fingers along the wood, feeling for anything else, the worn plank smooth under her fingers. Then, just as she went to get up, a light mark caught her eye and she scooted her body under the bench.

Melanie gasped. It was so faint she could barely see it. In fact, she'd missed it altogether last time. There, next to A.E.—were those initials? She could almost swear it said E.A. "Eloise Andrews," she whispered. "Oh my gosh. Gram." She shimmied out from under the bench and ran all the way to her car.

Forget the wallpaper, she was going straight to Addie's.

*

"Which do you want to hear?" Addie asked, pursing her lips reluctantly while heating up two giant, icing-covered cinnamon rolls for them and placing the pastries on china plates with bluebirds flying around the edges, the scent of vanilla and cinnamon filling the air. "Lou's side or Vera's?"

"It's important to me to understand Gram's decisions in all this." Melanie walked over to Addie's stove and scratched a slight burn mark by one of the burners, the soot getting under her nail.

Addie came in behind her and wiped it with a rag. "Pot caught on fire the other day," she said, scrubbing a bit harder to try to get the mark to fade completely. "I called the fire department. But I had it out before they got here."

Melanie eyed Addie, remembering what Josh had said about a fake fire. She'd been right about her being with it.

The old woman sat down in the padded chair next to a small side table holding a philodendron and a half-empty cup of tea. Melanie took a seat on the sofa, resting the cinnamon roll on her lap.

"Eloise was lost without Alfred," Addie said. "She cried in my childhood bedroom, telling me how she'd waited for his letter. Once, her housemaid had dropped the mail and it had fallen down the flood vent by the front door. Lou had sobbed, explaining how she thought she felt a letter in the vent. But I knew it was probably just her imagination."

"So she never got the letter," Melanie said in a whisper.

"If he ever sent one," Addie said.

"He did!" Melanie leaned forward, setting her plate on the side table. "He wrote her many letters, remember? I have them! In the first one, he said he'd written and she'd ignored it."

Addie covered her mouth with her weathered hands. "My God," she said through her fingers. "There was no way she'd ignore him. Your grandmother adored Alfred. Every time she was in town, Lou walked by the gorgeous house he'd built. She used to say it looked as though he'd built it to spite her because it was everything she'd ever wanted."

"But it was actually the opposite," Melanie said, breathless. "He built it *for* her."

"She was quick to point out that she loved your grandfather, and she wouldn't have changed that part of her life, but she always wondered about Alfred—why he hadn't written like he'd promised. It had broken her heart."

"What if the letter is still in the vent?"

"I doubt it was ever there, dear. It could've been lost in the post. The letter may have gotten misplaced in transit. Or, as much as your idealistic side would hate this, Alfred may have never actually sent it."

"But his letters imply that he did."

"Then why did he marry Vera?"

"He said that he'd married Vera because she was a wonderful woman and he was trying to move on." Melanie carried on and told Addie everything.

Addie shook her head, bewildered. "Lou said she'd seen him once, from across the main road, and called his name, but he'd ignored her."

"Or didn't hear her…" Melanie took a bite of her cinnamon roll, the sugary pastry melting in her mouth as she placed it back on the table.

"Poor Lou."

"There's only one way to find out if it is in that vent. I'm going over to Gram's old house."

"Someone else lives there now," Addie said, standing and heading into the kitchen. "Let me wrap your roll up for you."

"I have to try."

Addie handed her the pastry and nodded. "Go, child. See what you can find."

"Hi," Melanie said to the tall woman with bobbed brown hair and a kind smile at the door of her grandmother's childhood home. The sweeping staircase behind her inside was just as it had looked in Gram's old photos, the vibrant colors of reality making her feel as if the old black-and-white pictures had come to life in front of Melanie's eyes. "You don't know me—I bought the Ellis house on Sandpiper Lane—but my gram grew up here: Eloise Andrews."

"Oh?" the woman asked with interest.

"I have a very strange request. I wonder if you'd let me look inside your flood grate right there," she asked, pointing to the vent in the floor. "I'm hoping there may be a letter in it that belongs to my grandmother."

The woman swung the door wider. "Of course. Come on in. I'm Estelle."

"Thank you so much, Estelle!" Melanie entered the old plantation house, the space redone, the cool air-conditioning settling on her skin. "My grandmother was waiting for a letter and I was told that it may have fallen down there," she explained further.

"Well, have a look," Estelle said.

Melanie squatted down and tugged on the old grate, but it didn't want to budge, the thick iron seeming to protest against her pulling. "I think it's stuck," she said, giving her fingers a break, the ends of them red.

"What if we tried to pry it with something?" Estelle suggested. "Maybe a screwdriver?"

"That might work."

"Come with me." Estelle led Melanie down the hallway toward the kitchen at the back of the house. "I'm a sucker for social history," she said over her shoulder as Melanie followed her. "That's what drew me to this house."

"It's beautiful," Melanie said. "I've never been in it. My grandmother left this home in her early twenties and spent her married life on a farm in Alabama with my grandfather."

"Ah," Estelle said, pulling open a kitchen drawer and retrieving a flat-head screwdriver. They headed back to the front of the house.

Estelle slipped the tool under the lip of the grate and pried until the metal came loose from the seal it had created in the shellac of the hardwood floor. She lifted it out.

Melanie slowly sunk her hand down into the hole, stretching as far as she could reach, feeling around through the dust until the tip of her finger landed on something, and a bolt of excitement raced through her. Melanie squeezed her eyes shut and thrust her arm further, straining and pushing her fingers as far as they could go.

Suddenly, it was under her grip. She slid it toward her slowly, the tips of her fingers coming off of it and finding it again quickly before it slipped back into its resting place. Her breathing slow and steady, she moved her shaking fingers up the side of the vent until she could grab the paper with her other hand.

With a thumping heart, she peered down at the envelope between her fingers, noting the postmark: 1956. It was addressed to Gram with a return address from Alfred Ellis, 32nd Street Naval Station, San Diego, California. An electric buzz swam through her, her hands shaking.

"Unbelievable," Melanie whispered, her eyes lingering on it in wonder before she stood up and addressed Estelle. "Thank you so much for letting me look for this," she said, holding it to her chest.

"No problem at all. Maybe sometime we can get coffee and you can tell me about it."

"I'd love to," Melanie said. Then she got into her car and drove back to the Ellis house, her whole body trembling, the letter lying on the passenger seat, waiting to be read.

Chapter Twenty

Melanie took the envelope to the back porch and stopped short when she'd stepped outside. To her left was the most beautiful wooden porch swing, swaying in the coastal breeze by four ship's ropes. She went over to it, taking in the grain of the stained wood, the beveled edge of the handrail, and the soft baby-blue cushion on the bottom.

Holding the letter in her hand, she sat down on the swing, dragging her feet to keep herself steady until she could push off, the soft glide of it making her feel like she was floating. With the static sound of the wind coming off the shore filling her ears and the sun on her cheeks, she looked out at the chalky coastline, wishing she could have seen Josh when he'd come by.

She'd definitely have to thank him, so she decided to stop by his mother's house later. His work was so gorgeous that she would definitely offer to pay him…

But right now, she wanted to read Alfred's letter to her grandmother. Maybe she could find some clue as to what had happened.

November 6, 1957

To the love of my life,

*Eloise Andrews, I am hopelessly in love with you. I'll be back April 23rd,
and the minute I set foot in Rosemary Bay, I'm finding you, dipping
you right there in the street and kissing you for the whole world to see.
I want to marry you. Say yes.*

All my love,
Alfred

Melanie felt a mixture of emotions. She was thrilled to finally have
an answer as to whether or not her grandmother had been involved
with this man, but now the rest of Gram's life was in question. Did
she spend her evenings washing dishes at the kitchen sink, her eyes
on Gramps, wondering if there could've been a better life for her out
there? Did she hold on to what could have been, wishing her life had
turned out differently?

Melanie was incredibly sad for Alfred that he'd lost her, even
though it didn't make any sense because if they had found each other,
Melanie wouldn't have been here reading the letter. She wouldn't be
here at all. Yet she couldn't deny the pull on her heartstrings that his
marriage had failed as a result of it and he'd died alone here, the place
of his dreams slowly crumbling around him. And now, she too was
alone in that big house, as if in some cosmic way she was picking up
where he'd left off. The home was so quiet at night after she'd gone
to bed that it was eerie. And when Josh was there doing work, the
walls seemed brighter, as if they were glad for the company. But now,

the one person she enjoyed most in this town was going to be over a thousand miles away in New York, leaving her and the Ellis house to continue on as they always had.

Suddenly feeling like she couldn't let Josh go without at least telling him she appreciated the gorgeous swing he'd made, she got up and went to find him.

*

Melanie's breath caught when she saw the rental truck in the driveway of Josh's mother's house. The back was open and Josh was inside, shifting around boxes.

"What are you doing here?" he asked.

She shut her car door and walked over to him. "I wanted to say thank you for the swing."

"I promised I'd do it, so… it's done now." He wasn't making eye contact with her, sadness in his voice.

She jumped up into the back of the truck. "I'd like to pay you for it," she offered.

He lifted another box and set it on top of one of the others. "I don't need you to pay me. I need you to let me work." His tone was softer now, but that wall he was so great at building was back up. He kept shifting boxes, not looking at her.

"What's going on?" she asked, her head spinning to make sense of it all.

He twisted around, the dismay in his eyes clear when they finally met hers. "Why did you come here?"

"To say thank you."

"You're welcome," he said. "I've gotta get these boxes packed. I've stayed way too long and I need to go. Good luck with the house.

I hope you can finally let go of all the old stories and turn it into something great."

"The stories are real," she said.

He rolled his eyes. "You're impossible."

"I'm serious. I have proof."

He pursed his lips, shaking his head.

"Seriously. Alfred Ellis wasn't out of his mind after all. And neither is Addie. I found *another* letter," she said. "The one Alfred actually sent. And guess where I found it. In the vent in my grandmother's childhood home—the home that Addie told me to check." She moved over to him. "And my grandmother's initials *are* under that bench—I'd missed them the first time."

He sucked in a quiet breath, his gaze landing on her.

"So I have proof that Alfred and my grandmother's story is true." But then she guiltily snapped her mouth shut when she realized that by telling him this in all her excitement, she'd proven that Vera's connection to Alfred may also be true.

Josh seemed to be digesting something as well. He stepped over to her, his face coming into her personal space and making it hard to breathe. "Did you tell anyone about this?" he asked urgently, the intensity of his look making her nervous.

"Only Addie," she said.

His face suddenly frantic, he strode over to the truck, shut the back, and got in, starting the engine.

"Where are you going?" she called, as she ran to her car so she could follow him. From the look on his face, she wasn't sure what he was going to do.

He didn't answer, shutting the door with a slam. Then he peeled out of the driveway, engine rumbling, the truck coming inches from the side of her car.

Her hands trembling, Melanie threw the car in reverse and pulled out after him, following him down the side road as he went well above the speed limit. What was wrong with him?

She trailed him all the way back to her house, where he got out and hopped the steps two at a time to the front door, throwing it open and marching inside.

"What are you doing?" she yelled, running up the steps after him.

He didn't respond as he made his way through the parlor.

She followed him into the kitchen. "You can't just burst into my house," she said. "You aren't staying here anymore, remember?"

"Where are the letters?" he asked, throwing open kitchen drawers. "Give me the letters."

He continued opening doors, peering into her pantry, lifting up supplies to see if they were under anything.

"Why do you want them anyway?" she asked, trying to get him to focus on her, but when she grabbed his arm, he yanked it away. "What's going on?"

"Have you read them all?" he asked.

"Why?" she replied, his urgency sitting uncomfortably with her.

He stopped and faced her. "I need you to tell me where they are."

Melanie narrowed her eyes at him. "*Why?*"

"If you won't believe they're completely fabricated, then it's time to take matters into my own hands."

"They're *not* fake, Josh. Why do you need them?"

"It's incredibly important, okay?" His demeanor changed from angry to panicked. "Please, Melanie. Just let me see them."

Her curiosity won out, and she ran upstairs and got them. When she returned downstairs, Josh was on the back porch. She handed him the stack. "Want to tell me what all this is about?"

"There are things meant to be left alone," he said, pulling the last envelope from the stack.

To Melanie's horror, he ripped it in half. She gasped, trying to get it from him, but he stood up, tearing it again and then again. He continued destroying the letter while she swiped at his hand, tears filling her eyes. "You have no right," she said, her lip wobbling. "Give it to me!" She tried to grab the pieces but they were too small to get them all. Suddenly, he released them, all the paper scraps dispersing on the wind, flying away in every direction, blowing down on the beach.

Josh stared at her, looking just as dismayed as she did, apology in his eyes. But then he cleared it, tossed the stack of letters onto the swing, and walked toward the door, heading inside.

With shaking hands, Melanie gathered up the envelopes, tears spilling from her eyes. "Those were written to *my* grandmother," she seethed, following him in. "And now I'll never know what Alfred wanted to tell her."

"It's better that no one knows." He opened the front door and walked out.

"Don't ever set foot in this house again," she said, ignoring his comment completely, so angry with him that she could bite nails in two.

"No problem. I'm off to New York. Right now." He opened the truck door and peered back at her one more time. "See ya."

Melanie went inside and slammed the door shut, the sound of his engine and then the crunching of gravel as he pulled away filtering through the house. Sliding down to the floor, the letters in her fist, she put her head in her hands and cried, letting out all the emotions she'd built up since she'd gotten there.

Melanie sat in the silence, wondering how she was going to make it through this. "I don't understand why you're putting me through the ringer," she called out to her grandmother, hoping Gram could hear her. "It's too hard," she said, her voice withering on her quivering lips. The letters had made her feel for a brief moment like Gram was there with her again, whispering in her ear the whole time. But now, with the last letter gone, Josh had taken the only remaining shred of connection with her grandmother and torn it into a thousand pieces.

Finally allowing herself to crumble, she spent the next hour sobbing. She'd made it through Gram's funeral and the days after, when everyone back in Nashville had brought over covered dishes—the southern way to show their support. She'd gotten so much food that she'd had to give it away to neighbors. But she'd held it together the whole time. She'd kept her emotions in check through the sale of Gram's house, and in her lawyer's office as she'd gone through her inheritance. She'd worked so hard to be strong for so long, managing each step in the process. But now, it was finished. She sat alone, in an old house that no one else seemed to want, with barely enough money to cover the upkeep, and no way to make any income. Gram was gone. She'd never be there to reassure her or talk things through the way they used to do.

Frustrated, she got up, went into the kitchen, and threw the letters into a drawer. Then she left out the back door, headed for the beach. The bright blue sky and the squawk of gulls overhead seemed to mock her foul mood. As her bare feet sunk into the soft sand with every step, she considered Josh's reaction. Even if it were true about Alfred and his grandmother, surely people would understand if they knew the story. Why had Josh torn them up? It made no sense. She peered around for the scraps of paper, wondering what had been in that final letter, but they were long gone. Josh had said he'd read them all, so did he know something she didn't know? What did any of it matter now? He was gone too.

With a heavy heart, Melanie stared out at the lapping waves as they gurgled like champagne bubbles by her feet. This was a turning point. It was time to make some big decisions. She had to either put the house up for sale and cut her losses or throw herself into this renovation for no other reason than herself. The pros to staying were that she'd have something she could feel proud of when she was finished. She'd have a gorgeous piece of property, and she could open the bed and breakfast, meet interesting people, and be her own boss. The cons… She might go bankrupt trying to get the house in any kind of decent shape. She'd have to do it all by herself with no guidance from anyone else. Was she really ready to take this on?

Chapter Twenty-One

"Hey there, Melanie." A familiar voice sailed over a nearby dock at the edge of the gulf toward her as she took a morning stroll along the winding shore. Brenda waved as she walked around the wooden structure.

"Hi," Melanie greeted her from afar. "It was a surprise to hear my name called," she said loudly as Brenda made her way down the beach. "I'm not used to people knowing me around here."

"Well, it won't take long in this town before everyone knows your name." Brenda offered a friendly smile when she reached Melanie. "How's the house coming along?" It was clear that Brenda had to force the question out in a polite tone while biting back her distaste for it.

"It's getting there, although not as quickly as I'd hoped."

"I hear ya. Nothing ever goes as quickly as we hope. Mind if I walk with you?"

"Not at all." Melanie stepped up beside her, the two of them striding together. Brenda walked at a slower pace, which Melanie welcomed because the soft sand worked muscles that Melanie wasn't used to, putting a strain on her calves. "I needed some fresh air this morning."

"Me too." Brenda turned her face toward the wind. "Josh is off to New York, and he left in a hurry. Didn't even stay for breakfast."

"He's very hot and cold, isn't he?" Melanie noted. "I can't figure him out."

"Hot and cold?" Brenda's face crumpled in confusion, surprising Melanie. She'd assumed his mother knew all about his mood swings, but by the look on her face, it didn't seem so.

"One minute he's… sweet, and the next he's a bear."

"Really…" Brenda seemed to be searching for an answer to something in Melanie's face.

"It's as if he's afraid that I'll like him. If that makes any sense at all."

Brenda stopped and Melanie turned toward her.

"It makes total sense."

"Why?" Melanie asked.

Brenda locked arms with her and started walking again. "Let me tell you a little story…"

The wind picked up, pushing against them while they walked arm in arm. They'd passed the turn-off toward Melanie's way home, but she hardly noticed, interested in what Brenda had to say.

"My son was married for five years to Janie Jackson." She held her hair back with her fingers as the wind blew, making eye contact. "Janie grew up here, too. She became a successful local real estate agent, and eventually took a job with a prominent real estate development firm called Bowland Enterprises. While Rob Whitaker, the owner of the company, and Josh got along great, and Janie was quite happy with her new career, after she started that job, things became rocky for Josh and Janie. She started picking fights with him about little things, getting irritable. But he worked hard to save their marriage. Then one day, Josh came over and admitted to me that he had no idea why she was even with him. There was nothing left of their relationship, even after counseling and special date nights and trips away he'd prepared—anything he could do to fix it."

Melanie's heart ached for him. "How long ago was that?"

"About a year ago. When they finally split, he found out that Janie had been holding on, trying to dig up all she could find on my father's land that was being passed down to Josh. Janie wanted to know the legalities they faced if she tried to acquire it in a divorce."

"Oh my gosh," Melanie said. "That's terrible."

"Yes," Brenda said on a deep outbreath, the betrayal obviously hitting a nerve with her. "It turns out that Janie was having an affair with Rob, and the two of them were trying to acquire Josh's birthright to put up a retail chain, which is why Janie was holding off on ending things. She needed to be in their house to go through Josh's files until she found something."

"Wow," Melanie said, blown away by the news.

"So, Josh is a little skittish of relationships in any form."

"I can imagine."

"But I do find something interesting."

Melanie looked over at Brenda. "What's that?"

"Ever since the divorce, all I've seen is anger in my son. It was like he'd lost faith in life. So if you're seeing any of that sweetness that he's hidden away, you're doing something right."

A spark of hope bubbled up.

The two of them walked along the beach together, while Melanie digested this new information. The moments their lips were dangerously close, the times he'd smiled at her, the gentle feel of his arms around her—it all rushed in like a wave. And suddenly, it all made sense. Josh felt the same spark and he was pushing her away because he'd had to leave.

*

"What a jerk," Melanie's sister Kathryn said on the other end of the phone when Melanie told her what Josh had done with the letter.

"The thing is," Melanie said, fiddling with a scrap of wallpaper as she sat cross-legged on the floor in the parlor, the sunlight filtering in through the window and casting a long dusty ray across the boards. "I don't really think he *is* a jerk. I just saw his mother, and something's going on with him." She didn't want to say any more, knowing that Josh would hate being talked about like that.

"*I* think you don't want to admit to yourself that he might actually be a jerk. He hasn't been very nice since the beginning."

Melanie rubbed her lips together, remembering that salty kiss they'd shared.

"I can't believe that Gram and Alfred Ellis…" Kathryn trailed off. "Poor Gramps…"

"I know. It's all so surreal."

"Gram must have still felt something for him or she wouldn't have asked you to buy the house. I wonder what she thought about whenever she passed it," Kathryn asked.

"I just keep thinking, what if she'd gotten Alfred's letter? Her whole life would've been different."

"I think that things always end up the way they were meant to be," her sister said.

"So, Alfred was meant to be alone?"

Kathryn sat silent on the other end. "I don't know," she finally said, contemplatively. "It's sad, though, isn't it?"

"Yeah…"

"What are you gonna do?"

For the first time since she'd gotten here, Melanie didn't mind being alone. Maybe it was the revelation of how Josh might feel for her or the fact that she wouldn't stop looking for clues to Alfred's story, but she had an undeniable feeling that this moment was just a stop on the path to where she ultimately needed to be. She couldn't get there until she put one foot in front of the other and made her dreams happen. "I think I'm going to try to renovate the house and see where it leads me."

"Want me to come down there and help?" Kathryn asked.

Melanie peered around the bare room, the huge chandelier looking lonely all by itself. "I'd love it if you could," she replied.

"All right," Kathryn told her. "Let me see what I can do. I can probably drive down tomorrow night."

It would make all the difference in the world if Melanie had a familiar face here. Kathryn would be able to take her mind off everything she had going on. Even if only for a little while.

Melanie hadn't thought about Josh or the torn letter once since she'd spoken to her sister. She'd been occupied the entire morning with painting under the buzz of saws while the guys she'd called about the air-conditioning went to work on the ducts, installing air vents throughout the house. She'd also gotten in touch with the floor guy to schedule a time and, to her delight, a cancellation had opened up in his schedule. He'd be starting tomorrow.

One of the contractors from Josh's list had come to knock out the wall in the kitchen as well as demolish the old cabinets, and now he was painting the sanded and primed areas around the new bar he'd installed. The living and kitchen areas were really starting to come together.

"Your new counters and cabinets should come in tomorrow morning," he said, as he ran his paint roller under the water at the sink to rinse it out.

"That's wonderful," she said.

When the HVAC guys left, the air-conditioning finally working, and the contractor headed out, Melanie stood in the completely empty space. The kitchen counters and cabinets were gone, her new appliances standing solitary in the blank space. The house was a mess, but she felt a sense of accomplishment. She had taken the first of many steps toward her future.

The late afternoon sun cast an orange glow over the beach. Melanie sat on the bottom step of the back porch that Josh had built for her and dug her toes into the sand. She wondered where Josh was in his journey—how far had he gotten? If he came back for his truck at some point, she promised herself that she would have a word with him about how he'd left.

The coastal wind blew against her, ruffling her sundress. She pulled her hair back with her hand and turned her face to the sun, which sat low and brilliant in the sky. Then a familiar voice pulled her attention to the side of the house.

"Hey," Suzie said, walking over to her, Melanie noticing her red eyes as the woman approached. "Cole is with Eric," she said as she sat down. "We've had some not-so-great news from the doctor." Her fingers trembled as she set them on her knees.

"What is it?" Melanie asked. "You look worried."

"It's about Eric," she said. "He has a tumor in his stomach. Cancer. We're waiting for more tests to see if it's spread at all."

"Oh no," Melanie said, a wave of apprehension swelling in her gut.

Suzie's eyes glistened in the shimmering sunlight as she shook her head and turned toward the water. "I can't lose him," she said. "I'm so scared."

"Just take it one moment at a time," Melanie told her. "That's all you can do." The fear and anxiety that had filled her when Gram got sick inched back in without hesitation. "I spent three years taking care of my gram when she had cancer, and it's a roller coaster. If you try to take it all in at once, it's overwhelming. Just take it step by step."

"Yeah."

"I'm here for you."

"Thank you," Suzie said. "I just keep thinking about Cole. Josh has just left him and now Eric is sick. I know it's going to be a long battle to fight this thing, and Cole won't have a male influence in his life. While I'll do everything I can to keep normalcy for him, he'll feel the change, I'm sure, and he's already dealt with so much."

"Does Josh know yet?" Melanie asked, thinking that Josh may come home if he heard the news.

Suzie shook her head. "I haven't told him. We're still trying to figure everything out. But I came over to ask for your help."

"Anything."

"Cole really enjoyed being with you—he talks about it like crazy. I know you've got a lot going on with the house remodel, I just didn't know who else to ask with Josh gone… Would our little guy be able to come see you while we work out what Eric will be facing in terms of care? It would give Cole a less stressful environment."

"Of course," Melanie said immediately.

"It would only be during the day, while we discuss his treatment and get it all started. I'm not sure how sick he's going to be, but we'll cross that bridge when we come to it."

"How about *you?*" Melanie asked. "Do you need anything?"

Her eyes glistened over once more. "I don't even know what I need at this point."

"Well, if you need anything at all, I'm here," Melanie told her.

"Thanks." Suzie gave her a melancholy smile. "Can I bring Cole over in the morning at around nine? We're meeting with the doctor to talk about initial treatment."

"Absolutely." With the floors being redone and the cabinets and counters going in, Melanie would be able to get out of the house and focus on Cole. With a new sense of purpose, she decided she'd have to start thinking about things he'd like to do while he was with her. She'd do anything for that sweet little boy.

Chapter Twenty-Two

Melanie's eyes moved from the coffee maker to her phone when it vibrated. She set down her mug, grabbed her phone and saw a text from her sister, saying she'd be there this evening, and a rather long one from Josh:

Suzie told me about Eric. Thank you for helping out with Cole. He likes to hunt for seashells on the beach. He also likes to ride bicycles through town and stop at the general store for sodas. I don't let him get any with caffeine.

A pang of something shot through her as she read the text. Did she miss him? She texted back: *Thanks for the suggestions. I'll be sure to do those things with him.*

She got an immediate response: *Okay.*

She replied: *Did you make it to New York?*

A message floated back to her on the screen: *Yep. Getting unpacked now. Hey, I need to go.*

Just as well. She couldn't really talk to him about how he'd handled Alfred's letter over text, and there was more she wanted to say than just sharing pleasantries. She returned, *Okay*. Then she typed *Chat later* but thought better of it and deleted it.

She waited for a text in return, but he didn't come back to her.

At the resolutely blank screen, Melanie swallowed her disappointment, put her phone down and went to get ready for the day.

The old door buzzer sounded over the squeal of sanders from the crew working on the hardwoods. Melanie opened the front door to find Suzie standing with Cole.

"Hi!" Cole said. He covered his ears to drown out the noise while donning a blue and yellow racing backpack.

"Hello," Melanie said with a smile. "Don't worry, we aren't going to stay in the house today. I thought we'd walk down to the bike shop and rent some beach cruisers."

Cole's eyes grew round. "We are?" He hopped up and down.

Suzie gave her a grateful smile. "I'll be back to get him before dinner."

"Take your time," Melanie said.

Suzie gave Cole a squeeze. "I'll be back, okay?"

"Okay," Cole replied.

As Suzie walked back to her car and pulled away, Melanie waved goodbye and then patted her pockets. "I've got my phone and bank card," she said, stepping out onto the porch and shutting the door behind her. "Want to get out of here and find us a couple of bikes for an adventure?"

"Yes!" Cole took her hand and the two of them made their way to the sidewalk, heading into town. The sky was alight with the bright yellow sun, the birds squawking overhead. A lot of the debris from the storm had now been removed, and off in the distance, Rosemary Bay was beginning to look more recognizable. While there were still pockets of town giving away the fact that they'd been hit by the hurricane, with downed trees, blocked streets, and caution tape around broken power lines, it was amazing how quickly the town had rebuilt. Cars drove up and down Main Street, the stores had mostly opened, and there were people shopping and getting ice cream.

"Can we do a video chat with Josh?" Cole asked, looking up at her with those big brown eyes of his.

"We can try, I suppose," she replied. "He might be busy with his new job." She didn't want Cole to get his hopes up. If Josh saw Melanie was calling, she couldn't guarantee that he'd answer.

She pulled out her phone, and then clicked on Josh's number. The phone pulsed as they walked along, waiting for him to pick up. Then suddenly, to her relief, his face came onto the screen.

"Hey," he said, the harsh static of traffic in the background, two small lines between his eyes giving away the fact that he definitely wasn't expecting her call.

Melanie tilted the phone so both she and Cole could see the screen. "Hi," she returned. "Cole and I are walking into town to rent bikes."

"That sounds fun," he said, his voice animated for Cole's benefit.

Cole chatted with Josh the whole way, and Melanie let him, glad that the boy could have a little time with his friend. He said his goodbyes as they rounded the corner and stood in front of the bike shop.

"Which one are you going to get?" Melanie asked, running her finger over the handlebar of a small bright red bike, the first in line of an array of bicycles that spanned every color of the spectrum.

Cole sped over to a mint-green miniature beach cruiser with a navy-blue seat and handle grips. "I like this one," he said. "You should get that big one." The little boy pointed to a pale yellow bike with a front basket and wide leather seat.

"I think I will," Melanie said. "Shall we go in and rent them?"

"Yes!" Cole took her hand and they went inside.

Once Melanie had paid for the rentals, and the shopkeeper had unlocked the two bikes, Melanie and Cole hopped on.

"Where are we going?" he asked, the bike wobbling as he got a foothold on it.

"I heard that there's a kite festival going on down the beach. Want to ride over and check it out?"

"That would be fun!" Cole lifted off his bicycle seat and pedaled, the pedals going around as quickly as his little legs could push them.

Melanie increased her pace to keep up, the warm breeze blowing her hair behind her shoulders as she and Cole bumped along the sidewalk down the main road that paralleled the shore.

"Look!" Cole said.

Off in the distance, Melanie could make out the rainbow of kites pulling taut against their lines. "We're almost there." She pedaled harder to keep up with Cole.

When they got to the festival, Melanie secured their bikes to the rack with the locks that were in the basket of her bike, and they walked over to the mass of people who'd gathered to see the display. It looked like a parade in the azure sky—massive kites in varying colors and sizes loomed above them. Their canvas sides strained against the wind that kept them up in the air.

"I like that one," Cole said, his eyes on a giant puppy with its tongue flapping alongside the tails of the other kites with each gust.

"That's really cool," Melanie agreed, shielding her eyes from the blazing sun to see it. "We should get a kite and take it home."

Cole's eyes widened. "We should?"

"Sure." While kites weren't on her list of home décor items, she didn't mind doing a little something special for him. "Let's see what kinds they have."

The sales booth that had been set up on the beach had tons of kites hanging from the roof of the structure. Melanie fiddled with a few of the modest ones that were more reasonably priced. "What about this?" She held up a small triangle in dark blues.

Cole nodded politely, but she noticed his eyes on a yellow and orange fish-shaped kite. She peered up at it. The kite was way more than she'd been planning to spend... "You know which one I think is the best one here?"

"That one?" he asked, pointing to the fish.

"Definitely. We'll take that one," she said, and the booth worker pulled the fish down.

"Yeah!" Cole pumped his fists and jumped up and down.

"Should we try to fly it?"

Cole nodded vigorously, giggling the entire time.

"Okay, then. I'll need to buy that wooden spool and line. Could you assemble them for us, by chance?"

"Yes, ma'am," the man said, his fingers already working at an expert's pace to put it together for them.

With the kite in hand, Melanie and Cole walked over to an area of the beach where they'd have enough room to move around. She handed Cole the spool. "Hold it tightly," she said. Then she took the kite and walked it a few paces over until the line pulled against her. With a whoosh, she let it go and it sailed into the sky, making Cole laugh as he tensed to keep hold of the line.

"This is the most fun ever!" he said, as he watched the fish dipping and bobbing on the wind.

Melanie smiled, her heart full. Even if she'd only made his life better for a brief time, she was so thankful that she could.

After Suzie had picked up Cole, the weather was so nice that Melanie decided to walk down to Addie's to pop in and say hello. She walked over the silky sand, the gulf calm today, like she was. The sunshine above her and the occasional bird soaring in the sky made her feel like nothing could spoil this moment.

She knocked on the door.

"Well, fancy seeing you on my porch," Addie said. "I was just talking about you to Simon Banks. Come on in. I've just put some tea on."

"Who's Simon Banks?" she asked, stepping inside in response to Addie's beckoning.

"He's the town historian. I was telling him about your letters." She puttered into the small kitchen just off the living area, leaving Melanie in the doorway between the two rooms.

"Did he know about my gram or Alfred Ellis?"

Addie filled a teacup with hot tea. It clinked against its saucer as she handed it unsteadily to Melanie. "He'd heard a bit about their story," she said, pointing a finger at a little tray of sugar and milk that was sitting on the coffee table, offering it to her.

"What had he heard?" Melanie spooned a small bit of sugar into the tea and stirred it, then added milk.

"Well, apparently, Alfred and your grandmother had viewed the property that the Ellis house now sits on while he was here for the summer, back in 1956." She sat down in the chair opposite Melanie and tipped her head back, thought glazing over her eyes. "I still remember that summer. It seemed to stretch on all year—it felt like we could be kids forever. The navy ship had come in, and all the young men brought an air of excitement to this little village. We had dances and watched the boys play baseball at the park, we ate ice cream and dressed up like we were Hollywood stars. It was magical."

"That sounds amazing," Melanie told her, before sipping the sweet tea.

"Yes, but I digress," she said, still smiling at the wall as if the memory were there, playing out in front of her. "Simon remembered talking to them about it. Apparently, the dune that leads to the water used to be much higher—a storm took it out in the eighties. But it was called Lovers' Bluff. Simon still remembered how your grandmother's cheeks had turned crimson when he'd said that in front of Alfred."

"It's funny to imagine her in love with someone other than my grandfather. She seemed to really like Alfred. How long did they know each other?"

"He came into town in March, I believe, and he left in September."

"Wow, six months. It was a whirlwind romance, then."

"Like I said, that summer stands out for me. It felt like it was forever that those guys were here."

"What did Alfred live on while he was in Rosemary Bay? Did he work?"

"Some of it was paid leave, I'd imagine, and the rest of the time I suppose he used his savings. I know he didn't work because he spent every minute with Lou."

"My grandmother had a good life. She loved my grandfather, so things happen for a reason, right? But Alfred's story just makes me so sad."

"We don't always understand God's plan, do we?" Addie said, switching positions in her chair. "Sometimes I think we get in the way of our own path, falling in love or taking the long way around... God has to double-time it to get us back on track."

"So not everything is part of our life's plan?" Melanie challenged.

"Maybe not *our* life's plan, but it's all part of a bigger plan—a plan so large and all-encompassing that we can't see it because we're but a tiny grain of sand in the whole thing."

Melanie took another sip of her tea, quietly considering this idea.

"And I mentioned that key you have," Addie said. "I tried to describe it. Simon said you might want to see if it's to a safe deposit box."

"That's an idea," she said, suddenly hopeful she'd uncover another piece of the puzzle. She felt compelled to hear whatever it was Alfred wanted to say. Her heart ached for him. He'd been all alone in that big house, waiting and heartbroken...

"Simon is going to dig around a little bit and see what else he can find out," Addie said, interrupting Melanie's reverie.

Melanie nodded, glad to have even a tiny glimmer of hope that she'd find out something new that might shed light on this sad story. She considered what was in that letter Josh had torn up. What more could there be? She knew firsthand that both Vera and Gram had gone on to live full lives. They'd married, had families of their own, and that was that. What could it have said?

"Oh, Mel!" Melanie's sister Kathryn said, as she walked through the front door and stepped onto the newly sanded hardwoods. "You've been busy!" She set her bags down and gave her sister a hug before thrusting a bottle of rum with a bright yellow bow into her hands. "I figured you *need* this."

Melanie laughed, feeling an instant relief at seeing a friendly face. She raised her arms in the air, the bottle of rum hanging from her fist, and did a little twirl. "Do you feel that?" she sang. "Air-conditioning!"

Kathryn's smile widened. "It's amazing. And the wallpaper looks incredible!"

"There's so much more to do, though."

Kathryn put her hands on her denim-clad hips. "Where do you want to start?"

"For some reason, I've been pulled toward finishing the parlor. There's something about that room that draws me in." She peered through the large open double door to view the empty space. "Maybe it's because it has the chandelier that I know Alfred chose for Gram. I'd like to keep it but change out some of the pieces for starfish and driftwood—modernize it and make it beachier."

Kathryn smiled fondly at her sister.

"We need to hang the wallpaper in there. But first!" Melanie held up a finger. "Let's get your bags upstairs and then make a cocktail." She set the rum on the bottom step and they headed upstairs.

"Yes! I have piña colada mix in my suitcase." As they made their way up the old staircase, Kathryn turned back to address her sister. "I brought something else for you," she said.

"Tell me it's the butter pecan chocolate truffles I like so much."

"Better," Kathryn said with a laugh, as they rounded the corner at the top of the stairs.

"What could be better than that?" Melanie pushed open the door and set her sister's bag inside the room. Maybe they could go shopping for some furniture while she was here so she and Kathryn wouldn't have to sleep on an air mattress.

Kathryn unzipped her suitcase and pulled out an old book, handing it to Melanie. "This," she said. "We found it in those boxes of Gram's that were at Mom's."

Melanie delicately opened the leather-bound book, running her finger along the old cream-colored tape that held a photo to the page. She peered down at the image and squinted at the couple. It was a man she didn't recognize with a very young Gram. Their grandmother wore a white linen dress that tapered to her calves with an empire waist, showing off her figure. When Melanie realized the man had on a navy uniform, the hair on her arms stood up. The date was 1956, and the inscription in Gram's swooping pencil said, "A.E. before his deployment."

"Oh my gosh," Melanie said, throwing her hand over her gaping mouth. "That's Alfred Ellis." She held her breath as she peered into the gray eyes that were staring back at her, as if she were finally meeting the man whom she'd heard so much about. The small smile on his lips seemed to be greeting her, and a prickle ran down her arms.

"I figured." Kathryn looked on.

Melanie tucked the book under her arm and went over to the door. "Let's have those piña coladas. I'll unpack the blender."

Kathryn clapped her hands. "I'll grab the mix!"

Chapter Twenty-Three

Melanie was up before Kathryn. The sun was just coming up over the gulf, casting a blanket of diamonds on the surface of the water. She had a big day today: Cole was coming over to stay with them while she and her sister finished the wallpaper in the parlor and shopped for furniture.

She had no idea how long it would take her to strip the walls in the eight bedrooms upstairs or to renovate the bathrooms, even with Kathryn's help. She definitely needed to take a look at the list of contractors Josh gave her and get started scheduling the work. But at least her living space was coming together.

Her thoughts fluttered as if on the wind, her mind taking her back to Josh. She considered confronting him about tearing up the letter… Before she could second guess her decision, she pulled her phone out of her pocket and hit his number, putting the phone to her ear.

"Is everything all right?" he answered without even a hello.

"I suppose," she replied. "I wanted to ask you something."

He didn't respond.

Melanie kept going. "Why did you tear up the last letter that Alfred wrote to my grandmother?"

His steady breaths were the only indication that Josh was still on the line. He cleared his throat. "I tore up the letter because I didn't want you spreading rumors."

"But I found the first letter he sent at Gram's old house, and her initials are there beside his on the pier. That doesn't sound like a rumor to me. It sounds like a real story."

"How do you know that he didn't plant it all there? Can you really prove that the initials are your grandmother's?"

"My sister Kathryn is here. She brought a journal of Gram's with her, and you'll never believe what photo is on the first page. It's my grandmother and Alfred together on the pier, labeled in my grandmother's handwriting, not Alfred's. Now, do you want to tell me what's in that last letter?"

"Hello-o." Suzie's voiced floated over to Melanie, tearing her away from the conversation.

Cole ran toward her and threw his arms around her. "Who ya talking to?" he asked.

"Josh," she said, handing Cole the phone when he reached out for it.

The little boy put it to his ear. "Hi, Josh!" he said, walking into the yard.

"We have this final appointment before Eric has to go into surgery," Suzie said. "They want to get him in pretty quickly to see if they can get all the cancer while it's still early."

"How's he feeling?"

"Not very good. Cole thinks he has the flu."

"Are you going to tell him?" Melanie asked.

"I think we need to. I just don't know how…" Suzie looked out at the boy as he chatted to Josh.

"You gone fishin' yet?" Cole asked Josh, the phone pressed firmly to his little ear, his head down as he focused on Josh's answer.

"Without Josh here to console him, I'm not sure what we'll do. Cole and Josh just speak each other's language, and Josh can explain things to Cole in a way that neither I nor Eric can."

"Maybe you could have Josh there on video call when you tell Cole," Melanie suggested.

"Yeah," she said, thinking. "It's just not the same without him."

"Here you go," Cole said, beaming after talking to Josh, holding out Melanie's phone as he came back up from the yard.

"Thank you," Melanie said sweetly, taking her phone and slipping it back into her pocket.

"I'm going to head out," Suzie told them. Then she ruffled Cole's hair. "I'll be back to get you in a little bit. Don't have too much fun!" She gave him a wink.

Cole giggled.

"You know what I thought *might* be fun today?" Melanie asked Cole, patting the empty spot next to her on the porch swing before waving goodbye to Suzie as she disappeared around the corner of the house.

Cole climbed up and waited expectantly for her answer.

"I thought we could go down and see if the pedal boats are open."

"Yeah!" Cole wriggled around excitedly, rocking the swing.

The afternoon waves pawed at the shore behind them as Cole, Melanie, and Kathryn pedaled their boats around in the gulf. The waves were gentle today, just soft ripples that rolled onto the sand.

"We should try to pedal to that," Kathryn said from under her sun hat, as she pointed to a small peninsula jutting out into the water. "I'll bet we can find some really great seashells there."

"I'll race you!" Cole said, his tiny feet moving on the pedals, the boat pushing forward through the ebbing waves.

"You're on!" Kathryn said with a laugh.

Melanie pedaled up on one side of Cole while her sister took the other, the three of them pedaling as quickly as they could. Melanie eyed her sister and they let Cole pull ahead.

"He's gaining speed!" Melanie shouted to Kathryn. "Let's catch up."

Cole giggled uncontrollably, moving his legs faster than his little feet could stay on the pedals. "You can't catch me!" he called, as his head swiveled behind him to take stock of their location.

The sisters let Cole go ahead all the way to land where his boat was the first to slide onto the sand. "I did it! I won!" he said, jumping out and pumping his fists.

"You did!" Melanie said, getting out of her boat and pulling both hers and Cole's further onto shore to keep them from floating away.

Kathryn got out and did the same. "I see a shell already," she said, picking up a curled shell the color of burlap with a maroon stripe snaking through it. "Isn't this beautiful?"

Cole came over and peered down into her sister's hand, grains of white sand dropping back to earth through her outstretched fingers. "I want to find one," Cole said, touching it.

Melanie plucked it out of Kathryn's hand and held it against the clear sky to get a better look. She handed it to Cole. "Well, let's see what else we can find!"

Leaving the line of boats on a slant against the shore, the three of them set off on foot around the slip of a peninsula. The palm trees rustled in the wind, the gulf keeping time with its rhythmic movement. It was so peaceful out there on the beach, away from everything going on in Melanie's life. While she had a lot to be thankful for, and after the storm, the house repairs seemed to be going off without a hitch, she couldn't help wondering about Josh.

"I found a good one!" Cole called from a few paces away. He was squatting over the sand, dusting off a large shell in his little hand.

"Let's see it," Melanie said, moving over to him as Kathryn stopped her search and came over as well.

"Oh, look! It's a grey sea star," Kathryn said. "The storm must have washed it ashore."

"It's so pretty." Cole touched one of its points. "Is it still alive?" he asked.

"Doesn't look like it," Kathryn replied. "You see, when they're pushed out of their environment, they don't have what they need to survive, and they can't live. Unless someone comes along and helps them back into the water."

"Like when you don't have parents, it takes someone to help you or you won't have any food or love?" Cole asked, shocking Melanie at his poignant insight.

"Yes," Melanie answered softly.

"I miss Josh. I wish I could live with him."

Melanie stared at the little boy. "You do?"

Cole nodded. "But I can't because I already have Suzie and Eric. And sometimes my mom."

"Do you see your mom?" she asked carefully.

"Not very much. Only when she doesn't take her medicine."

Melanie cocked her head to the side, confused. "When she *doesn't* take her medicine?"

"Yes, she takes medicine that the doctor doesn't give her and it makes her sick. I saw it one time. Little pills."

So, his mother has a drug problem. Melanie nodded, forcing a smile. "Do you ever see your dad?"

"No. My mom can't remember his name."

"I see."

Suddenly, Melanie's problems with the house and Josh didn't seem so big after all. As she looked into Cole's innocent brown eyes, she wanted more than anything to make it better for him, and what she only now realized was that Cole didn't need someone to take him places; he needed to be surrounded by people in his life whom he could count on, to listen to him, ask him questions, and tuck him in at night. Suzie and Eric seemed great at that, but Melanie felt an overwhelming longing to be that for him as well.

"I have an idea," she said to him. "Let's go shopping after this. I need your help."

Chapter Twenty-Four

With the pedal boats turned back in and the bag of shells they'd found safely tucked away in her handbag, Melanie, Cole, and Kathryn walked into the town furniture shop.

"Okay," Melanie said. "One of the rooms in my house is going to be decorated just for kids. What kind of bed should I get for it? Could you find me a good one?"

Cole's chest puffed up with determination. "Yes," he said, his gaze moving around the store. He walked over to one of the four-poster twin beds, grimaced and moved on. Then he sat down on another small bed, bouncing before he decided against it and moved on to the next bed. But it was a whitewashed set of bunkbeds that caught his eye. He went racing over to them, climbing the ladder at the end and sitting on the top of it, his legs swinging over the side.

"This is the one," he said.

"You think?" she asked, already loving his choice.

"Definitely. I'd love to have this bed."

"Okay, then. Let's get it."

They put in the order for the bed and went back outside, where Melanie pointed to the toy shop across the street. "I'm going to need more than a bed in there. Can you help me pick out some toys? Then you can play with them until someone stays in that room."

"Yes!" he said, bouncing up and down and clapping his hands.

Crossing the street, they went inside, the shop window displays full of life-size stuffed animals, giant piano keyboards for kids to run on, drum sets, and puzzles with pieces the size of dinner plates. Cole spun the twirling rack of impulse items: yo-yos, harmonicas, riddle cubes, dice, card games, and drawing sets. He left it and ran to the back of the shop, tipping his head up to view the toys that stretched all the way to the ceiling. Then he went over and flopped into a seafoam-green corduroy beanbag, the thing nearly swallowing him up.

"We definitely need one of those," Melanie said with a grin. All she could see were his head and his little feet sticking out.

"One of these would be awesome," Cole agreed.

"Okay then. But why stop at one? Let's get two."

Cole's eyes grew round.

By this time, the shop owner had noticed them and came around the counter.

"We'll get two of these," Melanie said to the woman. "What else do we need, Cole?"

"Oooohh," he said, dashing toward the solar system display and grabbing a box. "What about one of these? This would be so cool…" He turned the box around to show Melanie a small round projector that displayed the planets on the ceiling. "They move around the sun!" he said, pointing to a photo on the back of the box.

"We'll take one of these too," Melanie told the clerk.

When they'd finished shopping, they filled the car with the beanbags, the projector, a rocking horse, a giant set of Lego, and a playhouse tent.

"This room's gonna be awesome," Cole said.

Melanie gave him a smile. "Thanks to you."

*

"I didn't know you were planning to have a children's room upstairs," Kathryn said after Suzie had picked up Cole. She carried the rocking horse upstairs, following Melanie.

"I thought I could take the two rooms at the end of the hall and cut a door between them, making them a suite," Melanie said over her shoulder, her arms full of the items Cole had chosen. "Then when Cole comes over, he'll have somewhere to play on rainy days."

"You're fond of him, aren't you?" Kathryn asked.

"He's such a sweet boy." Melanie pushed the door open with her foot and set the toys down on the empty floor, the yo-yo rolling away. Kathryn stopped it with her foot.

"He deserves more than the mess of a life he's been given." Kathryn positioned the rocking horse near the window that overlooked the gulf, the two of them peering out at the sparkles that danced on its surface.

"I know. And now the people that are the most supportive aren't able to give him their all. Josh left and Eric is dealing with his own battle…" Melanie took in a long breath and let it out slowly. "I'm not so sure what four-year-old boys enjoy doing from day to day, but something's pulling me to be a solid presence in his life."

Kathryn turned her way. "It's good to see you so passionate about things," she said. "You were so caught up in caring for Gram—and that's an honorable thing to do—but I worried about you. I worried you were getting lost."

Melanie nodded. "Lately, there are times when I feel like I've lost my way and I'm not really sure what my next move should be."

"I'll tell you what your next move should be," Kathryn said, grabbing her hands and spinning her around the empty room. "We need to get cleaned up and go out to dinner, to celebrate the fact that you will soon have furniture in this place!"

Melanie laughed. "I've still got a long way to go before this place is anywhere near furniture-ready."

"But it's ordered," Kathryn said, ever the optimist.

"Some of it," she clarified. "And it's supposed to be delivered in about a month or so, which means I'd better get a move on if I want to have anywhere to put it."

"We can brainstorm a brand-new to-do list over dinner. I'm without child and husband at the beach! I want seafood and cocktails."

"I remember what happened the last time we had dinner cocktails… I ended up with Josh spitting and sputtering at my front door, irritated that he had to even stand on the porch, let alone enter the house."

Kathryn huffed out a laugh. "I wonder what his deal is… Well, we won't let him ruin our evening." Kathryn stuck her face in front of Melanie's, pulling her out of her thoughts. "I'm your older sister and I call Smack on cocktails."

Melanie grinned. Smack was a game the two of them had made up as girls. Whenever one of them called Smack on something, it meant that if the other person didn't get to it first, the Smack-caller got to make an outlandish request that had to be carried out. It was a little like Truth or Dare without the Truth. "You can't call Smack on cocktails."

"I just did. And I don't have to wash my hair because I washed it this morning, but you do, so you'd better hurry. I'm totally getting to that bar first."

"Not if I call Smack on driving my car, and I have the keys."

"Ugh," she said, playfully frustrated. "Just wait until you're in the shower. I'll totally find them."

Unable to maintain the mock-serious facade, Melanie burst into laughter.

"I'm not joking," Kathryn said, still holding on to hers.

Melanie rolled her eyes with another chuckle. "I get the shower first."

"Speaking of keys," Kathryn said, sliding the old key Melanie had found off of the windowsill. "What's this one for?"

"It was with a bunch of random things in an old box Josh and I uncovered while checking for water damage. Remember Gram's friend Addie? I showed it to her, and she said it could be to a safe deposit box."

"It could be *anything*, really." Kathryn flipped the key over in her hand. "It also looks like a door key, or maybe it's for a lockbox of some sort?"

Melanie plucked it from her sister's fingers and held it up to the light. "So many mysteries with this house…" She set it back onto the windowsill.

"Why are you keeping it?" her sister asked.

"I don't know," Melanie replied honestly. "Maybe it holds a story…"

"The only thing I want to hold right now is a cocktail," Kathryn said with a grin. "Go get your shower!"

"Okay, okay," Melanie said, giggling. "I'm going."

"Kathryn?" Melanie called through the empty house, her voice echoing in the void. "Kathryn?" They had been getting dressed together, both of them in sundresses and wedge sandals, ready for some fun. Kathryn had finished before her, and now Melanie had no idea where she was. She checked the newly painted bedrooms upstairs—no Kathryn.

At a loss, she stood still on the upstairs balcony that overlooked the massive staircase and teardrop chandelier. Then suddenly, a faint noise got her attention. Her hearing perking, she tipped her head just so and heard it again, realizing it was a car horn outside. Melanie bounded down the steps and opened the front door to find her sister hanging out of the driver's-side window of her car.

"Found your keys!" she said from behind a large pair of designer sunglasses. "Smack."

"Ugh," Melanie replied, as she grabbed her handbag and headed out the door.

"So, what are you going to make me do?" she asked Kathryn as she climbed into the passenger side.

"I'm not sure," her sister answered. "I'd rather hold out and see what the situation offers once we get where we're going. Where *are* we going, actually?"

"I got us reservations at that beachside restaurant Mariner's Landing. I could do with their glass walls and shoreline views."

"Oh, fancy!" Kathryn said, changing course and heading toward the restaurant. "*I* could do with their Seahorse Rum Spritzer—remember that one with the coconut rum and lime?"

"I'd forgotten about that drink," Melanie said. Then her thoughts softened to the memory. "That was the last time we took Gram out for her birthday before she got really sick. She drank one and we had to stop her from getting a second."

"She was nearly dancing between the tables."

The memory warmed Melanie. "She was so full of life back then."

"I know." Kathryn turned onto a side street to take a shorter route, away from a line of debris that needed to be cleared. "That's how I remember her."

"I spent so long getting her through the end that I'd lost sight of the sparkle in her eyes."

Kathryn cut back over to the main road. "I'm sorry that I wasn't there a lot to help."

"Don't feel bad—you have a family and commitments of your own."

"Yeah, but you shouldn't have had to take the brunt of it all just because you're single. I've felt really guilty about leaving you with so much."

Melanie looked over at her sister, surprised by the direction the conversation had taken. "I had no idea that you felt that way. And you shouldn't. I was just fine."

"You take on a lot, Melanie. You just go and go, pushing yourself harder until you get it all done. You took care of Mom when she had her knee surgery and then you took care of Gram. You're fixing up this house just because Gram asked you to. But what about you? What can someone do for *you*?"

"I don't know," she answered honestly. "I'm so used to doing it all by myself that I don't really need anyone."

"You don't need anyone, or you don't have anyone—they're two different things."

Melanie bristled. "What's that supposed to mean?"

"I've thought of your Smack," Kathryn said, not answering Melanie's question. "You have to get a date with the first man who walks through the door of the restaurant."

"That's not fair," Melanie said, still shaking off her sister's comment. "What if he's married?"

"Okay, the first *single* man."

"You're so annoying," she said in their sisterly banter.

Chapter Twenty-Five

A white candle, in keeping with the minimalist white décor that surrounded them, flickered between Melanie and Kathryn while they nibbled on a smoked tuna dip appetizer and sipped the sugar sweetness of their Seahorse Rum Spritzers. The music of steel drums filled the air, and the evening sun came in at a slant through the signature glass wall that showcased the turquoise waters of the Gulf of Mexico like an enormous oil on canvas.

Mariner's Landing was a relaxed but sophisticated hotspot for those wanting an elegant menu with the casual beachside feel. It was The Place for people to be seen—its Instagram page boasted a collection of the country's rich and famous, smiling with their arm around its owner. The bar was full of glamorous vacationers tonight, their cheeks just a little too pink from too much sun and alcohol. The slight buzz of coastal nightlife hung in the air.

"A single guy still hasn't walked in yet," Kathryn noted with a playful huff.

"Thank God for that." Melanie stirred her cocktail with the striped straw that had once held a maraschino cherry and two slices of pineapple. She'd nibbled them off already. "Maybe I'll get lucky and no one will come through those doors."

"Ye of little faith," Kathryn said. "Your Prince Charming could come through right now. What if it's George Clooney?"

"I don't think he's single, is he?"

"Oh, look!" Kathryn pointed toward the door. "Here comes someone! And it looks like he's by himself."

The door opened and Melanie gasped. "What? Nooo…"

Josh strode in and took a seat at the bar. He was scrubbed up, his hair combed just so and clean-shaven, with a button-down shirt, the sleeves rolled to his elbows, and a pair of jeans frayed perfectly at the hem that fell over his leather flip-flopped feet.

"What's *he* doing here? I thought he was in New York."

"Go ask him," Kathryn said. "And while you're there, see where he wants to go on that date."

"You can't call Smack with him. We've tortured him enough."

"He can take it," she said.

"Isn't your Smack suggestion to ask a guy out for the purposes of finding me Prince Charming? Because I can save you the time. Josh is definitely *not* my Prince Charming." But her mind went back to his kiss, his strong embrace, the look of affection in his eyes…

"Just go talk to him," Kathryn urged.

Melanie considered how she and Josh had left their conversation this morning, with Cole carrying off her phone. It would be difficult to make small talk after she'd called to demand an explanation for tearing up the letter, but this wasn't the time or the place. As she hemmed and hawed, Josh caught sight of the manager and turned to greet him, his gaze opening up to the room and landing on her. She raised her eyebrows to question his presence.

The bartender traded him a beer for his credit card. Josh grabbed the bottle and walked over to them.

"Back so soon?" Kathryn asked with a grin, before sipping her cocktail.

"My truck was ready," he said, his eyes on Melanie. "And I wanted to check in on Cole anyway, so I got a quick flight in. He doing okay?"

"I'm not sure he knows about Eric yet," Melanie replied.

Josh nodded, thoughts evident on his face with the set of his jaw and the contemplation in his eyes.

"How long are you here?" she asked.

"Just long enough to see Cole and get my truck."

Melanie forced a nod, ignoring her disappointment.

Kathryn leaned in. "So, not long enough to explain why you'd destroy my sister's historic property?"

"What?"

"The letter," Melanie clarified. "But we don't have to talk about that now."

"Definitely not," Kathryn said. "You'll have plenty of time on your date."

"Our *what*?" Josh was looking more confused and flustered by the moment.

"Don't mind her," Melanie said, shooting daggers over at her sister. "She just sort of bet me that I'd have to date the next single guy that came through the door." She offered a weak smile.

Josh huffed, his gaze fluttering away from her.

Despite the fact that she hadn't planned to go out with him anyway, his response caused her to tense up. He didn't have to be so matter-of-fact about it. "Well," she said. "I don't need a date and I don't need an explanation about the letter anyway. I've got the town historian looking into it."

"What did you say?" he nearly growled, startling her.

Kathryn's eyes were the size of saucers, but Melanie wasn't going to let him scare her into submission. He couldn't treat people that way, and she was going to let him know about it. "What I do with my time is none of your concern."

"What else do you know about Alfred Ellis?" he asked. "Tell me right now, Melanie."

That was when she noticed it: his anger wasn't directed toward her. Was that fear she saw in his eyes? But she wasn't sure enough, so she stood her ground. "I don't have to tell you anything," she said, looking around, nervous they were making a scene.

He ground his teeth, his jaw bulging as his attention landed back on her. "I have to go see Cole," he said. "I thought I'd come in for a quick beer to settle my nerves before facing Eric, but I see this was the wrong place to come." He tore his eyes from her, and pushed the door open with all his might, striding out into the evening light.

"Good grief, that was intense," Kathryn said after he'd left.

"Yeah," Melanie agreed, shaken by the whole thing. "Can I just..." She got up, her thoughts in a muddle, and ran outside after him. "Josh!" she called to him as he got into his truck.

The vehicle's door was open; he twisted around to face her.

"Please tell me what's going on," she asked more calmly.

"Nothing's going on," he snapped. When he went to shut the door, she moved quickly, getting in the way. His chest filled with an irritated breath.

"Your expression certainly doesn't look like nothing."

"Don't meddle in things you know nothing about." He started the truck's engine and grabbed for the door handle, causing her to jump out of the way. Josh put the truck in reverse and Melanie stepped away, allowing him to leave.

"What was all that?" Kathryn asked when Melanie had gotten back inside.

"I truly have no idea." There was definitely a big piece of the puzzle missing that she had yet to figure out.

"Go ahead, do it," Kathryn urged her, as Melanie stood in front of the wall between the bathroom and the coat closet, the sledgehammer raised above her head. "Take out all your aggression toward Josh on that wall and whack it."

Melanie lowered the sledgehammer slowly until it hung by her side, the Seahorse Rum drinks they'd had tonight still giving her a little buzz. "Do we really need to have a bigger bathroom? I mean, with some new tile and a coat of paint, we could be done."

"True," Kathryn agreed. "But do you want to be *done* or do you want to be *amazed*? Taking the wall out from between the closet and bathroom will open up the space so much."

"You're right. If I'm being honest, I really want to swap out the old tile for a beachy hardwood, and encase the sink, hang some large artwork on the walls…"

"You know what needs to be done."

"Yes," she answered. Melanie adjusted her safety goggles and lifted the sledgehammer.

"Josh," Kathryn reminded her.

"Jjjjoooossshh!" she bellowed, as she slammed the end of the hammer into the wall, leaving a plume of dust and debris in its wake. Melanie peered at the black hole she'd made. "That felt great," she said, whacking the old plaster again.

Kathryn laughed. "Who needs a contractor? We've got you!"

Melanie laughed along with her.

"How many more walls are you taking out?" Kathryn asked with a cough, a happy seriousness settling over her.

"Two more," she answered. "Both upstairs."

The old buzzer rang on the door.

"Wonder who that is," Melanie said, handing Kathryn the hammer. She tried to brush the dust off her white face and arms, her clothes covered in it.

"It's a lost cause," Kathryn said. "Your hair is white right now. You're just gonna have to get the door like you are."

"Awesome," Melanie said, lifting her safety goggles and pushing her hair back with them.

"I'll keep going," Kathryn told her.

With her sister pounding away, Melanie continued to try unsuccessfully to brush herself off as she opened the front door. She stopped when she saw who it was. "Hi," she said to Josh, who stood opposite her.

"Hey." He had his hands in the pockets of his jeans and she could smell the faint scent of his aftershave. One corner of his lips rose ever so slightly as he took in the sight of her. "That's not how I left you in the parking lot earlier. You've been busy."

Kathryn thumped the wall again, sending a clap vibrating through the house.

"We're taking out the wall between the bathroom and the coat closet."

"Where's your mask?" he asked, concern causing those little lines to form between his eyes.

"Yeah, I think we definitely need them."

"And you're sure it's not a load-bearing wall?"

"I don't think it is."

"You don't *think* it is? Let me see." He breezed past her. "You could get hurt doing things like this without consulting people, you know," he said over his shoulder, as Kathryn continued to hit the wall.

Melanie grabbed his arm, stopping him in the hallway. "Are you here to bust my chops about how I renovate my house, or did you come for something else?"

He stared at her for a tick before answering. "I need to talk to you," he said. "This is the last chance I'll get because I've been to Eric and Suzie's, and now that I've got my truck, I'm not coming back any time soon."

Her stomach dropped at the thought. "What about Cole? Won't you come to see him?" she asked, her worry for the boy creeping in.

"Suzie's going to fly him up in a couple of months, as long as she can leave Eric."

Kathryn kept banging.

"Hang on, and I'll tell my sister we'll be outside."

Melanie told Kathryn, and despite her sister's suggestive eyebrow bouncing, she nodded before resuming her demolition. "Please don't feel like you have to do all the work," Melanie said.

"I like this," Kathryn yelled over the noise. "It's invigorating."

"Knock yourself out then," Melanie said. "Wait, don't actually…"

Kathryn laughed. "Go. See if you can squeeze a date out of Mr. Meanie."

Waving off the comment, Melanie headed out to the deck.

"Hey," he said when she got outside. He was pacing the deck, his hands in his pockets.

Melanie lowered herself down on the swing and gestured for him to sit next to her. "Your fidgeting is making me anxious," she said. "Tell me what's going on."

He sat down, his fingers spread on his knees, lips pursed, his expression intense. "I came by to ask you something." He looked into her eyes, and the vulnerability on his face had her holding her breath. "First, I wanted to say I'm sorry for ripping up that letter. I shouldn't have done that."

"Thank you for the apology. That means a lot."

"I got scared." He took in a deep breath and leaned back on the swing, rocking it, his gaze on the sky.

"What did the letter say, Josh?" she asked gently.

He blew air through his lips and sat back up. "I can't tell you."

"Why not? I won't say anything about it to anyone, I promise."

"I just can't risk it."

She wasn't going to beg him to trust her. "You said you were going to ask me something?"

"Yeah. I'd like you to keep those letters hidden. Please don't display them anywhere."

"Okay," she agreed, still not understanding his motives. "But if I agree to keep them hidden, can't you tell me what's in the final letter?"

"Maybe one day," he said, seemingly relieved. His shoulders had relaxed and he was visibly calmer. "I've gotta go," he said, standing up. "I'll… see ya." He stepped down the two stairs and onto the sand, heading toward the side of the house.

She waved goodbye, but something told her she wouldn't see him any time soon. "Wait!" she called after him, jumping up and running down the steps.

Josh turned around.

"Thank you for apologizing. And for helping me during the hurricane… I have to admit that seeing you tonight—I was glad you'd come back, even if only for a second. I'm gonna miss having you here."

His eyes locked on hers and his lips parted as if he were going to say something, that openness he so rarely allowed swimming all over his face. Watching him, Melanie prayed he'd admit to caring for her, like Brenda had said. "You're welcome," he answered instead, but by the thick silence that followed, she still wondered if he had more to say, willing him to tell her. "Just call me if you have any questions about anything…"

"Okay," she said.

Melanie watched him walk off, trying not to think about the quiet days ahead without him, the absence of his voice, and the way his face would float into her mind until she saw him again.

Chapter Twenty-Six

Melanie awakened to the sound of rain tapping at her window. After her encounter with Josh, she'd put him out of her mind while she and Kathryn had spent the last week taking care of Cole and working on the house. She'd done everything she could to keep from thinking of anything other than what needed to be done.

The contractors had finished tearing out the walls, the floor guys had come for the final varnish, and a few pieces of furniture had been delivered early. The Ellis house was finally starting to look like a home. While the exterior still needed a lot of work, and she had people coming to take care of it in the upcoming days, the house was generally livable, so Kathryn was heading home tomorrow.

Melanie got up and wrapped a blanket around her shoulders, then padded downstairs to have a cup of coffee in her shiny new kitchen. Through her window, the sky was gray, the gulf echoing the sentiment with a show of deep, stormy blue shimmying onto the shore.

Once the coffee pot had finished spilling its heady aroma into the air, she poured herself a cup and carried it over to the counter, where she noticed Gram's book that Kathryn had brought with her. She grabbed it, taking it over to her new farmhouse table. With the cooler air from the rain giving her a little chill under the air-conditioning, she draped the blanket over her legs and then opened the book, sipping her coffee, savoring the nutty warmth of it.

Melanie ran her fingers over the photo of Alfred and Gram. The two of them were standing side by side, but she could see the slight lean in Gram's demeanor, as if a cosmic force were pulling her toward Alfred. They looked so happy. She turned the page and saw a poem in Gram's handwriting. It read:

> *How peculiar is this life,*
> *That leaves its strings untied?*
> *That loosely bound weave of love,*
> *That delicious consuming ride.*
>
> *We throw our hands up,*
> *And squeal with delight,*
> *A glorious freefall of emotions,*
> *Merely to land with a resounding bump,*
> *Our tears the size of oceans.*
>
> *If only I could grab the twine,*
> *And hold with all my might,*
> *I may be able to lace it again,*
> *To keep the strings pulled tight.*

Melanie read Gram's words over again, and she couldn't help but feel that her grandmother had written this for Alfred. Was this house Gram's way of lacing things back together again somehow?

"Good morning," Kathryn said, coming into the kitchen and fixing her own mug of coffee. She sat down next to her sister and peered over at Gram's book.

"Anything good?" she asked.

"Yes," Melanie said, showing her the poem.

"That's beautiful." Kathryn sipped her coffee. "I didn't know that Gram wrote poetry."

"Apparently, there's a lot about Gram that we didn't know."

With the downstairs nearly finished, Kathryn and Melanie spent Kathryn's last day in Rosemary Bay finding inspiration for the bedrooms upstairs.

"I'd like to honor the historical feel of the home, but with each room having its own theme and name," Melanie said, as she inspected an antique vase in one of the shop windows. She went inside, Kathryn following, and picked up the glassware to get a better look.

"This is pretty," Melanie told her sister.

"That's part of our St. Vincent line," the woman at the register said, from behind reading glasses that were pulled down onto her nose.

"Oh, one of your rooms could be the St. Vincent Room," Kathryn suggested.

"I like that." Melanie walked over and set the vase on the counter. "I'll take this," she said. "What other pieces do you have?"

"There's that stained-glass picture over there," the woman said, pointing to a swirl of teal, dark blue, and white."

"Oh, that's stunning," Melanie said. She took a look at the price and it wasn't bad. "I'll take this too."

"Excellent. I'll get them wrapped up for you."

"Well, hello!" a recognizable voice called from the door, just as the bells jingled.

Melanie turned around to find Brenda walking in. "Hi," she said, happy to see her.

"How's it going?" Brenda asked.

"We're just putting the finishing touches on the house. This is my sister Kathryn," she said, introducing them. "And this is Josh's mother, Brenda." Melanie paid for the vase and stained glass.

The women shook hands.

"I'd love to see what you've done with the place," Brenda said, caution in her voice.

"You're welcome to stop by any time."

The clerk handed Melanie a gift bag with her items securely wrapped.

"We're heading that way now, if you'd like to come over," Kathryn offered. "I was going to suggest that we blend up the rest of our piña colada mix for lunch if you'd like to join us."

"My sister's on vacation, can you tell?" Melanie said with a grin.

"I could stop by for one drink…" Brenda said.

"Perfect. Besides Josh, you'll be our first official guest."

"It's looking great," Brenda said, peering around as she stood in the entryway. "I've always wondered what the interior of this place looked like. I feel a little like I'm betraying my mother for coming in. She so loathed Alfred Ellis that we dared not even look in the direction of this home for fear we'd get the evil eye."

"Well, this place makes me wonder if he wasn't such a bad guy… But it's my house now anyway, so don't feel bad being in here," Melanie said, skirting around the issue. She didn't know how much Brenda knew and she didn't want to break her promise to Josh.

Melanie took Brenda into the kitchen and offered her a barstool while Kathryn loaded up the blender.

"I'm glad you invited me to come over after hearing all the things Josh was telling me about you."

"Oh?" Melanie said, grabbing three plastic cups from the cabinet. "What did he say about me?"

"He told me about the storm and how he took you to see his land. He doesn't open up like that very much, so I was interested. And then when he said he was working here, I was definitely annoyed at first but also intrigued."

"He was just doing me a favor," she said. "I needed his help is all."

"He doesn't do favors like that. Ever. I think he likes you."

Kathryn poured their piña coladas, eyeing Melanie. "He doesn't seem to like her, the way he treats her," Kathryn said.

Melanie winced at her sister's forward comment, hoping that if she pursed her lips hard enough Kathryn would be quiet. But she wasn't so lucky.

"What?" Josh's mother said, clearly taken aback.

"Yes," Kathryn continued, rounding the counter before Melanie could step on her foot to hold her in place. "He tore up Melanie's letter."

"Letter?"

"Yeah, one of the ones Alfred wrote," Kathryn continued. "Here, let me get them."

Melanie intervened, grabbing her sister's arm. "Kathryn, she doesn't need to be bothered with—"

"It's fine—here, I'll get them." Kathryn grabbed the stack of letters from the kitchen drawer where Melanie had stashed them, thumbing through them. "These are incredible…" She set each of them out in date order, reading them all.

"Josh told me about a letter, and I explained to him that Alfred was an author of fiction…" Brenda peered down at them, her words withering as they came out. "There's one for every year."

"Yes, they're all in date order. Wait. Where's 1959?" Kathryn asked, grabbing the cup of piña colada from the counter.

"It's there somewhere," Melanie said, as she rinsed out the blender and set it aside to keep her nervous energy at bay. She wasn't sure what she was so worried about. Josh had already said he'd told his mother all about the letters. She took a drink of the sweet pineapple-coconut concoction. "I think 1959 was the one where he mentioned that he was still waiting for Gram or something…" Melanie said, coming around to stand next to Kathryn and Brenda.

"Look," her sister said, tapping each letter and pointing out the date.

"Wait a minute," she said, peering down at the final letter on the counter. She stared at it, her breath bated. "I had them out of order," she whispered, pawing for the last letter.

"What?" Kathryn grabbed it, excited before Melanie got a chance to read it.

"When Josh tore up the last letter in the stack, I must have had them out of order. 1959 is missing and that one…" She reached for it but didn't want to appear too panicked for Brenda's sake. "I haven't read that one," she said. "Do you mind?" Melanie held out her hand but both women seemed to notice her shaking fingers.

"Which means that now we can see what it says." Kathryn's eyes were already scanning the letter as Brenda looked on.

Melanie's heart raced, knowing that this was the letter that Josh had thought he'd destroyed. In a panic, she plucked it from Kathryn's hands, nearly crumpling it in her fist. "We don't have to read this now. We don't want to bore our first guest," she said, shoving it back into the drawer and then quickly moving to the other side of the counter to collect the other letters. "Let's just enjoy our drinks."

"Wait a minute," Brenda said. "I thought I saw my name. I'd like to read it if that's okay."

"I don't think it was…" Melanie said, but Kathryn and Brenda had already opened the drawer to take a peek.

"It *is* my name," Brenda said, snatching it out and reading it, her mouth dropping open and her eyes scanning at warp speed.

Melanie went around and leaned over her shoulder, feeling like she was betraying Josh, her pulse going a mile a minute.

April 23, 1968

My dearest Lou,

I know I have no reason to tell you this, but I always tell you my deepest thoughts and I'm struggling. It's been months now. I've grappled with the whole thing, really, not knowing how to handle this.

Vera knocked on my door. She said she needed to speak to me. She stood there with her little girl in a carriage and told me the child's name was Brenda. She went on to say that she would only come this once, and she never wanted to see me again. But my insistence to be honest with her had lingered in her mind, and she didn't want to go through life without telling me this huge thing. She begged me to promise that if she told me, I'd allow her to go on with her life and never contact her again. Of course, I agreed. I'd do anything she asked of me.

Then she lifted little Brenda from her buggy and handed her to me as tears streaked Vera's face, confusing me. I looked down at the pink-cheeked, milky-faced baby in my arms, the little one's powdery scent like coming home.

Vera told me that the child in my arms was my daughter.

She said I deserved to know but that I hadn't earned the right to have any part in our daughter's life. She's right, although I yearn to see the child grow into a young woman. I'm devastated. I will wonder about her—is she like me in any way…?

I feel as though my life has had no purpose since I walked off Willow Pier that day, leaving you behind. I'm left to wonder what would've happened had I stayed in Rosemary Bay. I wonder a lot whether you miss me sometimes, or do you feel you dodged a bullet letting me go? I pray you are happy, because all this pain would be worth your happiness.

Yours,
Alfred

Melanie gawked at the letter, the gravity of the situation hitting her. Brenda was Alfred Ellis's daughter. And Josh was his grandson. This was what Josh was determined to keep hidden.

"Oh my goodness, Brenda," Melanie said, her voice soft. "I'm sure this is a shock." She remembered Addie's warning: *Sometimes our secrets are better off buried.*

"Uh, yes." But then Brenda shook her head. "Unless this is nothing more than a foolish man's dream." She tossed the letter onto the counter as if dismissing it, but the shiftiness in her eyes gave away her fear. "I need to go," she said, so frazzled that she'd barely even touched her drink, leaving it in a pool of condensation.

Melanie didn't try to challenge the notion that the letters weren't real, but she knew that they most certainly were. And by Brenda's reaction, so did she.

Chapter Twenty-Seven

"You told my mother?" Josh belted through the phone.

Melanie squeezed her eyes shut. She'd gone back and forth after Brenda had left, deciding whether or not to tell him, but finally, she'd determined that it was the right thing to do. "It wasn't intentional. She came over to the house and saw the last letter on her own."

"She came over to the house?" he repeated, exasperated.

"She wanted to see what I've done with the place... You tore up the wrong letter, Josh."

The line fell silent.

"So, you're Alfred Ellis's grandson," she said quietly, while Kathryn sat beside her at the kitchen table for support.

"I am not." She couldn't see him, but she could tell he was spitting the words through clenched teeth. "There's no hard evidence that I am."

"I'm sorry that you had to find out this way," she said.

"My grandfather wasn't..." he whispered sadly, his words trailing off.

"Josh, I know this is a surprise, but it will all be okay—"

"No, Melanie," he said, abruptly. "No, it won't be okay. My land—the land I've been working for, the land I've come to New York to get what I need to build on—it has been passed down to male family members for generations. With no direct descendants for the land, it goes up for auction. It was in the will. If I'm Alfred's—"

"Oh my goodness, Josh," Melanie said, understanding the gravity of the situation.

"Who have you told?" he asked. "Remember, Melanie. Please. You can't forget a single person."

"Uh, Addie knows, and the person who owns my gram's house knows a little, and then there's the town historian and the librarian… and my sister Kathryn." She grabbed Kathryn's hand to steady herself.

"The developer's been calling and I haven't answered the calls," Josh said.

"How would they know anything had changed?"

"Janie. When Janie first started working at the company, she'd tried to convince me to sell the land and I wouldn't. Trying to change my mind, she told me Bowland would offer us millions. What she failed to explain was that when she left me, she'd get half."

"Do you think they'd use the letters to blackmail you—'sell or we let everyone know this secret?'" she asked, her hands shaking.

"I wouldn't put it past her," he said. "If Janie finds out, I could lose the land to her, but if I disclose that the land isn't legally mine so she can't get at it, then it goes up for auction and I lose it anyway."

"I'm so sorry," was all Melanie could say. "Is there anything I can do?"

"I don't know. Let me think…"

Kathryn leaned in. "Alfred Ellis didn't have a will, did he?" she whispered.

Melanie shrugged, struggling to make sense of the new information. Then something else occurred to her. *Wait.* If Alfred had a son, and he had a will, could she be facing the same issue as Josh? A small ache began to form behind her eyes. She squeezed them shut and rubbed them.

"Don't say anything else until I get there," said Josh. "I'm coming home. I need to talk to Janie to see what she knows, if anything."

A knock on the door jolted Melanie out of her thoughts. "Cole's here. I need to go. I won't say anything, I promise."

"I'll come straight to you when I get there."

"Okay."

While Melanie got off the phone and took in a few deep breaths to get herself together, Kathryn let Cole and Suzie in. Melanie had turned the parlor into a games room, with a chess board on the new driftwood center table that sat atop a sand-colored woven rug. Today, she'd replaced it with a tub of Lego, since it was still raining and they wouldn't be able to go outside. Cole immediately noticed, running over and opening the box, although he didn't have the same sparkle in his eyes that he usually did.

"We told him," Suzie said, tears brimming in her tired eyes. "Cole, I'm going to step outside with Melanie for a second."

"Okay," he called, as he dug through the Lego for a piece to add to the tower he'd started. Kathryn kneeled down to help him find the piece.

"It was too difficult not to tell him, with Eric going in and out of the hospital," Suzie continued once they were on the porch.

Melanie nodded, understanding completely how difficult this must be.

"When I called his mother to tell her what's going on, because I like to keep her updated with her son—maybe it's a silly idea, but she's still his mother," she whispered, one eye on the door, "she told me that she'd signed the papers to terminate her parental rights and Cole is now a ward of the state indefinitely. He's eligible for adoption. We haven't told him that yet."

"My goodness," Melanie said. "How will he take that news?"

"I'm not sure. There's so much change going on in his little life right now, with Eric sick, Josh gone, and now his mother…"

"I'll help any way I can."

"I know you will." Suzie gave her an unexpected hug. "Thank you for taking care of him."

"Of course." She dared not mention that Josh was coming back into town in case he couldn't see Cole, but she hoped he would. The little boy needed a friendly face during all this.

Cole and Melanie sat at the kitchen island in front of a pile of fishing line and seashells.

"What are we doing?" Cole asked.

"We're going to string these starfish and seashells onto the fishing line. Kind of like stringing popcorn for the Christmas tree—have you ever done that?"

Cole shook his head.

"You haven't? In that case, this winter, we'll definitely do that," she said, "but right now, we can practice, and then I'm going to add the strings of seashells to the chandelier in the parlor."

"That sounds fun. Can I help hang them?"

"Well, you'll have to go up really high on the ladder and I'm not sure Suzie would want me to let you do that."

"You can hold on to me." Cole picked up a piece of line and followed Melanie's lead.

"We'll see," she said, grinning down at him. "Let me show you how to make a little knot in the line to keep the shells from sliding down."

"How do you know how to do this?" Cole asked, following her lead, his little fingers fumbling on the line.

"My grandmother showed me how," she replied, helping him. "We used to make windchimes this way."

"I don't have a grandma," he said, blinking up at her with those big brown eyes. "I wish I had one. They always make you cookies and they smile a lot."

Melanie laughed. "They do," she agreed.

"You smile a lot," he noted, grabbing a small sand dollar.

"I try. Life throws a lot at you, and the only way to get through it is to find the good in things."

"Like this. This is good. Being with you is good."

A warm affection took over her as she looked down at Cole. "Thank you. I'm glad you think so."

"Josh is good. I miss him."

"I know you do."

"Why did he have to go so far away?"

"I'm not really sure," she said. There had to be other ways to get what he needed without moving to an entirely different state. "He has his reasons, I suppose."

Cole's bottom lip began to wobble suddenly. "I miss him so much," he said, setting the string of shells down and burying his head in Melanie's chest. "I just want him to come back home," he sobbed.

"Oh, honey, it's okay," she said, smoothing his hair and giving him a squeeze. Melanie's heart broke for the boy, and she knew that the minute she saw Josh, she needed to tell him.

Chapter Twenty-Eight

The next morning, Josh walked into the house unannounced.

The only reason Melanie was decent was because she'd gone out to breakfast with Kathryn before her sister had headed home.

"I'm sorry," she said, "but do you live here?" She pursed her lips to hide the fact that she was happy to see him, despite her concern over everything that had been going on.

"I did once," he said with a little smirk as his eyes met hers. "For about a week. You need to keep your front door locked. A crazy person can just walk in off the street."

"Yes, I see that now," she said, following him as he walked past the parlor.

"Wow, you've been busy," he said, eyeing the new addition to the chandelier. "The place is starting to look really nice."

"There's still quite a bit to be done," she said. "But the list of contractors you left me was invaluable. They all came as soon as they could fit me in and worked continuously to finish the interior."

"I'm glad to hear that." He went into the kitchen and poured himself a cup of coffee. "Want one?"

She huffed out an incredulous laugh at his making himself at home, but then sat down at the bar. "Yes." As he made her a cup, she decided to dive right into the heavy stuff to get it off her chest. "We need to talk about Cole."

He set her coffee down in front of her and then took a seat on the barstool beside hers. "What's wrong? Is he okay?"

She shook her head. "I don't think so." Melanie recounted their shell-stringing afternoon and how Cole had broken down.

Josh stared into his coffee, responsibility swimming around in his eyes. "When I decided to be a mentor to Cole, I didn't know we'd bond like we have. This isn't easy for me either."

"Is there no way to work closer to home so you can be there for him?"

Josh ran his hands through his hair in frustration. "I don't know. I want to... I just don't know how to make what I'm earning up in New York." He took a long, thoughtful draw of his coffee. "None of it will matter if I lose my land."

"What are you going to do?" she asked.

"The first thing I'm going to do is get rid of that letter. Please allow me to do that. Then, I'm going to see a lawyer. I've got an appointment at noon."

"You know," she said, not responding to his request, still unsure how she felt about destroying the letter, "it just occurred to me... Did Alfred Ellis have any kind of will?"

"I don't know, why?"

"He knew about your mother, right? And he probably knew about you too."

"Okay. What are you getting at?" he asked, before taking another sip of coffee.

"What if he had a will and left this property to his next of kin, but there wasn't one, so the house went on the market? What would happen then?"

"I have no idea," he said, raising a shoulder, concern on his face.

She felt bad for even mentioning it, but she mustered the courage, needing to know the answer. "If you lost your land, would you try to take the house from me?"

"Of course not," he said.

But she wondered if it really came down to it, and he had nowhere to live... "I wish you would've told me from the beginning so I wouldn't have said anything to anyone."

"I'm sorry I didn't trust you," he said. "I will from now on."

"Now on?" She gazed into his eyes. "Does that mean you plan to be friends?"

"Maybe," he said, but his smile gave him away. "We should stop to see my mom first, tell her we're going to see a lawyer. After that— whatever happens—we'll see Cole."

"Sounds like a plan."

Brenda opened the front door, the rims of her stunned eyes the same red as her nose. Rain was spitting down outside, making dark circles on the porch as she stared at her son, unsaid words written on her face. Josh wrapped his arms around his mother, squeezing her tightly. Melanie dropped her gaze to the floor of the porch, feeling terrible for all of this.

"Come in," Brenda finally said, letting her son go.

"I don't think a lot of people know," Josh told her, as they took a seat on the living room sofa. "It's a handful of people and even then, I'm not sure what they'd be able to prove."

Brenda pinched the bridge of her nose. "Janie just left."

Josh sat on the edge of the sofa, his shoulders tensing, surprise in his eyes. "What did she say?"

"Simon found a woman in town who was a nurse at the hospital when I was born. She said she remembered Mama mentioning Alfred and wishing he could see me."

"She told a nurse this with my grandfather there?"

Brenda wiped away more tears. "The nurse said he knew."

"Gramps was aware that you weren't his daughter?"

She nodded, her lip wobbling as she handed him her birth certificate. "I'd never had any reason to question Mama about why Dad's name wasn't on my birth certificate. She'd said once that he was in the war when I was born and he wasn't present, so they didn't list him. And they never told me otherwise. Dad just treated me as his own and there was no doubt in my mind that your gramps was my father." Another tear spilled down her cheek and she brushed it away with a shaking finger. "I wonder if it had even occurred to him that the land he left wasn't actually yours. I know he didn't think about it because he would've changed the wording of the will."

"So, what, Janie came over to try to stake her claim?" His voice rose, irritated.

"She said she was going to investigate the matter, that Bowland Enterprises wants the land, and if they can obtain it legally, she's going to help them do it."

"Damn it," he said under his breath. "I'll figure this out. I'm going to Thomas and Swift in town today to talk to a lawyer." He looked at his watch. "We should probably head out soon so we can get around any streets that are still blocked form the hurricane damage."

"I think we definitely need to see a lawyer," Brenda agreed. "I'm so sorry you have to deal with this. I wish I could fight your battle for you, but I can't. How will you handle this from New York?"

"I'm going to have to figure out a way," he said.

"Josh, son." Brenda's lips landed in a straight line as she looked at him. "You can build your own house. I can't imagine you need as much money as you claim to. What are you runnin' from?"

Josh's jaw tightened. "I need to be more than a handyman," he said. "I want to make something of myself. I have to if I want to be any good to anyone later."

"You are way more than a handyman," Melanie heard herself say. Both Josh and Brenda turned toward her.

Whether she really wanted to get into her inner thoughts or not, with their attention on her, she might as well just say what was on her mind. "You make a difference in people's lives," she said. "In my life. In Cole's. We're both miserable without you." She closed her mouth, not wanting to beg him to stay, but wishing with all her heart that he could.

He stared at her, pressure and longing on his face.

"If there are no more heirs to the property," one of the town's lawyers, George Swift, said to Josh and Melanie as he clicked a gold pen on the highly polished surface of his dark-wood desk, "then it falls to the next of kin. We'll need an affidavit from that next of kin and birth certificate."

"Uh, that's... the issue," said Josh. "My grandfather, Randall Claiborne, isn't listed as the father on my mother's birth certificate, so there's no way to prove if he's actually my grandfather. If my mother can't sign an affidavit, then what?"

One of George's eyebrows arched, as the man clearly worked to respond to this bit of local gossip as professionally as possible.

"What if someone were to contest it?" Josh pressed.

George cleared his throat and set the pen down. "Randall's will specifies that his land should pass to his next of kin, so it would pass to whomever the actual male heir is. The court can order DNA tests for other family members. If it comes out that your grandfather isn't actually your grandfather, then the land goes to the next of kin."

"My grandfather was an only child and has no living family."

"If Randall didn't have any other children of his own, and he has no living male family members, so no other administrator could come forward, his assets would be acquired by the state that would appoint a lawyer to handle it, and the assets would most likely be auctioned off."

Melanie needed to take the opportunity to ask the lawyer indirectly about the Ellis house. She had to know her legal right to it in the eventuality that Alfred Ellis did leave a will somewhere, stating the house should pass to his own heir. "And what if, say, someone bought an auctioned property, but subsequently an heir *was* found?" she asked carefully, so as not to give away the relationship between Alfred Ellis and Josh.

"The heir would have thirty days from the death of the owner to come forward. Otherwise, it would become property of the purchaser."

Knowing the Ellis house was in fact hers made Melanie breathe a sigh of relief. But it was short-lived.

"However," George added, his chair squeaking as he leaned forward, the thrill of battle in his eyes. "The heir could advise the court that he did not get his notice of sale and should be granted what we call an 'upset bid.' That would probably be granted."

Melanie turned to Josh but he didn't react. The set in his jaw and the fear in his eyes tugged at Melanie's heartstrings. Everything he'd been working for, all those memories from his childhood, the land he'd grown up visiting—all of it could be ripped right out from under him. She searched his face, looking for any answers as to what he was going to do, but he'd just glazed over.

"Thanks for answering our questions, George," Josh said, standing up and shaking the lawyer's hand.

"No problem. Let me know if you need anything else." George handed both Melanie and Josh one of his business cards. Melanie slid it into her handbag.

"Will do." Josh opened the clouded glass-paned door of the office and allowed Melanie to exit first. When they'd gotten through the small lobby and stepped out onto the sidewalk, he turned to her, looking suddenly exhausted. "I need a beer. Wanna go to Buster's?"

"Sure."

They walked along the tourist-filled street, the bright blue gulf to their left, a few shopkeepers still painting the exteriors of their stores after repairs from the hurricane. The clouds had moved offshore and the after-rain heat was thick in the air, settling in wet droplets on Melanie's skin, but she barely noticed, guilt consuming her. If she'd never pressed him on those letters, if she'd just left them alone… Addie had warned her about the secrets. And now Melanie had made a mess of things.

Josh opened the door of the bar, the cool air from inside tickling her skin. The interior was lively, the tables full of chatting tourists, beach music playing, the bar bustling with bartenders making lines of cocktails waiting for their servers to pick them up.

Josh said hello to the hostess who showed them immediately to a table for two that sat against the large window wall overlooking the bright coastline, a yellow surf warning flag rippling in the wind. She lit a candle between them and handed them the menu before heading back to her post. Josh held up a finger to the bartender, who seemed to understand the gesture.

"Want one?" Josh asked.

Melanie nodded, her gaze flickering to the dartboard where they'd first met, how he'd brushed her off at first but warmed up as the night went on. She remembered how the hint of his smile had settled upon her with a light buzz of electricity, not having any clue what that night would lead to.

Josh held up two fingers and the bartender popped the tops off of two local beers, setting them on the bar. Getting up to grab them, Josh returned and placed one in front of Melanie. She took a foamy sip, the aroma of hops and lemon filling her nose.

"What are you gonna do?" Melanie asked, continuing the conversation she knew was still playing out in his head since they'd left the lawyer's office.

"From the sound of it, there's not much I *can* do except put my bid on the land at auction and pray I can outbid Bowland Enterprises, which I doubt very seriously I can. They're a multi-million-dollar corporation." He tipped his beer up and gulped a few swallows.

"I'm sorry," Melanie said honestly. "This is all my fault. I should've kept quiet about things I didn't know enough about." The guilt ate at her, causing her lip to wobble. Not wanting to cry right there at the table, she tried to cover it up with a drink from her bottle.

"You didn't know it would end up like this. Sometimes things just become unraveled before we can stop them." Josh looked out at the sea, his eyes searching as if the answers were out there.

His comment made Melanie think of Gram's poem.

If only I could grab the twine,
And hold with all my might,
I may be able to lace it again,
To keep the strings pulled tight.

That was exactly how she was feeling right now. She could hardly manage, knowing she'd been the cause of Josh losing his birthright. Even if he won the auction, now he'd have to use the savings he'd been collecting to build his house just to buy the land. She had no idea how, but she was going to do anything she could to make it up to him.

Chapter Twenty-Nine

"Josh!" Cole said, running down the driveway as quickly as his pint-sized feet could take him. The little boy threw his arms around Josh, and when he did, the worry faded from Josh's face. He scooped Cole up into the air, spinning him around.

"Whatcha been up to?" Josh asked.

The little boy held on to Josh's ears, a smile plastered across his face. "Nothin' much. I dug a big hole in the woods so I can hide treasure."

"Sounds cool," Josh said, walking alongside Melanie with Cole atop his shoulders. "What treasure you gonna put in it?"

"The treasure I get when I find the pirate ship." Cole slid down off his shoulders, Josh catching him at his back and pulling him around the front of him, their movements so smooth that it was clear they'd done it before.

"You know about a pirate ship and you're not telling me?" He tickled Cole, making the boy squeal with laughter and wriggle out of his arms, darting away from him.

"You can help me look for it if ya want to," Cole said, still giggling. "I've got a map 'n' everything." He turned to Melanie. "You wanna come too? There might be pretty necklaces! Jewels and stuff."

"I'd love to," Melanie said, feeling a hundred times better now that Cole was around.

"Where's this map?" Josh asked.

"Right here." Cole pulled a haphazardly folded piece of printer paper from his pocket and opened it up, revealing a crayon-drawn map with a big red X in the middle. "See, there was a big storm," he said, squatting down and smoothing the paper on the ground, "and the ship crashed. Nobody survived and the boat got covered with sand. But the rubies and diamonds are all still there. We just have to find them."

Melanie was glad to see Cole wrapped up in his imagination and playing. She wondered how much he knew about his birth mother leaving, and about Eric's cancer. She hoped they could distract him for a few hours.

Cole folded the paper and placed it back into his pocket before grabbing Josh and Melanie's hands. "Let me show you where we're gonna put the treasure!"

The little boy led them to the woods next to his house. Suzie caught Melanie's eye from the window inside and waved to her. Melanie waved back just before Cole pulled her past the tree line. They meandered down a small path that wound its way deeper into the woods.

"Eric's been helping me dig," Cole told them as he led the way. "He says it makes him so tired, so it must be good exercise." He beamed up at the two of them. "We're almost done."

They walked a little further into the woods and came upon a small hole in the ground, covered by branches and leaves. The sun beamed down through the Spanish moss, the air thick with humidity but slightly cooler under the shade of the trees.

"Here it is!" Cole dropped their hands and lifted the branches to show off his work.

"Wow," Josh said, "you have been busy."

"When I find that treasure, I'll be ready!" Cole puffed out his chest. "The treasure is in these woods too!"

"It is?" Josh asked.

Cole nodded.

Josh squatted down to the boy's eye level. "Well, should we go and look for it then?"

Excitedly, Cole pulled the map back out and opened it up. "We need to find this big tree with the three low branches," he said, focused as he looked around.

"There are a few big trees over there," Melanie said, pointing to a patch of mature trees to their right.

Cole ran ahead of them, holding the map and studying it, and Josh and Melanie followed. "There!" he called, pointing to a tree with large branches jutting out toward the ground. He raced over to it and pounced onto the lowest branch, pulling himself up onto the next. "Nothing at the top of the tree," he announced, climbing back down.

"Maybe it's around the bottom," Josh said.

The three of them hunted for the treasure, moving leaves and looking under ferns. The heat had crept in, dusting Melanie's skin in little droplets, the breeze reaching them every now and again to relieve it. They continued the charade for a good five minutes straight before Josh stopped.

"I wish there was a treasure, but we just can't find one," Cole said, disappointed.

"We need a solid plan," Josh announced. "Hand me that map so I can take a look again?"

Cole peered up at him, the crumpled map in his two hands as he lifted it up to Josh.

"You know why the magic of the map isn't working? We're not ready," he told the boy with authority as he took in the map's directions. "What if Melanie and I come over tomorrow morning and bring a metal detector? Maybe then we can find it."

Melanie wasn't quite sure where Josh was going with the idea of bringing tools to search for a fantasy treasure, but when he smiled at her in solidarity, she played along. She was thankful for anything to take her mind off the guilt of Josh possibly losing his land, and she didn't mind at all spending another day with Josh and Cole.

The passenger-side window of Josh's truck was down, the salty air that had once been the smell Melanie associated only with vacation now feeling like part of her. "How are we going to find a treasure that isn't real?" she asked Josh on the way back to her house.

"I'll show you." He pulled into the hardware store and kept the engine running. "I'll be right back."

He ran into the store and returned minutes later with a couple small planks of wood and a few tools under his arm, as well as a bag full of hardware. "One more stop and then we'll head back to your house, I promise." They drove to Maryann's beach shop. "I'll need your help with this one," Josh told her before getting out of the car.

The shop looked quite different from the secured place Melanie had left that day before the storm had hit. Today, there were racks of brightly colored sarongs outside, with baskets of beachwear lining the entrance. Josh opened the door, ringing the bells as they entered. Maryann immediately greeted them with a wide grin, coming around the counter and swishing toward them, her arms stretched out.

"Hey, y'all!" she said, giving each of them a squeeze. "Fancy seeing you here, Josh. I thought you'd high-tailed it out of here."

"Yeah," he said. "I had to come back for some… business."

"You know what they say…" She waggled her eyebrows.

"No. What do they say?" he asked with a wry smile.

"When you can't leave something, your work isn't done. As much as you wanna get out of this town, maybe it's not ready to let you go yet."

He gave a half-smile. "Maybe."

"It sure would make everyone happy if you stayed."

"Thanks," he said, but Melanie's heart tugged at the uncertainty in his eyes.

"So, what brings y'all in?"

"We need to buy some jewelry. A lot of it," he said.

"All right. I've got that rack of necklaces over there…" She pointed to the row that Melanie had helped her pack up before the storm.

"I know you make a lot of the jewelry, right?" he asked.

Melanie remembered the small sign she'd seen next to the necklaces that day.

"Yeah, why?"

"Where can I get a few bags of costume jewels?"

"I've got some in the back. What are you looking for specifically?"

"I need emeralds, rubies, diamonds, and a few necklaces and rings thrown in. I want to make a treasure box for Cole and hide it in the woods. A pirate's treasure."

Melanie felt the swell of fondness hearing Josh's plan. What an adorably sweet thing to do.

Maryann clapped her hands together. "What a wonderful idea!" The woman rushed to the back room and returned with two large bags of mixed rhinestones in various colors. "Hang on," she said, thrusting them into Josh's hands. "I've got more!" She ran to the back again, this time coming in with a diamond tiara. "I'd made this for my niece's birthday and then she mentioned her pink dress, so I started over and made a second to match it. I'll throw this one in free of charge. I have a couple of large-stone rings over here that are pretty inexpensive…" She took them over to a display case.

"I'll take two of those," Josh told her. "And three of those jeweled necklaces."

With the jewels safely wrapped, Josh and Melanie headed out of the store. "Mind if I use an empty room at your place to build this treasure box?"

"Not at all," she said, as Josh pulled the truck out of the parking space, heading for the house, snippets of the gulf shimmering in the distance between the cottages as they drove. "I was just going to work on the business model for the bed and breakfast. I'm thinking things are looking good for a soft opening this winter."

"That's great," he said. "You've really worked hard."

"Thanks," she returned, tapping into his sudden seriousness. "I couldn't have done it without you."

Josh made a turn, and then his gaze darted over to her and back to the road. "I'm sorry I was such a bear when you met me. And I'm sorry I let my own fears about family secrets that you had nothing to do with get between us. You didn't deserve that."

"Thank you for the apology," she said, both surprised and delighted by his admission.

"I've had a rough time with my ex and I let it affect me. I thought if I pushed you away, it would be easier to leave and carry out my plans… She blindsided me, and left me trying to sift through our lives together to figure out why. Naturally, when your wife leaves you for a millionaire CEO and tells you that you aren't enough, it's a tough pill to swallow."

"I can imagine," Melanie said.

"It took me quite a while to realize that Janie's leaving had less to do with me and more to do with *her*. Even though she doesn't seem like it, she's an insecure person, and she has to tear people down to build herself up."

Melanie nodded, understanding. "I get that," she said. "I was engaged to a man named Adam, and when I decided to take care of my gram, he left me. For a long time, pushing him out of my mind was the easiest way to deal with losing him."

"And now?" he asked.

"I realized that if he couldn't stick by me, he wasn't the person I needed. It wasn't me, it was him. I'm not sure what made me realize it; the answer just sort of settled over me. What made *you* realize that it wasn't you who had the problem?"

"When I was with you, I felt purpose. And the more I fought it, the more I couldn't deny that what I was working so hard to achieve by leaving might not be what makes me the most content."

Happiness bubbled up, and she suppressed the smile that wanted to float across her face. "So you're saying I made it hard for you to leave?"

He came to a stop at the light and locked eyes with her. "It took all my strength."

The intensity in his eyes made it hard to breathe. "And now?"

"And now it feels like my well-laid plans are crumbling to the ground, and I don't know what I'm supposed to be doing. But I do know one thing: the very first place I wanted to go when I got into town was yours."

She allowed her delight to surface. "The *Ellis* house?" she teased.

He huffed out a grin and shook his head as the light turned green. "Not the Ellis house. *Your* house. I don't look at it the same anymore."

"I'm happy to hear that," she said. But her heart dipped at the reality of the situation. He'd finally, after all this time, opened up—but now there was a real possibility that without his land, he'd have no reason to stay in Rosemary Bay. When that was all she wanted.

Chapter Thirty

"Oh, you know what?" Josh said, his eyes rounding with his idea. "Could I take apart that old box we found? I'd love to use the rusty hinges and latch for Cole's treasure box."

"Sure," she said, pulling it out of the pantry and emptying the last few contents that were inside. She set an old map of the island and the photographs on the counter, along with the books, the pocket watch, and other items inside.

"Would you hand me the screwdriver?" he asked, as he moved his bottle of beer out of the way to reach across the kitchen island for it.

Melanie handed the tool to him and he disassembled the hinges on the old box.

"I should find a place to keep all this stuff," Melanie said, piling up the books and setting the old bible on top. "Wait, I have an empty container upstairs. I'll just grab it. Be right back."

She ran upstairs and grabbed a plastic bin that had held her toiletries until she'd been able to unpack them in the newly renovated bathroom. She'd just put all of Alfred's things in there... Pacing over to the windowsill, she went to grab the key that they'd found, but stopped when she realized it wasn't there. She remembered moving it to dust, and at the time it hadn't held much significance, but—of course—now that she wanted to file it away, it was nowhere to be found. She looked around the room, checking the floor and other areas she might have stashed it, like the little spot in her closet where she'd been keeping her jewelry, but it wasn't anywhere. With a sigh, she took the box back downstairs. She'd have to find it later.

While she loaded Alfred's things into the bin, Josh lined the hardware up on the treasure box. Once the hinges were on, he tested the lid, opening and closing it, securing the latch on the front of the natural wood box.

"All it needs now is a little stain and some distressing," he said.

"It looks gorgeous." Melanie handed him a plate with a slice of hot pizza that had just come out of the oven.

Josh moved the tools aside and went over to the sink to wash his hands. "He needs something to get excited about, you know?"

"Yeah." Melanie's heart ached for the little boy. "He's such a great kid. It's unbelievable what he's already gone through in his short life."

"I know." Josh dried his hands and returned to the other side of the bar, picking up his slice of pizza and taking a bite.

"He's up for adoption," Melanie said. "Do you think Suzie and Eric will adopt him?"

"They never planned to adopt," Josh replied. "They've been fostering kids for years. They feel like they can fill in the gap for those kids who are waiting for their forever home or for their parents to get it together."

There was a part of her that could see herself adopting Cole, but it seemed like such a fantasy. She had no clue about how to raise a child, and the new bed and breakfast would surely consume her time...

"What are you thinking about?" Josh's voice pulled her from her thoughts.

"Hm? Oh, I just wish he could find a great family," she replied.

Josh's phone went off on the bar, ripping both of them from the conversation.

"Great." He sucked in a breath and set his pizza down. "It's Janie."

Melanie shot a look to the pulsing phone, encouraging him to get it.

Josh swiped the phone off the bar, putting it to his ear. "Hello?" He took a step toward the open living area. "It didn't take long for you to pounce, did it?" His shoulders were tense, his frown set angrily as he listened. He strode back and forth, his gaze intense, as if his eyes could shoot lasers onto the floor. "Why did you bother calling me to tell me if you don't even have to go through me to get the land, Janie? Oh, out of courtesy," he snarled.

Melanie held her breath, worried for him as he stood silently, the phone to his ear.

Then, his whole body suddenly relaxed, his head dropping down. "Janie. Listen to me. You and I didn't work out, and that's okay. Relationships don't always go the way we hope. But this is my future we're talking about. Lost on a technicality. In all respects, my grandfather was my family, and he left that land to me." He ran his fingers through his hair, dejected. "If Bowland puts in an offer on that property, they'll be taking *everything* away from me—you know that, right?" He leaned against the wall, resting his head back, his gaze at the ceiling. "Not to mention that you won't be able to show your face in town. People will all know what you've done."

He heaved another breath. "Fine." Then he hung up the phone.

"I'm so sorry," Melanie said, walking over to him.

"I knew it was coming," he said. "She'd been calling me about buying it when she thought the land was mine. She's relentless and she doesn't care who she hurts, as long as she can make her new man Rob Whitaker happy. And word spreads quickly in this town."

"What are you going to do?"

He gritted his teeth and subtly shook his head before forcing a smile, resigning himself to the moment. "Well, right now, I'm going to eat my pizza, finish staining Cole's treasure box, and hang out with you. Got anything else to take my mind off of losing everything I've planned for?"

"I have leftover piña colada mix and half a bottle of rum."

"Perfect. Anything to distract me."

"Okay," she said with purpose. "Before she got sick, this is what Gram and I used to do whenever we wanted to get our mind off of things." Melanie went over to the radio and clicked it on. She cranked it up, the beachy music of steel drums and guitar filling the house. Throwing her arms above her head, she danced to the music, twirling and swaying her way over to Josh. She grabbed his hands, pulling him into the empty space in the living room.

Josh took charge and led her like a pro, spinning her around and moving perfectly in step with the music.

"You can dance?" she said, stunned, while they pulled apart and came back together in perfect unison.

"My mother thought lessons would make me more graceful on the football field," he said. "At seventeen, I was the laughing stock of my team—none of them let me live it down. But now it's coming in handy." He gave her another twirl before releasing her.

Melanie danced over to the refrigerator and grabbed the cocktail mix and the rum, setting them onto the counter. Josh came up beside her and filled the blender with ice.

"How much mix should I put in?" he asked, picking up the bottle of piña colada and turning it around in search of directions.

"I usually just pour in about this much," Melanie replied, placing a finger on the glass of the blender as a fill-line.

Josh poured in the mixture.

"Then just top it off with rum."

With the blender full, Josh placed the lid on and hit the button, the machine squealing over the radio. While the music played, making the house feel cheerier than it ever had, Melanie got down two glasses from the cabinet.

While Melanie moved his tools out of the way, Josh turned off the blender and checked it. "I think it needs more," he said, replacing the lid and turning it back on.

Suddenly, the lid shot off, flying across the counter and landing with a spinning thud. Neither of them noticed due to all the piña colada that was spraying them and the entire kitchen.

"Turn it off!" Melanie called out through surprised laughter, as she shielded Cole's treasure box from the alcoholic shower by throwing herself over it.

Josh felt around blindly as the liquid shot out of the top of the blender, finding the button on the machine and turning it off. They both stood dripping and sticky, the music still blaring around them. Melanie reached over and hit the power button on the radio.

"I guess I didn't put the lid on tightly that time," he said, licking piña colada off his lips. "Tasty, though."

Melanie laughed, tugging at her drenched shirt. "You don't have a change of clothes here," she said, pondering the idea.

"Well, I doubt I'd fit any of yours so there's only one option." He kicked off his flip-flops and grabbed the bottom of his shirt, pulling it over his head.

"Wait!" she said, in an attempt to prevent him from completely stripping down. She had to work to keep her eyes off his tanned bare chest. "What are you doing?"

"I'm going swimming." He walked toward the back door in his shorts. "Come on," he beckoned. "You can keep *your* shirt *on*." He gave her a wink and opened the door, the warm breeze blowing in.

"What should we do with this mess?" she asked, trying not to look as eager as she felt to rush into the waves with him.

"I'll get it all cleaned up when we get back in."

Melanie left the cocktail-covered kitchen behind and followed Josh outside, over the dunes to the beach. "Last one in the water has to do a shot of rum when we get back!" He took off through the soft sand, and Melanie ran after him, pushing herself as hard as she could, barely keeping up. Just before he got completely in the water, she grabbed his leg, the two of them falling with a splash.

"Ha!" she said when she'd come up for air. "We tied."

"We did not," he said with a laugh. He shook his hair to keep it from dripping into his face, beads of water shimmering on his toned biceps.

"You said last one in the water, but we're both in the water," she pointed out, crossing her arms, and making his grin grow wider.

"Fine," he conceded. He seemed as though he was working to keep his gaze on her face, a mixture of amusement and fondness swimming around in his eyes. "Still sticky?"

"I think I'm good now," she said as the waves bobbed around her, making her feel like a human buoy. "How about you?"

"I might need one more dip."

He dove under the waves and to her shock, Melanie felt him grab her legs and lift her into the air as he came up, causing her to squeal. "One more dip for you too!" he said, tossing her into the water with a splash.

She came up, wiping the salty spray off her face. "Oh, you're in for it!" She blinked to clear her eyes while pushing against the waves to get to him.

Josh darted out of the way as she swiped at him. "Are you going to pick *me* up and throw me in the water?" he teased.

"No, but I can do this!" She threw herself against him, knocking him backwards, both of them falling into the surf. His arms wrapped around her and when they came up, he was looking down at her as water sheeted over both their faces.

"Careful, I'll do it again," she said, to avoid all the flutters she was feeling.

"Promise?" he said softly, a smirk forming at the corners of his mouth. Then he leaned in and pressed his lips to hers. His warm, salty kiss had a hint of rum and coconut, and she could've kissed him forever, but he pulled back, leaving her breathless. "What do you say, we clean up the kitchen, heat up the rest of the pizza, and make more piña coladas. Then sit out on the back porch until we fall asleep?"

A fizzle of excitement ran through her and she couldn't hide her happiness. "That sounds amazing," she said.

"My grandmother used to say that life could carry you out like an undertow. But that shouldn't stop you from swimming like crazy," Melanie said as she pushed against the deck with her bare foot, the swing she and Josh were sitting on sailing forward. She'd jumped in the shower and changed into dry clothes, but the salt in the air still sat on her skin.

Josh, bare-chested, looked out at the gulf, his shirt hung over the railing, drying in the breeze. He took a drink of his frosty piña colada, his cheeks pink from sun and the rum. "I feel like all I do is swim against the tide," he admitted. "I try to keep myself from doing it. I make plans and attempt to stick to them, but it doesn't work. It's very frustrating."

"Maybe the plans you're making aren't what's meant for you," she said, the advice rolling off her tongue just like it used to do for Gram, surprising her. She'd never been the one to offer advice—goodness knows, she certainly wasn't the picture of how to live a life to its fullest. "You know, I'm the opposite. I feel like I haven't planned a thing in my life, and it all still falls apart." She laughed at the idea before she noticed his eyes on her, the fondness in them sobering.

He turned toward her, locking her gaze. "What if our plans *and non-plans* have all crumbled, not because they aren't meant for us, but because we haven't found the person to support us when it all falls to pieces?"

Without warning, her mind went to Alfred Ellis, and that theory made total sense. Like a whisper from out on the gulf, it had sailed into her mind. It wasn't a lightning bolt or a white horse riding in. It was just a perfect moment, with the orange sun sinking on the horizon and the lapping of the waves. Slowly, she turned back to Josh and asked, "How do you know when you've found that someone?"

"Because they make you feel like everything you've done until now has been to lead you here." He set his drink down on the railing and then gently took hers, placing it next to his own.

"*Here?*" she asked.

"Here." Josh leaned in, placing his lips next to her ear, and whispered, "And here," making the hairs on her arms stand up. His mouth moved to her cheek. "And here." And then finally, his lips brushed hers, sending an electric current right through her body. "And here." He reached around her, pulled her in and kissed her, her emotions flooding through her like a tidal wave. She put her arms around his neck and kissed him back, their lips fitting together like perfect puzzle pieces.

She was the first to pull back. "I'm afraid you'll try to push me away again," she admitted, her heart in real danger of being shattered beyond repair if he did.

The skin between his eyes creased as he looked off into the distance, pensive. Then he refocused on her. "I don't know…"

Her heart fell into her stomach. But his hand was on her face, pulling it back into his view.

"You didn't let me finish," he said. "I don't know what my plan is now. I don't have a clue what I'm supposed to do with my life. But I'm pretty sure of one thing: I can't stay away from you. In New York, I'd lie in bed, staring at the ceiling, your face flooding my mind. I wondered if you were okay and whether you needed any help… I kept thinking about your smile… I love your smile."

"Don't go back to New York," she told him in a whisper.

"Okay."

The finality in the way he answered gave her a sense of relief like nothing she'd felt before, and she knew that even though neither of them had an inkling of what was coming next, they could get through it together.

Chapter Thirty-One

"Got your map?" Josh asked Cole as they headed through the line of pine trees for the thick woods, a metal detector Josh had borrowed from his mother swinging in his hand while Melanie carried a shovel.

Melanie and Josh had been up since before the sun, burying the treasure box full of Maryann's jewels, and twenty dollars' worth of gold coins he'd gotten at the token machine in the local arcade. They'd hidden it under the tree with three low limbs, meticulously covering over it with dirt and arranging moss to make the ground look undisturbed. It had worked out perfectly, because Suzie and Eric had a doctor's appointment first thing, so when Suzie called late last night to ask Melanie if she could watch Cole this morning, they'd come right over.

When they got to the woods, Cole pulled the map out and smoothed it out on a tree. "I think we need to go this way," the boy said, the yellow rain boots he'd put on in a hurry when they'd arrived crunching the leaves as he walked.

Josh fired up the metal detector, the *tweep tweep* of it the only sound between the three of them as they made their way into the forest. "I think we're picking up a signal," Josh said, sweeping the metal detector in a totally different place than where they'd buried the box. The beeping went crazy. "Hey, Mel, can you bring the shovel over here?"

Melanie couldn't hide her grin when he called her Mel. She hurried over with the shovel.

"If the treasure is there, I'm gonna spend all the money inside," Cole said excitedly.

Josh set the metal detector down and began moving the soil with the shovel. "What will you buy?" he asked, concentrating on the area where the detector had picked up a signal.

"I'm going to pay for all of Eric's doctors," Cole said proudly.

Josh stopped digging. "What?"

"Suzie told me he's really sick, and I heard them talking about how much the doctors cost. The insurance doesn't cover everything."

Melanie's heart sank for little Cole. He was too young to be worrying about insurance copays. "We'll make sure they have what they need," she said.

"Well, maybe you won't have to. What's there, Josh?" Cole asked.

Josh moved the soil around some more, unearthing something. He reached down and sifted through the soil. "You're the proud owner of…" He picked up the object. "An old key ring." He held up a metal ring with a little anchor pendant on it.

Cole's eyebrows went up. "Hey, I'll take it!"

Josh brushed the key ring off and dropped it into Cole's palm. Then he picked the metal detector back up. "Let's head to the tree we found from your map yesterday and see if there's anything there."

Cole held out the map and they all headed toward the tree with three branches. As expected, when they got under it, the metal detector went crazy.

"Oh my goodness!" Cole exclaimed, jumping up and down. "There's something there!"

"Sometimes, if you believe, you might just find a little magic," Josh told him, as he handed the little boy the shovel. Together, Josh and Cole worked to get the treasure box out of the ground.

"It's a real pirate's treasure!" Cole said, his eyes wide and a giant grin across his face. With a gasp, he opened the lid, revealing the coins and jewels. He put the tiara on his head and danced around. "We did it! We found the treasure!" He threw his arms around Josh and squeezed him tightly. "Thank you for helping me!" Then he ran over to Melanie and took off the tiara, placing it on her head. "You look real pretty," he said.

"Thank you," Melanie said, adjusting it.

"I'm glad you came."

"Me too," she said. And she couldn't think of any two people she'd rather be spending the day with.

"Let's hear your good news," Melanie said, as she and Josh took a seat around Suzie and Eric's small kitchen table. Cole was already at the table, wearing four beaded necklaces and two gemstone rings from the treasure box he'd so excitedly shown his foster parents the minute they'd walked through the door.

"Eric has been cleared for surgery," Suzie said. "And they're hopeful that they can get all of it. The chemo will continue, and the outlook is really good."

"Oh, Eric, I'm so happy to hear that," Melanie said.

"Thanks," Eric replied, looking relieved. "It's been terrifying but I'm hoping things will look up soon."

"We should celebrate," Suzie said. "When do you go back to New York, Josh?"

Josh looked over at Melanie. "I'm not sure," he said, clearly think-ing it over. "I have some scheduling to figure out." He perked up and turned back to Suzie. "When did you want to celebrate? I'll be there."

"Why don't we do an early dinner tonight?" Suzie suggested. "We can do a big seafood boil. Eric, are you up for dinner tonight or will that be too much on you?"

"I'd love to have dinner with y'all," Eric said.

"All my favorite people in one spot!" Cole danced around the linoleum floor, his beaded necklaces swinging with his movement.

Melanie squatted down to Cole's level. "How about if I bring all the fixin's to make s'mores?"

"Yeah!" Cole pumped his fists in the air and then gave her a big squeeze.

The blue and orange flame flickered up from the small fire pit on the deck out back of Suzie and Eric's house. Cole and Melanie held long marshmallow-roasting skewers that she'd bought for Kathryn's birthday a few years back. Each one had a giant marshmallow on the end of it. Josh, Suzie, and Eric had settled in the Adirondack chairs around the fire.

"I can't believe she'd do that," Eric said, when he'd heard about Janie's plans to take Josh's land.

Melanie put two graham crackers on a plate and added a square of chocolate before helping Cole transfer his hot marshmallow onto it.

"I could work for the next ten years and not have enough to put down on a piece of property of that size," Josh said, shaking his head, a bottle of beer resting on his knee. "At auction, the cost will be astronomical."

Cole held his s'more between his tiny fingers and crawled onto Josh's lap. "I can give you some of my jewels to pay for it," he said.

"Aw, buddy, that's really nice of you," Josh told him, setting the bottle of beer down to give the little boy more room on his lap. "It's okay. I just need to figure out a new plan. Just like we did finding your treasure."

Cole nodded, his face crumpled in understanding. "Anywhere's good."

"What do you mean?" Josh asked the boy gently.

"It doesn't matter where I live," he said, "as long as I have the people I love."

Josh looked at him, Cole's words clearly making an impact. "You know what? You're totally right." His eyes found Melanie's and he smiled, all the stress she'd seen in his face wiped away. And it was the best sight she'd seen since she'd gotten to Rosemary Bay.

Chapter Thirty-Two

Melanie sat on the step of her back porch, her fingers trailing the grains of the wood underneath her. The morning air blew softly across her face, the overcast sky having not yet burned off for the day. She held Gram's journal that Kathryn had brought her and breathed in the briny air, thinking about Josh. He'd stayed on the air mattress last night. Having him in the house had made her feel whole—she couldn't explain it, but for the first time in that house, she'd slept like a baby with his arms wrapped around her.

"Good morning," Josh said, coming up behind her.

She twisted around to greet him, and a fizzle ran through her at the sight of his disheveled hair and overnight stubble. He handed her a cup of coffee.

"Thanks," she said, taking the mug.

He sat down next to her. "What's that?"

"It's my gram's journal," she said. "There's not a whole lot in it…" She opened the book and flipped through the pages.

"May I?" he asked, reaching for it.

Melanie handed him the journal and when she did, a very thin envelope fell from the back of the book. It caught on the wind and she jumped up to step on it before it blew away. "What is this?" she asked no one in particular, as she bent down and pulled it from under her bare foot.

The tissue-thin envelope was sealed and when she held it toward the sky, she could see her gram's writing on a paper inside it. She brought it over to Josh.

"Should I open it?" she asked.

"Up to you," he said.

As she held the envelope in her hands, a new sense of calm settled over her at the thought of reading her grandmother's words. She recalled the last time she'd read a letter from Gram. How far she'd come…

Gently, she slipped her finger under the flap of the envelope, pulling the seal loose and sliding out the thin paper, opening it in her hand. Sitting down next to Josh, she gasped. "It's to Alfred," she said in a whisper.

He leaned in next to her. His spicy scent mixed with the salty air was like coming home. "What does it say?"

Dear Alfred,

After a lifetime of silence, I felt it would give me closure to finally write this letter before we meet on the other side, and if you weren't going to do it, I would. There were moments when I almost spoke to you that run like a highlight reel in my mind. I saw you once across the street and your name was on my lips. You didn't look my way so I kept quiet. I can still remember the ache rolling around in my gut, wanting to throw my arms around you and put my hands on your face, kiss your lips. But I knew you weren't mine anymore, and I belonged to someone else. I swallowed the lump in my throat and cleared my tears, staring at you until you disappeared around the corner.

And the house you'd built—I would never go by it until it was empty. The pain was too great, and if I saw you in the window, I wouldn't have had the strength to stay away. My husband didn't deserve that. He was a wonderful man. He gave me everything I needed and more. I know that time should've healed what was broken when you didn't come for me, but a piece of my heart has remained unfilled, with a constant feeling that we've left something unfinished. There was a piece of me that had remained on the pier that day.

Life is a strange journey. Even though we never got to have our shot at it together, and I have so many unanswered questions, I've felt you with me along the way.

My hope is that somehow our love will spread its wings and continue on without us. I certainly think that while brief, our love was big enough to last forever.

Until we meet again,
Eloise

Silently, Melanie peered up at the sky, the sun just beginning to peek through the haze. There they were: the grandchildren of Alfred and Eloise, sitting on the back porch of the house that had been built out of that love. *Somehow our love will spread its wings and continue on without us...* She turned to Josh, her thoughts clicking into place.

"Quit your job," she told him.

His eyes widened. "What?"

"Stay here."

"What are you talking about?"

"I don't want you to leave again," she told him. "I want you to help me run the bed and breakfast."

"What?" he asked again with a chuckle, disbelief in his face laced with a sparkle that she couldn't deny.

She closed the letter in the journal and took his mug of coffee, setting it down. "Stay!" she said, pulling him up by his hands. "Stay right here. We can do this together. You and I. Say yes!"

Josh scooped her up into his arms, twirling her around and making her laugh. She hadn't ever really felt alive until that moment, and it was intoxicating, like a piece of her had been missing her whole life. Perhaps it had been…

"So is that a yes?" she asked, wrapping her arms around his neck.

Josh set her down and took her face in his hands. "Yes," he said, before pressing his lips to hers in the sweetest kiss.

"I brought over some peach cobbler," Addie said at Melanie's door as she held out a steaming, buttery pie, the sugary fruit lifting out of it and the scent circling them. Melanie had been arranging a few of the rooms and doing laundry in her new washing machine while Josh went to see his mother to give her the good news, and then call his employer in New York.

"That's so kind of you," Melanie said. "Come in."

"I won't stay," Addie said, "but I wanted to tell you that I heard back from Simon Banks. He called around, and First National in town has safe deposit boxes."

"Oh?" she asked, holding the pie in her arms.

"You'll never believe this." Addie leaned heavily on her brightly colored cane.

"What is it?"

"Box 0113 belonged to Alfred Ellis."

Melanie almost dropped the pie, the possibility of finding out more of Alfred's story thrilling her.

Addie reached out to steady it. "It wasn't properly inventoried after Alfred's death, so whatever he had in it is still there."

"Will they let me open it?" she asked, her heart pattering.

"Simon already thought of that. He petitioned the court to give you access to it, although you won't be able to keep what's in it, since we can assume you aren't listed in Alfred Ellis's will, if he even had one. But it's worth finding out what's in it, so you'd better go get your key."

Melanie gritted her teeth. "I have to find it first. I can't remember where I put it."

"Lord have mercy, child," Addie said, shaking her head with an exhale. "Where did you have it last?"

"It was on the windowsill in the bedroom upstairs, but now it's gone. I must have picked it up to clean and absentmindedly put it somewhere. I'll check all my shorts pockets and the washing machine."

"Well," Addie said, clearly trying to defuse any distress, "there might not be a thing in that box, so it could be just as well."

"Yes," Melanie said, but inside, she was dying to have that key. "Thank you for the pie. You're welcome to come in and have a slice."

"Thank you, dear, but I'm out for my daily walk and at my age, exercise trumps pie. Gotta stay healthy."

"Okay," Melanie said. "Another time, then."

"Maybe after you find what's in the box, you can fill me in."

"All right," she said. "Deal."

Melanie had searched three rooms for the key so far when the doorbell buzzed yet again. Wondering who in the world it could be now, she brushed her hands on her shorts and went down to answer it, holding her breath when she encountered Janie standing on the other side.

"Is Josh around?" she asked with no introductions. She pushed her designer glasses onto her head to make eye contact. "I heard he was staying here." She gave an appraising glance over Melanie's head into the entryway.

"He's not in at the moment," Melanie said, standing in the doorway as if she were guarding the house from Janie's negative energy.

"Yes, I am," Josh said, walking up the drive behind Janie. "What do you want?" he spat.

Janie spun around to face him. "I want to be civil and tell you to your face that we're obtaining rezoning permits and putting in an offer on the Claiborne parcel."

"You mean my land." His gaze gripped her with utter disgust.

Janie let out a bitter chuckle. "I don't think it's yours anymore."

"How much are you offering?"

"One point five million—our ceiling offer."

Melanie's heart plunged.

Josh took an angry step toward Janie. "You're heartless."

"It's business, Josh. Doesn't the fact that I'm telling you personally count for anything?"

"It tells me what a cold person you really are."

She shrugged, pursing her shiny red lips in an indifferent pout. "Suit yourself," she said. "At least I can be a bigger person in all this."

He let out a resentful laugh.

"Whatever." Janie stormed off without another word, breezing past him and climbing into her Lexus, speeding away.

"I'm so sorry, Josh," Melanie said as the two of them stood in the silence that Janie had left, the only sound the shushing gulf behind the house.

"Nothing ever turns out like we plan, does it?"

"It doesn't seem like it," she agreed.

"I hate that the land that was given to me in honor and love is the source of this awful disagreement. And now it'll be some strip mall..." He took in a deep breath.

With an empathetic nod, Melanie opened the door wider to let him into the house, both of them at a loss for words.

"There's nothing better than warm peach cobbler with vanilla ice cream on top," Josh said, as he dipped his fork into a slice of Addie's pie. "It almost makes me forget about Janie's visit." He offered Melanie a knowing grin.

She was happy at his attempt to be lighthearted. They'd decided to see if Addie's pie could give them any inspiration for what Josh should do. Melanie smiled back, taking a bite, the sugary sweetness mixed with the tartness of the peach exploding in her mouth.

Just then, the new washer made a loud clang and let out an odd vibrating noise.

Josh set down his fork. "Hang on, I'll take a look," he said, quickly assessing the situation and getting up.

"I hope there's nothing wrong with it," Melanie said, standing and pacing up beside him.

"Stay," he urged. "Enjoy your pie. I'll take care of it."

Melanie sat back down and took another bite of her pie. As she savored the vanilla flavor of the cold ice cream against the warm buttery pie crust, she gazed out the window at the sunshine. *Gram, please don't let the washer be broken*, she said in her head. *I've come this far. Do you have anything you can tell me about what happens next?*

To her relief, the washer went back to its normal humming sound.

"The sheets you're washing had all gone to one side and knocked the drum off track. I readjusted it and moved the sheets around."

"Thank goodness," she said.

"Any idea what this is?" He held up the 0113 key. "I found it under the washer."

Melanie sucked in a breath. "Yes!" she said, throwing her arms around him, the surprise of it making him laugh.

He handed it to her.

"It's from the box you found in the closet. And it opens Alfred's safe deposit box at First National. We should go see what's in it right now!" She grabbed her plate, scraping the last few crumbs into the trash and setting it in the sink. "Come with me."

"Wait," he said, stopping her.

Melanie pausing to hear what he had to say.

"So far, Alfred's things haven't really *helped* us. They've made our lives more difficult, really."

"Okay," she said, waiting for his point.

"Nothing good has come of them," he reiterated.

"That's not entirely true. Finding his things taught me about my gram."

"Right, but did that information help your life? Was it really a great thing to know that the love of her life slipped through her fingers and she missed out on being with him?"

Melanie considered this, unable to answer.

"And it certainly hasn't worked out well for me. I'm just saying… Do you really want to know what's in that box?"

She set the key on the counter, suddenly unsure, Addie's voice coming into her mind as a whisper: *Sometimes our secrets are better off buried.* Perhaps she should learn from experience. "Maybe I should think about it first."

Josh pulled out the chair next to his. "Yes. Right now, I say we have more pie."

Chapter Thirty-Three

Melanie walked slowly to allow Addie to keep up. The old woman plodded along the sidewalk between their houses with her brightly colored cane, the evening swells out on the water like a tidal lullaby. The sun had begun its descent, but it was slow to meet the horizon in the summer months, still reaching out with its beams as if it was protesting the arrival of night.

"The whole town tried, I heard, but it took a girl from out of town to get Josh to stay," Addie said with a smile, as she paced slowly beside Melanie on her nightly walk. Melanie had filled her in on everything when Addie had asked her to come along, which she didn't mind doing at all, since Josh had had to run some errands.

"I worry about us," Melanie blurted, as they made their way back to her house.

Addie slowed to a stop, twisting her head and looking up at Melanie.

"He can stay at the Ellis house with me, and he can work there, but every time he drives out of town and passes his grandfather's land, he'll be reminded of losing it. It's *my* fault he's lost it. Will he eventually resent me?"

Addie blew a thoughtful breath through her lips. "Knowing Josh, I can't imagine he would think that way."

"It could sit in the back of his mind…" She turned her face to the sunshine and closed her eyes, letting the rays warm her skin in an attempt to calm this new worry that had surfaced. "We've been through so much already," she said. "It's like everything's been against us. And if we don't work out, where will he go?"

"You definitely have been through quite a bit," Addie said with an empathetic smile. "But you aren't thinking about it the right way. You two have *been through it*—together. And you've made it. There's no guarantee about the future, but if you never try, you might be missing out on a lifetime of happiness."

Melanie's thoughts went to Alfred and Gram and the lifetime they'd missed out on. "You know what? You're right. Thank you, Addie." She gave the old woman a hug.

"It's no problem." Addie nodded toward the Ellis house where Josh was standing by his running truck. "Looks like you've got some living to do *right now*."

Melanie couldn't hide her happiness at seeing him standing there. She sent him a questioning look but he only smiled back at her. "I suppose I should go," she said. "Will you be okay walking back home?"

"Of course, dear. Go. Your prince is waiting."

Melanie laughed, giving Addie another squeeze and then walking over to Josh.

"I need you to get in and then close your eyes," he said when she'd reached him.

"Okaaay," she replied, wondering what he had in store for her.

"You can't open them."

"I won't," she promised, climbing in.

Josh jogged around to his side of the truck and got in.

*

"Listen," Josh said, covering Melanie's eyes as he walked behind her through the thick summer heat. "Do you hear that?"

"Yes," she said, honing in on the sound of the crickets, the crunch of brush under their feet, and rushing water. They'd ridden for ages—so long that she'd dozed off, having to keep her eyes shut. "What's that other sound?" she asked, noting the soft hum in the distance.

"A generator."

"A generator?"

"Yep. I needed one for this. Open your eyes."

"We're on your land," she said, taking in the strings of lights now strung in the trees near the waterfall, the porch swing full of pillows hanging from one of them, the small platform covered in a tablecloth with candles flickering.

"My whole life, I've had memories on this land, but before I let it go, I needed to have a memory with you here."

A hollow feeling settled over her. "This is beautiful," she said, an undeniable sadness present between them. "But you shouldn't be put in this position. I'm so sorry."

"We'll have plenty of time to worry about it. Right now, I want to create a memory that will last a lifetime." He clicked on the radio, soft music playing around them. He took her hands and walked her over to a clearing under the lights.

"These were the errands you were running?" she asked, reaching up and putting her arms around his neck, the two of them swaying to the music.

"Yep," he said, grinning down at her.

"You surprised me with this. I didn't know you were the romantic type."

He laughed and then dipped her. "Only with the right person," he said once he'd righted her.

A burst of excitement swam through her when she realized that this moment, under the trees and the lights, the cool air blowing toward them off the waterfall, his arms around her—she'd been waiting for this her whole life and she hadn't even known it. It was as if she'd finally taken in a gulp of air after holding her breath for years.

"Hungry?" he asked once the song ended. "I've got fresh fruit in the cooler."

"Oooh. What kind?"

"Mangos and pineapple." He took her hand and led her over to the picnic area he'd set up.

She lowered herself down, the vanilla scent from the candles floating up around them. "That sounds amazing," she said.

"I also have champagne." He reached into the cooler and pulled out the bottle, popping the cork. The foam bubbled over as he grabbed a flute from his bag.

"This is quite different from the last time we were here."

"I haven't ruled out swimming," he said, pulling her bikini from the bag to show her.

"You've thought of everything."

He handed her a fizzing glass of champagne and sat down. With the candlelight flickering in his serious eyes, he gazed at her. "I don't normally just do this sort of thing…" he said. "But you're worth it."

"Thank you," she said, the guilt she had over causing him to lose this gorgeous piece of property rising up again.

"What's wrong?" Josh asked, completely in tune to her and noticing right away.

"I told Addie that I'm worried we won't survive this," she said.

"Survive what, candles and champagne? I think we'll manage," he teased, but she didn't laugh, her fear winning out.

"You know what I mean. Losing this." She waved her arm around at the trees.

He followed her gesture with a thoughtful pout. "I'll let you in on a little secret." He leaned closer to her, the cedarwood and vanilla scent of him layered with the vanilla of the candles. "I got to New York and I sat in my empty apartment, wondering what I was even doing. I couldn't get you off my mind, and the more I tried to push you away, the worse it got. That doesn't happen to me." He gazed into her eyes. "Losing this land is unthinkable, but if it's a step toward my future and what's *meant* for me, I'll take it, because I've never felt more sure of anything until I met you. Thanks for giving me time to admit it."

Melanie leaned in and gave him a kiss, the music playing around them, making it all feel like magic. Then she pulled back. "No more secrets," she said. "We'll get through it together."

"No more secrets," he agreed.

Chapter Thirty-Four

Melanie padded down the steps of the Ellis house to the savory, salty smell of crispy bacon and scrambled eggs. When she got to the kitchen, Josh twisted around from the stove, a spatula in his hand.

"Good morning," he said, reaching over and handing her a cup of coffee. "It's still hot. I was going to get you up in just a second but you must've read my mind."

"This looks delicious," she said, reaching up to give him a kiss on the cheek before settling in at the bar so she could talk to him. She set her coffee down, noticing the 0113 key that was still sitting there on the counter. She picked it up and fiddled with it.

Josh brought over two plates and sat next to her, his eyes on the key. He set her plate in front of her and handed her a fork. The steaming pile of eggs made her stomach growl.

"I wonder what's in that safe deposit box," she said, digging into the eggs.

"Probably nothing," he replied. "Or something terrible."

"What could possibly be that terrible after what we've been through?"

He ate a bite and swallowed. "What if we find out we're cousins or something?"

Melanie threw her head back and laughed. "Then best we find out now rather than later."

He shivered dramatically, making her laugh again. He snapped off a piece of bacon and popped it into his mouth before picking up the key and holding it to the light. "It couldn't be anything that bad, right?"

"Whatever is in there, we can get through it together," she replied.

"We could leave it be and go on with our lives…"

"What's the fun in that?" she said with a wide smile.

"Your glass-half-full mentality is what gets you into trouble, you know. If you recall, nothing Alfred Ellis left behind has helped us in any way."

"I know," she said, thoughtful. "But I feel him here. My gram told me that ghosts only talk to us when they have something to say." She took the key from Josh's fingers. "What if he's got one last thing to tell us?"

"Like we're invading his privacy and he wants us to leave for good?"

She stared down at the key. "No more secrets you said, right? Whatever's in there, if it's something terrible, let's get it out into the open so we can handle it before it tears us apart."

"All right," he relented. "We'll call Mom and then see if we can get a court order to get into the box after breakfast. No family has ever come forward—he doesn't have any. I think we can convince the judge to issue a letter appointing you as personal representative of the estate. At the very least, with that, we can view the contents of the box. Are you sure you want to do it?"

"Absolutely," Melanie said.

*

"We could chuck the key in the bushes and make a run for it. Never look back," Josh said, as he and Melanie neared the door of First National bank with the deed to the Ellis house showing occupancy, the court order that the judge had granted and signed after hearing their story, and their driver's licenses.

"Where's your sense of adventure?" Melanie teased, but in her head, she pleaded with Gram to let this be something wonderful and not awful.

Josh opened the door for her and they walked into the chilly air of the bank, pacing past the cherry-wood furniture and wingback chairs to the teller.

"So you've got the Ellis key. We're all wondering what's in there," the woman said, scratching her beehive with a pencil as she peered at the screen of her computer through her brightly colored readers. "I'll need you to fill out some paperwork and then you can come on back. You do know you can't take anything out, since he didn't give you permission, right?"

Melanie nodded.

Josh stopped her, putting his hand on her arm. "You sure you want to do this?" he asked. "Last chance to let it go. Once we know what's in there, there's no turning back."

"I know your family has spent years avoiding this man, but I feel it in my gut—he has something to tell me. And I want you there with me when I find out."

He took in a deep breath. "Okay," he said. "Let's go."

They filled out the paperwork, showed their IDs and headed into the vault, where the manager of the bank clicked open the first lock of the little door to Alfred's safe deposit box. Melanie slowly slipped her key into the other one. She got a wild shiver when it fit in the keyhole as smooth as silk. She turned the key and opened the door, pulling the metal box from inside and setting it on the table. Her heart racing, she stared at the closed box, knowing that once she saw what was inside, it would be done. She also braced for the moment when she'd open it and find nothing—it could go either way.

Josh took her hand.

Slowly, she lifted the lid, her eyes going immediately to a velvet ring box. She lifted it out and opened it. Her mouth hung open at the sight of the enormous diamond solitaire, surrounded by a band of diamonds. She slipped the platinum jewelry out of its holder and slid it onto her finger—a perfect fit. "Wow," she said, peering down at it. "I don't think I've ever seen anything this beautiful." She took it off and noticed the inscription: *Eloise, Love is forever.*

Her vision clouded with her tears. "He bought it for Gram and she never got to wear it." Slowly, she put it back into the box, knowing she couldn't keep it. She wiped a tear that spilled down her cheek as Josh put a supportive arm around her.

Setting it aside, she pulled a manila envelope from the box and opened it, scanning the document that was inside. "It's a will."

"A will?" Josh leaned over her shoulder.

Her heart in her throat, terrified that Alfred had left the house to someone else and she'd find herself in a mess of a legal battle to keep it, she read the legal jargon, but as her eyes moved over the words, she realized quite quickly that this had nothing to do with the house.

"What is it?" Josh asked.

She clutched the will to her chest. "Your mom has reason to believe that she's Alfred's daughter, right? And we might even have DNA for testing on Alfred's old things."

"Yes," he said, guarded, his gaze fluttering over to the bank manager who was standing at the door, pretending not to listen.

"Alfred has left a gift to his descendants, who"—she turned the paper around, pointing to the clause—"shall receive the gift upon the death of the undersigned. That would be *you*." She pulled out another sealed envelope that read, *Only to be opened by beneficiary of the will.*

He stared at her unblinking, clearly trying to process this. "What's the gift?" he asked, taking the envelope and holding it up to the light.

"I don't know. It's probably the ring. That could be the receipt."

He picked up the ring box and opened it, the diamond sending a dancing light around the room. "I'm not sure I want anything from him, so I'll be happy to give you the ring."

"I'd love that," she said, the inscription rolling around in her mind: *Love is forever.* "Look at this." She flipped to another page. "It's an affidavit of paternity."

Blinking to clearly wade through his questions, Josh focused on the form. He traced the name at the bottom. "Vera Wilson. That's my grandmother's name."

"This is saying that Alfred is your mother's father, and Vera's signed it."

"Yes," he said, thinking. "We'll have to go back to the judge to get a letter of testamentary so we can *keep* what's in the box. Remember what he said—that could take thirty days or more."

Melanie could absolutely wait thirty days to get Gram's ring. She placed the ring and the documents back into the box and closed the lid, feeling like she was shutting the last message from Gram in the darkness of the box, eager to have it back.

Chapter Thirty-Five

Melanie stared at the mass of boxes in the entryway, elated. "We've unpacked *all* of them," she said to Josh, grinning up at him. "You're officially moved in." They'd spent the last two weeks getting everything back home from New York and settling in at the bed and breakfast together.

The walls had all been painted, their bright white surfaces and large windows framing the aquamarine gulf outside. The furniture was all in, the navy-blue and teal pillows dotting a clean and crisp interior. Coastal coffee table books lined the whitewashed built-ins and the tables surrounded by white wicker chairs. The candles were lit and the lamps all on. The only thing they had left to do was to break down the last of Josh's moving boxes.

"I cannot believe I'm living in the Ellis house," he said with a laugh. He picked her up and spun her around. "Let's celebrate."

"What do you want to do?" she asked, wrapping her arms around his neck.

"We could go to Barney's and have drinks," he suggested.

"Or we could grill out, eat fresh fish and oysters until we're stuffed, and then sit on the porch swing until the stars come out." Just the idea of sitting on the newly painted decking—blue like the dark stripe in the sea—with the pots of pink peonies they'd gotten to add even more color the space would be amazing.

"That sounds wonderful," he said, "but I don't feel like it's big enough for this celebration."

Melanie trailed off, thinking, but was distracted when Josh's phone rang in his pocket.

He answered it. "Yes," he said to the unknown caller. "Mm hm. Excellent. We'll be there in five minutes." He hung up the phone, pulling her close. "How about we go get your grandmother's ring?" he asked. "That ought to be big enough of a celebration, yes?"

"It cleared?" she asked, her mouth hanging open in excitement.

"They rushed it."

"Yes!" she squealed before giving him a big kiss. "I can't wait to have it. I feel like it's Gram's last message to me." She looked up at him. "Thank you for giving it to me," she said seriously.

"You're more than welcome," he said. "Let's go."

The familiar contents of the box sat on the bank table in front of Melanie and Josh.

"You'll want to keep this receipt to insure the ring," Josh said, waving the unopened envelope in the air. He put his finger under the flap and opened it, pulling out the piece of paper with dollar amounts inscribed.

"I'll insure it today," she said, but Josh didn't seem to hear her.

His eyes were on the paper in his now shaking hands. "This isn't a receipt," he said, his face unreadable. Was that panic or surprise she saw in his eyes?

"What is it?" she asked.

He swallowed and let out a ragged breath, not looking up from the page.

"It's the gift, right?" she asked. *Gift* was a good word, she reminded herself. It couldn't be anything terrible. She prayed it wasn't.

"Yeah," he said in a whisper. "It's a gift." He finally tore his eyes from the document and looked up at her. "The gift is the remainder of Alfred Ellis's bank account," he said. "Three million dollars—his family inheritance."

They stared at each other, stunned.

Like a whisper, Gram's voice filtered into her ear. *If he has something to say...*

In that moment, Melanie realized that Alfred was giving his grandson the life he'd never had. Alfred had just made it possible for Josh to keep his land, live in his grandfather's house as long as he wanted, and be in the company of someone from the family Alfred had never been able to be a part of. And best of all, the Ellis house was full: full of life, full of laughter, and full of hope.

Love really was forever.

Epilogue

"Addie!" Melanie said, swishing up to the old woman in her vintage 1950s A-line, off the shoulder chiffon wedding dress, as she let the woman in through the front door of The Ellis House bed and breakfast, where they were all gathering after her wedding to Josh. She and Josh were both Ellises now, by blood *and* marriage.

In a simple ceremony at the white church downtown, lined with magnolias and pink roses, with just close friends and family, Melanie and Josh had married. While Melanie had taken Josh's name, Claiborne, she felt like an Ellis for sure. The house, finally finished, was dripping in flowers, the chandelier in the parlor gleaming and bright, the wallpaper restored, and the rooms now full of guests. She could feel both Alfred and her grandmother all around her.

But Melanie wasn't the only one who had taken Josh's name in the last year.

"Hi Addie!" Cole said, rushing in and helping the old woman through the door. "Did you see my fancy shoes?" he asked her, before she'd barely gotten across the threshold, tapping his patent leathers proudly.

The adoption had gone through just after Melanie and Josh had gotten engaged, and Eric had come home after a successful surgery, which was such a wonderful surprise for them all. Josh didn't want the surprises to end there, however; he'd wiped Eric and Suzie's medical bills with part of his inheritance from Alfred.

And now, with white balloons, flowers, and candles filling the house, and a band out back by the biggest wedding cake of the season, according to the local bakery, all the guests had been invited, along with everyone in town, to the reception. The bed and breakfast had been a wonderful place to celebrate their big day, but Melanie couldn't wait for the surprise that was coming *after* the reception.

"Wow, where is this?" she'd asked after the ceremony, as she peered down at a photo of a white house with double front porches, paddle fans, and rocking chairs along both the top and bottom levels, on Josh's phone. The stately home had double chimneys, and she could see the hint of a swimming pool with twinkle lights nestled in the greenest grass out back.

"Less than an hour away," he'd said. "It's our new home."

Josh had been busy building their dream house on his land. He hadn't let Melanie and Cole in on any of it until tonight, the entire honeymoon a total surprise.

"I had it completely decorated and we'll be spending our first evening as a family there tonight. There's a pool, a basketball court for Cole, a fire pit, and a stone path leading to the waterfall, which we can view from the balcony of our master bedroom."

Melanie had actually gasped—a long breath of utter surprise.

"And then Suzie and Eric are coming to get Cole," he'd whispered into her ear, in a deliciously romantic suggestive tone.

And now, while she mingled with the guests, the lingering excitement of seeing their new home and spending the evening around the fire, watching Cole splash in the pool under the twinkling lights above it, followed her with every step.

Addie joined the crowd that was gathered in the kitchen and living rooms, spilling out into the back yard. Maryann was there, and Eric and Suzie, all the guys that had worked on the house, Steven and the other friends who'd been sending Josh off that first night over darts, Kathryn and Toby along with Ryan, and her mom chatting with Brenda—everyone was celebrating.

"Thank you all for coming," Josh said to settle the crowd. "We're so glad you all could be here to share this day with us."

Melanie walked over and stood next to her husband, Cole following. She put her arm around her new son, Gram's diamond glistening on her hand beside a matching wedding band that Josh had commissioned.

Josh pulled Cole into his side with a loving little squeeze and then put one arm around Melanie. "As many of you know, this house has been a labor of love. When I first met my gorgeous wife, I thought she was crazy for buying it. But what she taught me was that when it feels like everything—literally everything—is going wrong, sometimes, without our knowledge, it's actually going very, very right." Josh leaned down and gave Melanie a kiss to the cheers of the crowd. "Enjoy the food and drinks today as we celebrate!"

Melanie wiped a tear of happiness that had come up unexpectedly as she looked around at her beautiful home, full to the brim with friends, family, and travelers who had come for a week of sun and sand, her heart full. And while she couldn't see them, she knew that Gram and Alfred were somewhere among the crowd.

A Letter from Jenny

Hi there!

Thank you so much for reading *The Beach House*. I really hope you found it to be a summery, heartwarming getaway!

If you'd like me to drop you an email when my next book is out, you can sign up here:

www.bookouture.com/jenny-hale

I won't share your email with anyone else, and I'll only email you when a new book is released.

If you did enjoy *The Beach House*, I'd love it if you'd write a review. Getting feedback from readers is amazing, and it also helps to persuade other readers to pick up one of my books for the first time.

Until next time,
Jenny xo

    7201437.Jenny_Hale

    jennyhaleauthor

    @jhaleauthor

    jhaleauthor

    www.itsjennyhale.com

Acknowledgments

I am grateful to my husband Justin, who has provided support for every single one of my projects over the years, held strong when I had yet another idea to further my journey, and allowed me to follow my heart, wherever it takes me.

To my friends and family, I thank you from the bottom of my heart for all your positivity and encouragement.

I am so appreciative of the creative community here in Nashville, and I feel so lucky to be among such inspiring people who lift me up and give me amazing opportunities to expand my creativity.

Huge kudos to the folks at Bookouture and my lovely editor Christina Demosthenous, who waits patiently as I give her new layers of story upon every edit. She keeps it all running smoothly.

To all those who have paved my path for success, I will be forever grateful.

Made in the USA
Las Vegas, NV
25 June 2021